Praise for *New York Times* bestselling author Linda Howard

"You can't read just one Linda Howard!"
—*New York Times* bestselling
Catherine Coult...

"This master storyteller tak...
—*RT Book...*

"Ms. Howard can wring s... tension
out of her characters t... ...sfied you
are when you fini... ...nt more."

"Linda Howard k... ...aders want."
—*Affair... ...ur*

Praise for *New York Times* bestselling author Stephanie Bond

"This is a series the reader will want to jump on in the very beginning. It's witty, sexy, and hilariously funny."
—*Writers Unlimited* on *Body Movers*

"I devoured this book and loved it!"
—*Fresh Fiction* on *Body Movers*

"*Body Movers* is signature Stephanie Bond, with witty dialogue, brilliant characterization, and a wonderful well-plotted storyline."
—*Contemporary Romance Writers*

"The exciting start of a new series."
—*Romance Reviews Today* on *Body Movers*

Linda Howard is an award-winning author of many *New York Times* bestsellers, including *Up Close and Dangerous, Drop Dead Gorgeous, Cover of Night, Killing Time, To Die For, Kiss Me While I Sleep, Cry No More* and *Dying to Please.* She lives in Alabama with her husband and two golden retrievers. Visit her online at lindahoward.com.

New York Times Bestselling Authors

LINDA HOWARD
and
STEPHANIE BOND

Under the Mistletoe

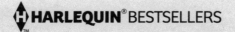

ISBN 13: 978-0-373-60666-5

Under the Mistletoe

Copyright © 2008 Harlequin Books S.A.

The publisher acknowledges the copyright holders of the individual works as follows:

Bluebird Winter
Copyright © 1987 by Linda Howington

Naughty or Nice?
Copyright © 1998 by Stephanie Bond, Inc.

Recycling programs
for this product may
not exist in your area.

This edition published by arrangement with Harlequin Books S.A.

For questions and comments about the quality of this book, please contact us at CustomerService@Harlequin.com.

Printed in U.S.A.

CONTENTS

BLUEBIRD WINTER

Linda Howard

CHAPTER ONE

IT WASN'T SUPPOSED to happen like this.

Kathleen Fields pressed her hand to her swollen abdomen, her face drawn and anxious as she looked out the window again at the swirling, wind-blown snow. Visibility was so limited that she couldn't even see the uneven pasture fence no more than fifty yards away. The temperature had plummeted into the teens, and according to the weather report on the radio, this freak Christmas Day blizzard was likely to last the rest of the day and most of the night.

She couldn't wait that long. She was in labor now, almost a month early. Her baby would need medical attention.

Bitterness welled in her as she dropped the curtain and turned back to the small, dim living room, lit only by the fire in the fireplace. The electricity and telephone service had gone out five hours ago. Two hours after that, the dull ache in her back, which had been so constant for weeks that she no longer noticed it, had begun strengthening into something more, then laced around to her distended belly. Only mildly concerned, she had ignored it as false labor; after all, she was still three weeks and five days from her due date. Then, half an hour ago, her water had broken, and there was no longer any doubt: she was in labor.

She was also alone, and stranded. This Christmas snow, so coveted by millions of children, could mean the death of her own child.

Tears burned her eyes. She had stolidly endured a bad marriage and the end of her illusions, faced the reality of being broke, alone and pregnant, of working long hours as a waitress in an effort to keep herself fed and provide a home for this baby, even though she had fiercely resented its existence at the beginning. But then it had begun moving inside her, gentle little flutters at first, then actual kicks and pokes, and it had become reality, a person, a companion. It was *her* baby. She wanted it, wanted to hold it and love it and croon lullabies to it. It was the only person she had left in the world, but now she might lose it, perhaps in punishment for that early resentment. How ironic to carry it all this time, only to lose it on Christmas Day! It was supposed to be a day of hope, faith and promise, but she didn't have any hope left, or much faith in people, and the future promised nothing but an endless procession of bleak days. All she had was herself, and the tiny life inside her that was now in jeopardy.

She could deliver the baby here, without help. It was warm and somehow she would manage to keep the fire going. She would survive, but would the baby? It was premature. It might not be able to breathe properly on its own. Something might be wrong with it.

Or she could try to get to the clinic, fifteen miles distant. It was an easy drive in good weather...but the weather wasn't good, and the howling wind had been getting louder. The roads were treacherous and visibility limited. She might not make it, and the effort would cost her her own life, as well as that of her child.

So what? The words echoed in her mind. What did her life matter, if the baby died? Would she be able to live with herself if she opted to protect herself at the risk of the baby's life? Everything might be all right, but she couldn't take that chance. For the baby's sake, she had to try.

Moving clumsily, she dressed as warmly as she could, layering her clothing until she moved like a waddling pumpkin. She gathered water and blankets, an extra nightgown for herself and clothes for the baby, then, as a last thought, checked the telephone one more time on the off-chance that service might have been restored. Only silence met her ear, and, regretfully, she dropped the receiver.

Taking a deep breath to brace herself, Kathleen opened the back door and was immediately lashed by the icy wind and stinging snow. She ducked her head and struggled against the wind, cautiously making her way down the two ice-coated steps. Her balance wasn't that good anyway, and the wind was beating at her, making her stagger. Halfway across the yard she slipped and fell, but scrambled up so quickly that she barely felt the impact. "I'm sorry, I'm sorry," she breathed to the baby, patting her stomach. The baby had settled low in her belly and wasn't kicking now, but the pressure was increasing. It was hard to walk. Just as she reached the old pickup truck a contraction hit her and she stumbled, falling again. This contraction was stronger than the others, and all she could do was lie helplessly in the snow until it eased, biting her lip to keep from moaning aloud.

Snow was matting her eyelashes when she finally struggled to her feet again and gathered up the articles she had dropped. She was panting. *God, please let it be a long labor!* she prayed. *Please give me time to get to the clinic.* She could bear the pain, if the baby would just stay snug and safe inside her until she could get help for it.

A dry sobbing sound reached her ears as she wrenched the truck door open, pitting her strength against that of the wind as it tried to slam the door shut. Clumsily she climbed into the truck, barely fitting her swollen stomach behind the wheel. The wind slammed the door shut without her aid, and for a moment she just sat there, entombed in an icy, white world, because snow covered all the windows.

The sobbing sound continued, and finally she realized she was making the noise.

Instantly Kathleen drew herself up. There was
nothing to gain by letting herself panic. She had to
clear her mind and concentrate on nothing but driving, because her baby's life depended on it. The baby
was all she had left. Everything else was gone: her
parents; her marriage; her self-confidence; her faith
and trust in people. Only the baby was left, and herself. She still had herself. The two of them had each
other, and they didn't need anyone else. She would
do anything to protect her baby.

Breathing deeply, she forced herself to be calm.
With deliberate movements, she inserted the key in
the ignition and turned it. The starter turned slowly,
and a new fear intruded. Was the battery too cold to
generate enough power to start the old motor? But
then the motor roared into life, and the truck vibrated
beneath her. She sighed in relief and turned on the
wipers to clear the snow from the windshield. They
beat back and forth, laboring under the icy weight
of the packed snow.

It was so cold! Her breath fogged the air, and she
was shivering despite the layers of clothing she wore.
Her face felt numb. She reached up to touch it and
found that she was still covered with snow. Slowly
she wiped her face and dusted the flakes from her
hair.

The increasing pressure in her lower body made

it difficult for her to hold in the clutch, but she wrestled the stubborn gearshift into the proper position and ground her teeth against the pressure as she let out the clutch. The truck moved forward.

Visibility was even worse than she had expected. She could barely make out the fence that ran alongside the road. How easy it would be to run off the road, or to become completely lost in the white nightmare! Creeping along at a snail's pace, Kathleen concentrated on the fence line and tried not to think about the things that could happen.

She was barely a quarter of a mile down the road when another contraction laced her stomach in iron bands. She gasped, jerking in spite of herself, and the sudden wrench of the steering wheel sent the old truck into a skid. "No!" she groaned, bracing herself as the truck began going sideways toward the shallow ditch alongside the road. The two right wheels landed in the ditch with an impact that rattled her teeth and loosened her grip from the steering wheel. She cried out again as she was flung to the right, her body slamming into the door on the passenger side.

The contraction eased a moment later. Panting, Kathleen crawled up the slanting seat and wedged herself behind the steering wheel. The motor had died, and anxiously she put in the clutch and slid the shift into neutral, praying she could get the engine started again. She turned the key, and once again the truck coughed into life.

But the wheels spun uselessly in the icy ditch, unable to find traction. She tried rocking the truck back and forth, putting it first in reverse, then in low gear, but it didn't work. She was stuck.

Tiredly, she leaned her head on the steering wheel. She was only a quarter of a mile from the house, but it might as well have been twenty miles in this weather. The wind was stronger, visibility almost zero. Her situation had gone from bad to worse. She should have stayed at the house. In trying to save her baby, she had almost certainly taken away its only chance for survival.

HE SHOULD EITHER have left his mother's house the day before, or remained until the roads were clear. Hindsight was, indeed, very sharp, unlike the current visibility. His four-wheel-drive Jeep Cherokee was surefooted on the icy road, but that didn't eliminate the need to see where he was going.

Making a mistake made Derek Taliferro angry, especially when it was such a stupid mistake. Yesterday's weather bulletins had warned that conditions could worsen, so he had decided to make the drive back to Dallas right away. But Marcie had wanted him to stay until Christmas morning, and he loved his mother very much, so in the end he'd stayed. His strong mouth softened as he allowed himself to think briefly of her. She was a strong woman, raising him single-handedly and never letting him think she'd have it any other way. He'd been elated when she had met Whit Campbell, a strong, laconic rancher from Oklahoma, and tumbled head over heels in love. That had been...Lord, ten years ago. It didn't seem that long. Marcie and Whit still acted like newlyweds.

Derek liked visiting the ranch, just across the state line in Oklahoma, and escaping the pressures of the hospital for a while. That was one reason he'd allowed Marcie to talk him into staying longer than his common sense told him he should. But this morning the urge to get back to Dallas had also overridden his common sense. He should have stayed put until the weather cleared, but he wanted to be back at the hospital by tomorrow. His tiny patients needed him.

The job was compelling, and he never tired of it. He had known he wanted to be a doctor from the time he was fifteen, but at first he'd thought about being an obstetrician. Gradually his interest had become more focused, and by the time he was midway through medical school his goal was set. He specialized in neonatal care, in those tiny babies who came into the world with less of a chance than they should have had. Some of them were simply premature and needed a protective environment in which to gain weight. Others, who were far too early, had to fight for every breath as their underdeveloped systems tried to mature. Every day was a battle won. Then there were those who needed his surgical skills after nature had gone awry, and still others who were beyond help. Every time he was finally able to send a baby home with its parents, he was filled with an intense satisfaction that showed no signs of lessening. It was also why he was now creeping, almost blindly, through a blizzard instead of waiting for better weather. He wanted to get back to the hospital.

The snow completely covered the road; he'd been following the fence lines, and hoping he was still on track. Hell, for all he knew, he was driving across someone's pasture. This was idiocy. He swore under his breath, holding the Cherokee steady against the gusting, howling, swirling wind. When he got to the next town—*if* he got to the next town—he was going to stop, even if he had to spend the night in an all-night grocery…provided there was an all-night grocery. Anything was better than driving blindly in this white hell.

It was so bad that he almost missed seeing the bulk of an old pickup truck, which had slid into a ditch and was now resting at an angle. In one sense seeing the old truck was good news: at least he was still on the road. He started to go on, thinking that whoever had been driving the truck would have sought more adequate shelter long ago, but a quick uneasy feeling made him brake carefully, then shift into reverse and back up until he was alongside the snow-covered bulk. It would only take a minute to check.

The snow had turned into icy, wind-driven pellets that stung his face as he opened the door and got out, hunching his broad shoulders against the wind that tried to knock him off his feet. It was only a few steps to the truck, but he had to fight for every inch. Quickly he grabbed the door handle and wrenched it open, wanting to verify that the truck was empty so he could get back into the Cherokee's warm interior. He was startled by the small scream from the woman who lay on the seat and then jerked upright in alarm when the door was opened so suddenly.

"I just want to help," he said quickly, to keep from frightening her more than he already had.

Kathleen gasped, panting at the pain that had her in its grips. The contractions had been intensifying and were only a few minutes apart now. She would never have been able to make it to the clinic in time. She felt the numbing blast of cold, saw the big man who stood in the truck's open door; but just for the moment she couldn't reply, couldn't do anything except concentrate on the pain. She wrapped her arms around her tight belly, whimpering.

Derek realized at a glance what was happening. The woman was completely white, her green eyes vivid in her pale, desperate face as she held her swollen belly. A strong sense of protectiveness surged through him.

"It's all right, sweetheart," he murmured soothingly, reaching into the truck and lifting her out in his strong arms. "You and the baby will be just fine. I'll take care of everything."

She was still whimpering, locked in the grip of the contraction. Derek carried her to the Cherokee, sheltering her from the brutal wind as much as he could. His mind was already on the coming birth. He hadn't delivered a baby since he'd been an intern, but he'd been on hand many times when the newborn was expected to have difficulties.

He managed to open the passenger door with her still in his arms, and gently deposited her on the seat before hurrying around to vault in on his own side. "How far apart are the contractions?" he asked, wiping her face with his hands. She lay slumped against the seat now, breathing deeply at the cessation of pain, her eyelids closed.

Her eyes opened at his touch, the wary eyes of a wild animal in a trap. "Th-th-th-three minutes," she said, her teeth chattering from the cold. "Maybe less."

"How far is the hospital?"

"Clinic," she corrected, still breathing hard. She swallowed and wet her lips. "Fifteen miles."

"We won't make it," he said with awful certainty. "Is there anyplace around here where we can shelter? A house, a restaurant, anything?"

She lifted her hand. "My house…back there. Quarter mile."

Derek's experienced eyes took note of the signs.

She was exhausted. Labor was tiring enough, without being alone and terrified, too. Stress had taken its toll. He needed to get her warm and comfortable as soon as possible. Her eyes closed again.

He decided not to chance turning the truck around and getting off the road; instead he put the Cherokee in reverse, guiding himself by the fence line beside him, because he couldn't see a damned thing out the back window. "Tell me when I get to your driveway," he ordered, and her eyes fluttered open in response.

A minute or so later another contraction curled her in the seat. Derek glanced at his watch. Just a little over two minutes since the last one. The baby certainly wasn't waiting for better weather.

A rusted mailbox on a leaning fence post caught his attention. "Is this your driveway?" he asked.

She lifted her head, and he could see that her white teeth were sunk into her bottom lip to hold back her groans. She managed a short nod, and he shifted into low gear, turning onto the faint trail by the mailbox and praying for time.

CHAPTER TWO

"THE BACK DOOR'S open," Kathleen whispered, and he nodded as he steered the Cherokee as close to the steps as he could.

"Don't try to get out on your own," he ordered as she reached for the door handle. "I'll come around and get you."

Kathleen subsided against the seat, her face pale and taut. She didn't know this man, didn't know whether she should trust him, but she had no choice but to accept his help. She was more frightened than she'd ever been in her life. The pain was worse than she'd expected, and added to it was the numbing fear for her child's life. Whoever the man was, right now she was grateful for his company.

He got out of the Cherokee, bending his head against the wind as he circled the front of the vehicle. He was a big man, tall and strong; he'd handled her weight easily, but his grasp had been gentle. As he opened the passenger door, Kathleen started to swing her legs around so she could slide out, but again he stopped her by scooping her up in his arms.

"Put your face against my shoulder," he instructed, raising his voice so she could hear him
over the howling wind. She nodded and buried her
face against his coat, and he turned so that his back
blocked the wind from her as he carried her the few
feet to the back door. He fumbled for the doorknob
and managed to turn it, and the wind did the rest,
catching the door and slamming it back against the
wall with a resounding crack. A small blizzard of
snow entered with them.

Swiftly he carried her through the small, time-
worn ranch house until he reached the living room,
where the fire still burned low in the fireplace. She
felt as though hours had passed, but in reality it had
been only about an hour since she had fought her
way to the truck.

Still with that powerful, controlled gentleness,
he placed her on the sagging old couch. "I've got
to get my bag, but I'll be right back," he promised,
smoothing her hair back from her face. "Don't try
to get up—stay right here."

She nodded, so tired that she couldn't imagine
going anywhere. Why did he want his luggage right
now? Couldn't it wait?

Another contraction. She curled up on the couch,
giving gasping little cries at the fierceness of the
pain. Before it ended he was beside her again, his
voice soothing but authoritative as he told her to take
quick, short breaths, to pant like a dog. Dimly she re-

membered reading instructions for breathing during labor, and the same description had been used. She tried to do as he said, concentrating on her breathing, and it did seem to help. Perhaps it just took her mind off the pain, but right then she was willing to do anything.

When the contraction had eased and she slumped exhausted on the couch, he said, "Do you have extra wood for the fire? The electricity is off."

She managed a wan smile. "I know. It went off this morning. I brought extra wood in yesterday, when I heard the weather report—it's in the wash room, just off the kitchen."

"You should have gone to the clinic yesterday," he said crisply as he got to his feet.

She was tired and frightened, but fire still flashed in her green eyes as she glared up at him. "I would have, if I'd known the baby was going to come early."

That got his attention; his black brows snapped together over his high-bridged nose. "You're not full term? How early are you?"

"Almost a month." Her hand went to her stomach in an unconscious gesture of helpless concern.

"Any chance your due date was miscalculated?"

"No," she whispered, her head falling back. She knew exactly when she'd gotten pregnant, and the memory made her go cold.

He gave her a crooked smile, and for the first time she noticed how beautiful he was, in a strong,

masculine way that was almost unearthly. Kathleen
had gotten into the habit of not looking directly at
men, or she would have seen it before. Even now,
something in his golden brown eyes made her feel
more relaxed. "This is your lucky day, sweetheart,"
he said gently, still smiling at her as he took off his
thick shearling coat and rolled up his sleeves. "You
just got stranded with a doctor."

For a moment the words didn't make sense; then
her mouth opened in silent disbelief. "You're a doctor?"

He lifted his right hand as if taking an oath. "Li-
censed and sworn."

Relief filled her like a warm tide rushing through
her body, and she gave a small laugh that was half
sob. "Are you any good at delivering babies?"

"Babies are my business," he said, giving her another of those bright, tender smiles. "So stop worrying and try to rest while I get things arranged in
here. When you have another contraction, remember
how to breathe. I won't be long."

She watched as he brought in more wood and
built up the fire until it was blazing wildly, adding
warmth to the chilled room. Through the pain of another contraction, she watched as he carried in the
mattress from her bed and dumped it on the floor in
front of the fire. With swift, sure movements he put
a clean sheet on it, then folded towels over the sheet.

He rose to his feet with powerful grace and approached her. "Now, let's get you more comfortable," he said as he removed her coat. "By the way, my name is Derek Taliferro."

"Kathleen Fields," she replied in kind.

"Is there a Mr. Fields?" he asked, his calm face hiding his intense interest in her as he began taking off her boots.

Bitterness filled Kathleen's face, a bitterness so deep it hurt to see. "There's one somewhere," she muttered. "But we aren't married any longer."

He was silent as he removed her thick socks, under which she also wore leotards that she'd put on when she realized she would have to try to get to the clinic. He helped her to her feet and unzipped her serviceable corduroy jumper, lifting it over her head and leaving her standing in the turtleneck sweater and leotards.

"I can do the rest," she said uneasily. "Just let me go into the bedroom for a nightgown."

He laughed, the sound deep and rich. "All right, if you think you can manage."

"Of course I can manage." She had been managing much more than that since Larry Fields had walked out.

But she had barely taken two steps when another contraction bent her double, a contraction so powerful that it was all she could do to gasp for breath. Involuntary tears stung her eyes. She felt his arms around her; then he lifted her and a moment later placed her on the mattress. Swiftly he stripped off her leotards and underwear, and draped a sheet over her; then he held her hand and coached her breathing until the contraction eased.

"Rest for a minute now," he soothed. "I'm going to wash my hands so I can examine you. I'll be right back."

Kathleen lay tiredly on the mattress, staring up at the water-stained ceiling with swimming eyes. The heat from the fire flickered against her cheeks, bringing a rosy glow to her complexion. She was so tired; she felt as if she could sleep for the rest of the day, but there wouldn't be any rest until the baby was born. Her hands clenched into fists as anxiety rose in her again. The baby had to be all right. It had to be.

Then he was back, kneeling at the foot of the mattress and lifting the sheet that covered her. Real color climbed into her face, and she turned her head to stare into the fire. She had never really been comfortable with intimacy, and even her visits to the doctor had been torturous occasions for her. To have this man, this stranger, touch her and look at her...

Derek glanced up and saw her flushed face and expression of acute embarrassment, and a smile flickered around his mouth as amused tenderness welled up in him. How wary she was of him, despite being forced to put her welfare in his hands! And rather shy, like a wild creature that wasn't accustomed to others and didn't quite trust them. She was frightened, too, for her child, and of the ordeal she faced. Because of that, he was immensely gentle as he examined her.

"You aren't fully dilated," he murmured. "The baby isn't in such a hurry, after all. Go with your contractions, but don't push. I'll tell you when to push. How long ago did the contractions start?"

"My back was hurting all last night," she said tiredly, her eyes closing. "The first real contraction was at about ten o'clock this morning."

He glanced at his watch. She had been in labor a little over five hours, and it would probably last another hour or so. Not a long labor, especially for a first pregnancy. "When did your water break?"

He wasn't hurting her, and her embarrassment was fading. She even felt drowsy. "Umm…about one-thirty." Now she felt his hands on her stomach; firm, careful touches as he tried to determine the baby's position. Her warm drowsiness splintered as another contraction seized her, but when she breathed as he'd instructed somehow it didn't seem as painful.

When she rested again, he placed his stethoscope against her stomach and listened to the baby's heartbeat. "It's a strong, steady hearbeat," he reassured her. He wasn't worried about the baby's heart, but about its lungs. He prayed they would be mature enough to handle the chore of breathing, because he didn't have the equipment here to handle the situation if they couldn't. Some eight-month babies did just fine; others needed help. He looked out the window. It was snowing harder than ever, in a blinding sheet that blocked out the rest of the world but filled the house with a strange, white light. There was no way he could summon emergency help, and no way it could get here, even if the phones were working.

The minutes slipped away, marked by contractions that gradually grew stronger and closer together. He kept the fire built up, so the baby wouldn't be chilled when it finally made its appearance, and Kathleen's hair grew damp with sweat. She tugged at the neck of her turtleneck sweater. "It's so hot," she breathed. She felt as if she couldn't stand the confining fabric a minute longer.

"A nightgown wouldn't be much of an improvement," Derek said, and got one of his clean shirts from his luggage. She didn't make any protest when he removed her sweater and bra and slipped the thin, soft shirt around her. It was light, and much too big, and it felt wonderful after the smothering heat of the wool sweater. He rolled up the sleeves and fastened the buttons over her breasts, then dampened a washcloth in cool water and bathed her face.

It wouldn't be too much longer. He checked again to make certain he had everything he needed at hand. He had already sterilized his instruments and laid everything out on a gauze-covered tray.

"Well, sweetheart, are you about ready to get this

show on the road?" he asked as he examined her again.

The contractions were almost continuous now. She took a deep breath during a momentary lull. "Is it time?" she gasped.

"You're fully dilated now, but don't push until I tell you. Pant. That's right. Don't push, don't push."

She wanted to push. She desperately needed to push. Her body arched on the mattress, a monstrous pressure building in her, but his deep voice remained calm and controlled, somehow controlling her. She panted, and somehow, she didn't push. The wave of pain receded, the pressure eased, and for a moment she rested. Then it began again.

It couldn't last much longer; she couldn't bear it much longer. Tears seeped from her eyes.

"Here we go," he said with satisfaction. "I can see the head. You're crowning, sweetheart. It won't be but another minute. Let me make a little incision so you won't be torn—"

Kathleen barely heard him, barely felt him. The pressure was unbearable, blocking out everything else. "Push, sweetheart," he said, his tone suddenly authoritative.

She pushed. Dimly, she was astounded that her body was capable of exerting such pressure. She gave a thin cry, but barely heard it. Her world consisted only of a powerful force that squeezed her in its fist, that and the man who knelt at her spread knees, his calm voice telling her what to do.

Then, abruptly, the pressure eased, and she sank back, gasping for breath. He said, "I have the baby's head in my hand. My Lord, what a head of hair! Just rest a minute, sweetheart."

She heard a funny sound, and alarm brought her up on her elbows. "What's wrong?" she asked frantically. "What are you doing?"

"I'm suctioning out its mouth and nose," he said. "Just lie back—everything's all right." Then a thin, wavering wail rose, gaining in strength with every second, and he laughed. "That's right, tell us about it," he encouraged. "Push, sweetheart, our baby isn't too happy with the situation."

She pushed, straining, and suddenly she felt a rush, then a great sense of relief. Derek laughed again as he held a tiny but furious scrap of humanity in his hands. "I don't blame you a bit," he told the squalling infant, whose cries sounded ridiculously like those of a mewling kitten. "I wouldn't want to leave your soft, warm mommy, either, but you'll be wrapped up and cuddled in just a minute."

"What is it?" Kathleen whispered, falling back on the mattress.

"A beautiful little girl. She has more hair than any three babies should have."

"Is she all right?"

"She's perfect. She's tiny, but listen to her cry! Her lungs are working just fine."

"Can I hold her?"

"In just a minute. I'm almost finished here." The umbilical cord had gone limp, so he swiftly clamped and cut it, then lifted the squalling baby into her mother's anxious arms. Kathleen looked dazed, her eyes filling with tears as she examined her tiny daughter.

"Put her to your breast," Derek instructed softly, knowing that would calm the infant, but Kathleen didn't seem to hear him. He unbuttoned her shirt himself and pushed it aside to bare one full breast, then guided the baby's mouth to the rich-looking nipple. Still the baby squalled, its tiny body trembling; he'd have to do more than just give it a hint. "Come on, honey," he coaxed, reaching down to stroke the baby's cheek just beside her mouth. She turned her head reflexively, and he guided the nipple into her mouth. She squalled one more time, then suddenly seemed to realize what she was supposed to do, and the tiny mouth closed on her mother's breast.

Kathleen jumped. She hadn't even reacted to his touch on her breast, he realized, and looked closely at her. She was pale, with shadows under her eyes, and her dark hair was wet with perspiration. She was truly exhausted, not just from the physical difficulty of labor and giving birth, but from the hours of anxiety she'd suffered through. Yet there was something glowing in her face and eyes as she looked at her baby, and it lingered when she slowly looked up at him.

"We did it," she murmured, and smiled.

Derek looked down at her, at the love shining from her face like a beacon, and the attraction he'd felt for her from the start suddenly solidified inside him with a painful twist. Something about her made him want to hold her close, protect her from whatever had put that wary, distrustful look in her eyes. He wanted her to look at him with her face full of love.

Stunned, he sank back on his heels. It had finally happened, when he had least expected it and had even stopped looking for it, and with a woman who was merely tolerating his presence due to the circumstances. It wasn't just that she had other things on her mind right now; he could tell that Kathleen Fields wanted nothing to do with a man, any man. And yet the thunderbolt had hit him anyway, just as his mother had always warned him it would.

Teaching Kathleen to love wouldn't be easy, but Derek looked at her, and at the baby in her arms, and knew he wouldn't give up.

CHAPTER THREE

KATHLEEN COULDN'T REMEMBER ever being so tired before; her body was leaden with exhaustion, while her mind seemed to float, disconnected from the physical world. Only the baby in her arms seemed real. She was vaguely aware of the things Derek was doing to her, of the incredible confidence and gentleness of his hands, but it was as if he were doing them to someone else. Even the painful prick of the sutures he set didn't rouse her, nor did his firm massaging of her stomach. She simply lay there, too tired to care. When she was finally clean and wearing a gown, and the linen on the mattress had been changed, she sighed and went to sleep with the suddenness of a light being turned off.

She had no idea how long it was before he woke her, to lift her carefully to a sitting position and prop her against him while the baby nursed. He was literally holding both her and the baby, his strong arms supporting them. Her head lay on his broad shoulder, and she didn't have the strength to lift it. "I'm sorry," she murmured. "I can't seem to sit up."

"It's all right, sweetheart," he said, his deep voice reaching inside her and soothing all her vague worries. "You worked hard. You deserve to be a little lazy now."

"Is the baby all right?" she managed to mumble.

"She's eating like a pig," he said, his chuckle hiding his worry, and Kathleen went back to sleep as soon as he eased her back onto the mattress. She didn't even feel him lift the baby from her and refasten her gown.

Derek sat for a long time, cradling the baby in his arms. She was dangerously underweight, but she seemed remarkably strong for her size. She was breathing on her own and managing to suckle, which had been his two biggest worries, but she was still too tiny. He guessed her weight at about four pounds, too small for her to be able to regulate her own temperature because she simply didn't have the body fat necessary. Because of that, he had wrapped her warmly and kept the fire in the fireplace hotter than was comfortable.

His calm, golden brown eyes glowed as he looked down at her tiny face, dominated by the vague, huge blue eyes of the newborn. Premature infants had both an aged and a curiously ageless look to them, their doll-like faces lacking cuddly baby fat, which revealed their facial structure in a fragile gauntness. Even so, he could tell she was going to be a beauty, with her mother's features and even the same thick, black hair.

Every one of his tiny, frail patients got to him, but this stubborn little fighter had reached into his heart. Maybe it was because he could look at her and see her mother in her, because Kathleen was a fighter, too. She had to be; it wasn't easy to go through a pregnancy alone, as she obviously had. And when she had gone into labor too early, instead of remaining here where *she* would be safer, she had risked her own life in an effort to get to the clinic where her baby could have medical care.

He couldn't help wondering about the absent Mr. Fields, and for the first time in his life he felt jealousy burning him, because the unknown man had been, at least for a while, the recipient of Kathleen's love. Derek also wondered what had happened to put that wariness in her eyes and build the walls in her mind. He knew they were there; he could sense them. They made him want to put his arms around her and rock her, comfort her, but he knew she wouldn't welcome his closeness.

The baby squeaked, and he looked down to see that her eyes were open and she was looking at him with the intensely focused expression of someone with bad eyesight. He chuckled and cuddled her closer. "What is it, honey?" he crooned. "Hungry again?" Because her stomach was so small, she needed far more frequent feedings than a normal newborn.

He glanced over at Kathleen, who was still sleeping heavily. An idea began to form. One of Derek's characteristics, and one that had often made his mother feel as if she were dealing with an irresistible force rather than a child, was his ability to set long-term goals and let nothing sway him from his course. When he wanted something, he went after it. And now he wanted Kathleen. He had been instantly attracted to her, his interest sparked by the mysterious but undeniable chemical reaction that kept animals mating and procreating; humans were no exception, and his own libido was healthy. Her pregnancy hadn't weakened his attraction, but rather strengthened it in a primitive way.

Then, during the process of labor and giving birth, the attraction had changed, had been transmitted into an emotional force as well as a physical one. They had been a team, despite Kathleen's reserve. The baby had become his; he was responsible for her life, her welfare. She had exited her mother's warm body into his hands. He had seen her, held her, laughed at her furious squalling, and put her to her mother's breast. She was, undeniably, *his*. Now his goal was to make the baby's mother his, too. He wanted Kathleen to look at him with the same fiercely tender love she'd shown to her child. He wanted to father the next infant that grew inside her. He wanted to make her laugh, to ease the distrust in her eyes, to make her face shine with happiness.

No doubt about it, he'd have to marry her.

The baby squeaked again, more demandingly. "All right, we'll wake Mommy up," he promised. "You'll help with my plan, won't you? Between the two of us, we'll take such good care of her that she'll forget she was ever unhappy."

He woke Kathleen before the baby began to squall in earnest, and carefully propped her in a sitting position so she could nurse the child. She was still groggy, but seemed more alert than she had before. She held the baby to her breast, stroking the satiny cheek with one finger as she stared down at her daughter. "What time is it?" she asked dreamily.

He shifted his position so he could see his wristwatch. "Almost nine."

"Is that all? I feel as if I've been asleep for hours."

He laughed. "You have, sweetheart. You were worn out."

Kathleen's clear green eyes turned up to him. "Is she doing all right?"

The baby chose that moment to slurp as the nipple momentarily slipped from her lips. Frantically the tiny rosebud mouth sought the beading nipple again, and when she found it she made a squeaky little grunting noise. The two adults laughed, looking down at her.

"She's strong for her size," Derek said, reaching

down to lift the miniscule hand that lay on Kathleen's ivory, blue-veined breast. It was such a tiny hand, the palm no bigger than a dime, but the fingernails were perfectly formed and a nice pink color. Sweat trickled at his temple, and he could see a fine sheen on Kathleen's chest, but at least the baby was warm enough.

Kathleen tried to sit up away from him, her eyes sharpening as she considered his reply, but her body protested the movement, and with a quiet moan she sank back against his muscled chest. "What do you mean, she's strong for her size? Is she doing all right or not?"

"She needs an incubator," he said, wrapping his arm around Kathleen and supporting her soft weight. "That's why I'm keeping it so hot in here. She's too small for her body to regulate its own temperature."

Kathleen's face was suddenly white and tense. She had thought everything was fine, despite the baby being a month early. The sudden knowledge that the baby was still in a precarious position stunned her.

"Don't worry," Derek soothed, cradling her close to him. "As long as we keep her nice and warm, she shouldn't have any trouble. I'll keep a close watch on her tonight, and as soon as the weather clears we'll get her to a cozy incubator." He studied the fragile little hand for a moment longer, then tenderly replaced it on Kathleen's breast. "What are you going to name her?"

"Sara Marisa," Kathleen murmured. "Sara is—was—my mother's name. But I'm going to call her Risa. It means 'laughter.'"

Derek's face went still, and his eyes darkened with barely contained emotion as he looked at the baby. "How are you spelling it? S-a-r-a or S-a-r-a-h?"

"S-a-r-a."

It was still the same name, the name that had become synonymous, in his mind, with love. He had first seen mind-shattering, irrevocable love in Sarah Matthews's face when he had been fifteen, and he had known then that he would never settle for anything less. That was what he wanted to feel, what he wanted to give, what he wanted in return. Sarah's love was a powerful, immense thing, spilling over into the lives of everyone near her, because she gave it so unselfishly. It was because of her that he was a doctor now, because of her that he had been able to finish college at an accelerated pace, because of her that he had a warm, loving extended family when before there had been only himself and his mother. Now this new life was leading him into the sort of love he'd waited for, so it was only fitting that she should be named Sara. He smiled when he thought of Sara holding her namesake. She and her husband, Rome, could be the baby's godparents, though they'd probably have to share the honor with Max and Claire Conroy, two other very special friends and part of the extended family. He knew how they would all take to Kathleen and the baby, but he wondered how Kathleen would feel, surrounded by all those loving strangers. Anxious? Threatened?

It would take time to teach Kathleen to love him, and all the people who were close to him, but he had all the time in the world. He had the rest of his life.

The baby was asleep now, and gently he took her from Kathleen's arms. "Risa," he murmured, trying her name on his tongue. Yes, the two of them together would overwhelm Kathleen with love.

Kathleen dozed on and off the rest of the night, and every time she woke she saw Derek with her daughter in his arms. The picture of the tall, strong man holding the frail infant with such tender concern gave her a feeling she couldn't identify, as if something expanded in her chest. He didn't let down his guard for a minute all night, but kept vigil over the child, kept the room uncomfortably warm, and held Kathleen so she could nurse her whenever that funny, indignant little squeak told them the baby was getting hungry. Sometime during the night he removed his shirt, and when she woke the next time she was stunned by the primitive beauty of the picture he made, sitting crosslegged before the fire, the powerful muscles of his damp torso gleaming as he cuddled the sleeping baby to him.

It struck her then that he wasn't like other men, but she was too sleepy and too tired to pursue the thought. Her entire body ached, and she was in the grip of a powerful lassitude that kept her thoughts and movements down to a minimum. Tomorrow would be time enough to think.

It stopped snowing around dawn, and the wild, whistling wind died away. It was the pale silence that woke her for good, and she gingerly eased herself into a sitting position, wincing at the pain in her lower body. Derek laid the baby on the mattress and reached out a strong arm to help her.

"I have to go—" she began, stopping abruptly as she wondered how she could phrase the urgent need to a stranger.

"It's about time," he said equably, carefully lifting her in his arms.

Her face turned scarlet as he carried her down the dark, narrow hallway. "I don't need any help!" she protested.

He set her on her feet outside the bathroom door and held her until her legs stopped wobbling. "I put a couple of candles in here last night," he said. "I'll light them, then get out of your way, but I'll be just outside the door if you need me."

She realized that he didn't intend to embarrass her, but neither was he going to let her do more than he deemed wise. There was a calm implacability in his face that told her he wouldn't hesitate to come to her aid if she became too weak to take care of herself. It was difficult to remember that he was a doctor, used to bodies of all sizes and shapes. He just didn't seem like any doctor she'd ever met before.

To her relief, her strength was returning, and she didn't need his help. When she left the bathroom, she walked down the hall under her own power, though he kept a steadying hand under her arm just in case. The baby was still sleeping peacefully on the mattress, and Kathleen looked down at her daughter with a powerful surge of adoration that shook her.

"She's so beautiful," she whispered. "Is she doing okay?"

"She's doing fine, but she needs an incubator until she gains about a pound and a half. The way she's been nursing, that might take only a couple of weeks."

"A couple of weeks!" Kathleen echoed, aghast. "She needs hospital care for a couple of weeks?"

His eyes were steady. "Yes."

Kathleen turned away, her fists knotting. There was no way she could pay what two weeks in a hospital would cost, yet she couldn't see that she had a choice. Risa's life was still a fragile thing, and she would do anything, anything at all, to keep her child alive.

"Does the clinic that you were going to have the facilities to care for her?" he asked.

Another problem. She swallowed. "No. I...I don't have any medical insurance. I was going to have her there, then come home afterward."

"Don't worry about it," he said. "I'll think of something. Now, sweetheart, lie down and let me take a look at you. I want to make sure *you're* doing all right."

It had been bad enough the day before, when she was in labor, but it was worse now. It had been a medical emergency then; now it wasn't. But, again, she had the feeling he would do exactly as he intended, regardless of any objections she raised, so she stared fixedly at the fire as he examined her and firmly kneaded her abdomen.

"You have good muscle tone," he said approvingly. "You'd have had a lot harder time if you hadn't been as strong as you are."

If she was strong, it was the strength given by years of working a small grubby ranch, then long hours of waiting on tables. Spas and gyms were outside her experience.

"What do we do now?" she asked. "Wait?"

"Nope. You're doing well enough to travel, and we can't afford to sit around until the phones are fixed. I'm going to start the Jeep and get it warm, and then I'm taking both you and the baby to a hospital."

She felt instant panic. "You want to take the baby *out?*"

"We have to. We'll keep her warm."

"We can keep her warm here."

"She needs a hospital. She's doing all right now, but things can change in the blink of an eye with a preemie. I'm not going to take that chance with her life."

Kathleen couldn't control a mother's natural fear of exposing her fragile child to the elements. There was no telling which roads were closed, or how long it would take them to reach a hospital. What if they ran off the road again and got in a wreck?

Seeing her panic build, Derek reached out and firmly took her hand. "I won't let anything happen," he said calmly, as if he had read her thoughts. "Get dressed while I start the Jeep and fix something for breakfast. Aren't you hungry? You haven't eaten a bite since I found you yesterday."

Only then did she realize how empty she was; it was odd, how even the thought of hunger had been pushed from her mind by all that happened. She changed in her icy bedroom, hurriedly pulling on first one pair of pants after another, and growing more and more frustrated as she found that they were too small. Finally she settled on one of the first pairs of maternity pants she had bought, when she had been outgrowing her jeans. Her own body was unfamiliar to her. It felt strange not to have a swollen, cumbersome stomach, strange to actually look down and see her toes. She had to move carefully, but she could put on socks and shoes without twisting into awkward contortions. Still, she didn't have her former slenderness, and it was disconcerting.

After pulling on a white cotton shirt and layering

a flannel shirt over it, she pulled a brush through her tangled hair and left the bedroom, too cold to linger and worry about her looks. Wryly, she admitted that he had successfully distracted her from her arguments; she had done exactly as he'd ordered.

When she entered the kitchen, he looked up from his capable preparations of soup and sandwiches to smile at her. "Feel strange not wearing maternity clothes?"

"I am wearing maternity clothes," she said, a faint, very feminine despair in her eyes and voice. "What feels strange is being able to see my feet." Changing the subject, she asked, "Is it terribly cold outside?"

"It's about twenty degrees, but the sky is clearing."

"What hospital are you taking us to?"

"I've thought about that. I want Risa in my hospital in Dallas."

"Dallas! But that's—"

"I can oversee her care there," Derek interrupted calmly.

"It's too far away," Kathleen said, standing straight. Her green eyes were full of bitter acknowledgment. "And I won't be able to pay. Just take us to a charity hospital."

"Don't worry about paying. I told you I'd take care of you."

"It's still charity, but I'd rather owe a hospital than you."

"You won't owe me." He turned from the old wood stove, and suddenly she felt the full force of his golden brown gaze, fierce and compelling, bending her to his will. "Not if you marry me."

CHAPTER FOUR

THE WORDS RESOUNDED in her head like the ringing of a bell. "Marry you?"

"That's right."

"But...*why?*"

"You'll marry me so Risa can have the care she needs. I'll marry you so I can have Risa. You're not in love with someone, are you?" Numbly she shook her head. "I didn't think so. I guess I fell in love with your daughter the minute she came out of you, into my hands. I want to be her father."

"I don't want to get married again, ever!"

"Not even for Risa? If you marry me, you won't have to worry about money again. I'll sign a prenuptial agreement, if you'd like. I'll provide for her, put her through college."

"You can't marry me just because you want my baby. Get married to someone else and have your own children."

"I want Risa," he said with that calm, frightening implacability. Alarm began to fill her as she realized that he never swerved from the course he had set for himself.

"Think, Kathleen. She needs help now, and children need a lot of support through the years. Am I such a monster that you can't stand the thought of being married to me?"

"But you're a stranger! I don't know you and you don't know me. How can you even think of marrying me?"

"I know that you loved your child enough to risk your own life trying to get to the clinic. I know you've had some bad luck in your life, but that you're strong, and you don't give up. We delivered a baby together. How can we be strangers now?"

"I don't know anything about your life."

He shrugged his broad shoulders. "I have a fairly uncomplicated life. I'm a doctor, I live in an apartment, and I'm not a social lion. I'm great with kids, and I won't mistreat you."

"I never thought you would," she said quietly. She had been mistreated, and she knew that Derek was as different from her ex-husband as day was from night. But she simply didn't want another man in her life at all, ever. "What if you fall in love with someone else? Wouldn't that tear Risa's life apart? I'd never give up custody of her!"

"I won't fall in love with anybody else." His voice rang with utter certainty. He just stood there, watching her, but his eyes were working their power on her. Incredibly, she could feel herself weakening inside. As his wife, she wouldn't have the bitter, day after day after day struggle simply to survive. Risa would have the hospital care she needed, and afterward she would have all the advantages Kathleen couldn't give her.

"I couldn't…I couldn't have sex with you," she finally said in desperation, because it was her last defense.

"I wouldn't want you to." Before she could decide if she should feel relieved or insulted, he continued, "When we sleep together, I want you to think of it as making love, not having sex. Sex is cheap and easy. Making love means caring and commitment."

"And you think we'll have that?"

"In time." He gave her a completely peaceful smile, as if he sensed her weakening and knew he would have things his way.

Her throat grew tight as she thought about having sex. She didn't know what making love was, and she didn't know if she would ever *want* to know. "Things…have happened to me," she said hoarsely. "I may not ever—"

"In time, sweetheart. You will, in time."

His very certainty frightened her, because there was something about him that abruptly made her just as certain that, at some point in the future, she would indeed want him to make love to her. The idea was alien to her, making her feel as if her entire life had suddenly been rerouted onto another track. She had had everything planned in her mind: she would raise Risa, totally devoted to her only child, and take pleasure in watching her grow. But there was no room for a man in her plans. Larry Fields had done her a tremendous favor by leaving her, even if he had left her broke and pregnant. But now, here was this man who looked like a warrior angel, taking over her life and shaping it along other lines.

Desperately she tried again. "We're too different! You're a doctor, and I barely finished high school. I've lived on this scrubby little ranch my entire life. I've never been anywhere or done anything—you'd be bored to death by me within a month!"

Amusement sparkled in his amber eyes as he walked over to her. "You're talking rubbish," he said gently, his hand sliding under her heavy hair to clasp her nape. Before she could react he had bent and firmly pressed his mouth to hers in a warm, strangely intimate kiss; then he released her and moved away before she could become alarmed. She stood there staring at him, her vivid green eyes huge and confused.

"Say yes, then let's eat," he commanded, his eyes still sparkling.

"Yes." Her voice sounded dazed, even to herself.

"That's a good girl." He put his warm hand on her elbow and led her to the table, then carefully got her seated. She was uncomfortable, but was not in such pain that it killed her appetite. Hungrily they ate chicken noodle soup and toasted cheese sandwiches, washed down with good strong coffee. It wasn't normal breakfast fare, but after not eating for so long, she was delighted with it. Then he insisted that she sit still while he cleaned up the kitchen, something that had never happened to her before. She felt pampered, and dazed by all that had happened and she had agreed to.

"I'll pack a few of your clothes and nightgowns, but you won't need much," he said. "Where are the baby's things?"

"In the bottom drawer of my dresser, but some of her clothes are in the truck. I didn't think to get them yesterday when you stopped."

"We'll pick them up on the way. Come into the living room with the baby while I get everything loaded."

She held the sleeping child while he swiftly packed and carried the things out. When he had finished, he brought a tiny, crocheted baby cap that he'd found in the drawer, and put it on Risa's downy head to help keep her warm. Then he wrapped her snugly in several blankets, helped Kathleen into her heavy coat, put the baby in Kathleen's arms, and lifted both of them into his.

"I can walk," she protested, her heart giving a huge leap at being in his arms again. He had kissed her....

"No going up or down steps just yet," he explained. "And no climbing into the Jeep. Keep Risa's face covered."

He was remarkably strong, carrying her with no evident difficulty. His strides were sure as he waded through the snow, avoiding the path he'd already made because it had become icy. Kathleen blinked at the stark whiteness of the landscape. The wind had blown the snow into enormous drifts that almost obliterated the fence line and had piled against the sides of the house and barn. But the air was still and crisp now, the fog of her breath gushing straight out in front of her.

He had turned the heater in the Jeep on high, and it was uncomfortably warm for her. "I'll have to take off this coat," she muttered.

"Wait until we've stopped to get the things out of your truck or you'll get chilled with the door open."

She watched as he went back inside to bank the fires in the fireplace and the wood stove, and to lock the doors. She had lived in this house her entire life, but suddenly she wondered if she'd ever see it again, and if she cared. Her life here hadn't been happy.

Her confusion and hesitancy faded as if they had never been. This place wasn't what she wanted for Risa. For her daughter, she wanted so much more than what she had had. She didn't want Risa to wear patched and faded clothes, to marry out of desperation, or to miss out on the pleasures of life because all her free time was spent on chores.

Derek was taking her away from this, but she wouldn't rely on him. She had made the mistake of relying on a man once before, and she wouldn't do it again. Kathleen decided that as soon as she had recovered from giving birth, and Risa was stronger, she would get a job, save her money, work to better herself. If Derek ever walked away from her as Larry had done, she wouldn't be left stone broke and without the means to support herself. Risa would never have to go hungry or cold.

FIVE HOURS LATER, Kathleen was lying on a snowy-white hospital bed, watching the color television attached to the wall. Her private room was almost luxurious, with a full bath and a pair of comfortable recliners, small oil paintings on the wall, and fresh flowers on her bedside table. The snowstorms hadn't reached as far south as Dallas, and from the window she could see a blue sky only occasionally studded with clouds.

Risa had been whisked away to the neonatal unit, with people jumping to obey Derek's orders. Kathleen herself had been examined by a cheerful obstetrician named Monica Sudley and pronounced in excellent condition. "But I never expected anything different," Dr. Sudley had said casually. "Not with Dr. Taliferro taking care of you."

Dr. Taliferro. Her mind had accepted him as a doctor, but somehow she hadn't really understood it until she had seen him here, in his own milieu, where his deep voice took on a crisp tone of command, and everyone scrambled to satisfy him. She had only seen him wearing jeans and boots and a casual shirt, with his heavy shearling coat, but after arriving at the hospital he had showered and shaved, then changed into the fresh clothes he kept in his office for just such situations. He had seen to Risa, then visited Kathleen to reassure her that the trip hadn't harmed the infant in any way.

He had been the same, yet somehow different. Perhaps it was only the clothes, the dark slacks, white shirt and blue-striped tie, as well as the lab coat he wore over them and the stethoscope around his neck. It was typical doctor's garb, but the effect was jarring. She couldn't help remembering the firelight flickering on his gleaming, muscled shoulders, or the hard, chiseled purity of his profile as he looked down at the child in his arms.

It was also hard to accept the fact that she had agreed to marry him.

Every few hours she put on a robe and walked to the neonatal unit, where Risa was taken out of the incubator and given to her to be fed. The sight of the other frail babies, some of them much smaller than Risa, shook her. They were enclosed in their little glass cubicles with various tubes running into their tiny naked bodies, while little knit caps covered their heads. Thank God Risa was strong enough to nurse!

The first time she fed her daughter, she was led to a rocking chair in a small room away from the other babies, and Risa was brought to her.

"So you're the mother of this little honey," the young nurse said as she laid Risa in Kathleen's eager arms. "She's adorable. I've never seen so much hair on a newborn, and look how long it is! Dr. Taliferro had us scrambling like we were having an air raid until we had her all comfy. Did he really deliver her?"

Faint color burned along Kathleen's cheekbones. Somehow it seemed too intimate to discuss, even though giving birth was an everyday occurrence to the staff. But the young nurse was looking at her with bright, expectant eyes, so she said uncomfortably, "Yes. My truck slid off the road during the blizzard. Derek came by and found me."

"Ohmigod, talk about romantic!"

"Having a baby?" Kathleen asked skeptically.

"Honey, digging ditches would be romantic if Dr. Taliferro helped! Isn't he something? All the babies know whenever he's the one holding them. They never get scared or cry with him. Sometimes he stays here all night with a critical baby, holding it and talking to it, watching it every minute, and a lot of his babies make it when no one else gave them much of a chance."

The nurse seemed to have a case of hero worship for Derek, or maybe it was more than that. He was incredibly good-looking, and a hospital was a hothouse for romances. It made Kathleen uneasy; why was she even thinking of marrying a man who would constantly be pursued and tempted?

"Have you worked in this unit for long?" she asked, trying to change the subject.

"A little over a year. I love it. These little tykes need all the help they can get, and, of course, I'd have walked barefoot over hot coals to get to work with Dr. Taliferro. Hospitals and clinics from all over the nation were fighting to get him."

"Why? Isn't he too young to have built a reputation yet?" She didn't know how old he was, but guessed he was no older than his midthirties, perhaps even younger.

"He's younger than most of them, but he finished college when he was nineteen. He graduated from med school at the top of his class, interned at one of the nation's best trauma centers, then studied neonatal medicine with George Oliver, who's also one of the best. He's thirty-two, I think."

It was odd to learn so much about her future husband from a stranger, and odder still to find he was considered a medical genius, one of those rare doctors whose very name on the staff listing gave a hospital instant credibility. To hide her expression, she looked down at Risa and gently stroked the baby's cheek. "He sat up all night holding Risa," she heard herself say in a strange voice.

The nurse smiled. "He would. And he's still on the floor now, when he should be home sleeping. But that's Dr. Taliferro for you—he puts the babies before himself."

When Kathleen was back in her room, she kept thinking of the things the nurse had told her, and of the things Derek had said to her. He wanted Risa, he'd said. Was that reason enough to marry a woman he didn't love, when he could marry any woman he wanted and have his own children? Of course, he'd also said that eventually he expected to have a normal marriage with her, meaning he intended to sleep with her, so she had to assume he also intended to have children with her. But why was he so certain he'd never fall in love with someone and want out of the marriage?

"Problems?"

The deep, quiet voice startled her, and she looked up to find Derek standing just inside the door, watching her. She'd been so engrossed in her thoughts that she hadn't heard him.

"No, no problems. I was just…thinking."

"Worrying, you mean. Forget about all your second thoughts," he said with disquieting perception. "Just trust me, and let me handle everything. I've made arrangements for us to be married as soon as you're released from the hospital."

"So soon?" she gasped.

"Is there any reason to wait? You'll need a place to live, so you might as well live with me."

"But what about blood tests—"

"The lab here will handle them. When you're released, we'll get our marriage license and go straight to a judge who's an old friend of mine. My apartment is near here, so it'll be convenient for you to come back and forth to feed Risa until she's released. We can use the time to get a nursery set up for her."

She felt helpless. As he'd said, he had handled everything.

CHAPTER FIVE

KATHLEEN FELT AS IF she'd been swept up by a tornado, and this one was named Derek. Everything went the way he directed. He even had a dress for her to wear for the wedding, a lovely blue-green silk that darkened her eyes to emerald, as well as a scrumptious black fake-fur coat, shoes, underwear, even makeup. A hairdresser came to the hospital that morning and fixed her hair in a chic, upswept style. Yes, he had everything under control. It was almost frightening.

He kept his warm hand firmly on her waist as they got the marriage license, then went to the judge's chamber to be married. There, Kathleen got another surprise: the chamber was crowded with people, all of whom seemed ridiculously delighted that Derek was marrying a woman he didn't love.

His mother and stepfather were there; dazedly, Kathleen wondered what his mother must think of all this. But Marcie, as she had insisted Kathleen call her, was beaming with delight as she hugged Kathleen. There were two other couples, two teenagers and three younger children. One of the couples consisted of a tall, hard-looking man with graying black hair and a wand-slender woman with almost silver-white hair and glowing green eyes. Derek introduced them as Rome and Sarah Matthews, very good friends of his, but something in his voice hinted at a deeper relationship. Sarah's face was incredibly tender as she hugged him, then Kathleen.

The other couple was Max and Claire Conroy, and again Kathleen got the feeling that Derek meant something special to them. Max was aristocratic and incredibly handsome, with gilded hair and turquoise eyes, while Claire was quieter and more understated, but her soft brown eyes didn't miss a thing. The three youngsters belong to the Conroys, while the two teenagers were Rome and Sarah's children.

Everyone was ecstatic that Derek was marrying, and Marcie couldn't wait to get to the hospital to visit her new grandchild. She scolded Derek severely for not contacting her immediately, but stopped in mid-tirade when he leaned down and kissed her cheek, smiling at her in that serene way of his. "I know. You had a good reason," she sighed.

"Yes, Mother."

"You'd think I'd eventually learn."

He grinned. "Yes, Mother."

The women all wore corsages, and Sarah pressed an arrangement of orchids into Kathleen's hands. Kathleen held the fragile flowers in shaking fingers as she and Derek stood before the judge, whose quiet voice filled the silent chamber as he spoke the traditional words about love and honor. She could feel the heat of Derek's body beside her, like a warm wall she could lean against if she became tired. They made the proper responses, and Derek was sliding a gold band set with an emerald surrounded by small, glittering diamonds on her finger. She blinked at it in surprise, then looked up at him just as the judge pronounced them man and wife, and Derek leaned down to kiss her.

She had expected the sort of brief, warm kiss he had given her before. She wasn't prepared for the way he molded her lips with his, or the passion evident in the way his tongue probed her mouth. She quivered, her hands going up to grab his shoulders in an effort to steady herself. His hard arms pressed her to him for a moment, then slowly released her as he lifted his head. Purely male satisfaction was gleaming in his eyes, and she knew he'd felt her surprised response to him.

Then everyone was surrounding them, laughing and shaking his hand, and there was a lot of kissing and hugging. Even the judge got hugged and kissed.

Half an hour later Derek called a halt to the festivities. "We'll have a real celebration later," he promised. "Right now, I'm taking Kathleen home to rest. We have to be back at the hospital in a couple of hours to feed Risa, so she doesn't have a lot of time to put her feet up."

"I'm fine," she felt obliged to protest, though in truth she would have appreciated the chance to rest.

Derek gave her a stern look, and she felt inexplicably guilty. Sarah laughed. "You might as well do what he says," the older woman said in gentle amusement. "You can't get around him."

Five minutes later Kathleen was sitting in the Jeep as he expertly threaded his way through the Dallas traffic. "I like your friends," she finally said, just to break the silence. She couldn't believe she'd done it; she had actually married him! "What do they do?"

"Rome is president and CEO of Spencer-Nyle Corporation. Sarah owns Tools and Dyes, a handcraft store. Two stores now, since she just opened another one. Max was a vice president at Spencer-Nyle with Rome, but about five years ago he started his own consulting business. Claire owns a bookstore."

His friends were obviously very successful, and she wondered again why he had married her, because she wasn't successful at all. How would she ever fit in? "And your mother?" she asked quietly.

"Mother helps Whit run his ranch, just across the Oklahoma border. I'd spent Christmas with them, and was on the way back to Dallas when I found you," he explained.

She didn't have anything else to ask him, so silence reigned again until they reached his apartment. "We'll look for something bigger in a few weeks, after your doctor releases you," he said as they left the elevator. "I've shoved things around and made closet space, but feel free to tell me to rearrange anything else you'd like moved."

"Why should I change anything?"

"To accommodate you and Risa. I'm not a bachelor any longer. I'm a husband and a father. We're a family—this is your home as much as mine."

He said it so simply, as if he were impervious to all the doubts that assailed her. She stood to the side as he unlocked the door, but before she could move to enter the apartment he turned back to her and swept her up in his arms, then carried her across the threshold. The gesture startled her, but then, everything he'd done that day had startled her. Everything he'd done from the moment she met him had startled her.

"Would you like a nap?" he asked, standing in the foyer with her still in his arms, as if awaiting directions.

"No, just sitting down for a while will do it." She managed a smile for him. "I had a baby, not major surgery, and you said yourself that I'm strong. Why should I act like a wilting lily when I'm not?"

He cleared his throat as he carefully placed her on her feet. "Actually, I said that you have great muscle tone. I don't believe I was admiring your strength."

Her pulse leaped. He was doing that to her more and more often, saying little things that made it plain he found her desirable, or stealing some of those quick kisses. Five days earlier she would never have found those small advances anything but repulsive, but already a secret thrill warmed her whenever he said or did anything. She was changing rapidly under his intense coddling, and, to her surprise, she liked the changes.

"What are you thinking?" he asked, tapping her nose with a fingertip. "You're staring at me, but you aren't seeing me."

"I was thinking how much you spoil me," she replied honestly. "And how unlike me it is to let you do it."

"Why shouldn't you let me spoil you?" He helped her off with her coat and hung it in the small foyer closet.

"I've never been spoiled before. I've always had to look out for myself, because no one else really cared, not even my parents. I can't figure out why you should be so kind, or what you're getting out of our deal. You've done all this, but basically we're still strangers. What do you want from me?"

A faint smile touched his chiseled lips as he held out his hand. "Come with me."

"Where?"

"To the bedroom. I want to show you something."

Lifting her brows in curiosity at his manner, Kathleen put her hand in his and let him lead her to the bedroom. She looked around. It was a cheerful, spacious room, decorated in blue and white and with a king-size bed. The sliding closet doors were mirrored, and he positioned her in front of the mirrors with himself behind her.

Putting his hands on her shoulders, he said, "Look in the mirror and tell me what you see."

"Us."

"Is that all? Look at yourself, and tell me what I got out of our deal."

She looked in the mirror and shrugged. "A woman." Humor suddenly sparked in her eyes. "With great muscle tone."

He chuckled. "Hallelujah, yes. But that's only part of it. That's not to say I'm not turned on by your fantastic legs and gorgeous breasts, because I am, but what really gets me is what I see in your face."

He'd done it again. She felt her entire body grow warm as her eyes met his in the mirror. "My face?"

One arm slid around her waist, pulling her back to lean against him, while his other hand rose to stroke her face. "Your wonderful green eyes," he murmured. "Frightened and brave at the same time. I sometimes see hurt in your eyes, as if you're remembering things you don't want to talk about, but you don't let it get you down. You don't ask me for anything, so I have to guess at what you need, and maybe I overdo it. I see pleasure when I hold you or kiss you. I see love for Risa, and compassion for the other babies. I've turned your life upside down, but you haven't let it get to you. You've just gone along with me and kept your head above water. You're a survivor, Kath. A strong, valiant, loving survivor. That's what I got out of the deal. As well as a great body, of course, and a beautiful baby girl."

The eyes he had described were wide as Kathleen heard all those characteristics attributed to herself. He smiled and let his fingers touch her lips. "Did I forget to mention what a kissable mouth you have? How sweet and soft it is?"

Her mouth suddenly felt swollen, and her lips moved against his fingers. "I get the picture," she breathed, her heart pounding at her aggressiveness. "You married me for my body."

"And what a body it is." He bent his head to nuzzle her ear, while his hands drifted to her breasts and gently cupped them. "While we're being so honest, why did you marry me? Other than to give Risa all the advantages of being a doctor's daughter."

"That was it," she said, barely able to speak. She was stunned by his touch to her breasts, stunned and scared and shocked, because she was aware of a sense of pleasure. Never before had she enjoyed having a man touch her so intimately. But her breasts were sensitive now, ripe and full of milk, and his light touch seared through her like a lightning bolt.

"Forget about what I can give Risa," he murmured. "Wasn't part of your reason for marrying me because of what I can give you?"

"I...I can live without luxury." Her voice was low and strained, and her eyelids were becoming so heavy she could barely hold them open. Her mind wasn't on what she was saying. The pleasure was so intense it was interfering with her breathing, making it fast and heavy. Frantically she tried to tell herself it was only because she *was* nursing Risa that her breasts were so warm and sensitive, and that, being a doctor, he knew it and how to exploit it. He wasn't even touching her nipples, but lightly stroking around them. She thought she would die if he touched her nipples.

"You look gorgeous in this dress, but let's get you out of it and into something more comfortable," he whispered, and his hands left her breasts. She stood pliantly, dazed with pleasure, as he unzipped the lovely dress and slipped it off her shoulders, then pushed it down over her hips to let it fall at her feet. She wore a slip under it, and she waited in a haze for him to remove it, too, but instead he lifted her in his arms and placed her on the bed, moving slowly, as if trying not to startle her. Her heart was pounding, but her body felt liquid with pleasure. She had just had a baby; he knew she couldn't let him do *that*…didn't he? But he was a doctor; perhaps he knew more than she did. No, it would hurt too much.

Perhaps he had something else in mind. She thought of his hands on her naked skin, of feeling his big, muscled body naked against her, and a strange excitement made her nerves throb. Slowly the thought filled her mind that she trusted him, truly trusted him, and that was why she wasn't afraid. No matter what, Derek would never hurt her.

His eyelashes were half-lowered over his eyes, giving him a sensually sleepy look as he slipped her shoes off and let them drop to the floor. Kathleen watched him in helpless fascination, her breath stilling in her lungs when he reached up under her slip and began pulling her panty hose down. "Lift your hips," he instructed in a husky voice, and she obeyed willingly. When the nylon was bunched around her knees, he bent and pressed a kiss to her bare thighs before returning to his pleasant task and removing the garment.

Her skin felt hot, and the bed linens were cool beneath her. She had never *felt* so much before, as if the nerve endings in her skin had multiplied and become incredibly sensitive. Her limbs felt heavy and boneless, and she couldn't move, even when his hands stroked her thighs and pleasure shivered through her. "Derek," she whispered, vaguely surprised to find that she could barely speak; she had slurred his name, as if it were too much effort to talk.

"Hmm?" He was bent over her, the warmth of his body soothing her as he lifted her with one arm and stripped the cover back on the bed, then settled her between the sheets. His mouth feathered over her breasts, barely touching the silk that covered them.

Incredible waves of relaxation were sweeping over

her. "You can't make love to me," she managed to whisper. "Not yet."

"I know, sweetheart," he murmured, his deep voice low and hypnotic. "Go to sleep. We have plenty of time."

Her lashes fluttered down, and with a slow, deep sigh she went to sleep. Derek straightened, looking down at her. His body throbbed with the need for sexual relief, but a faint, tender smile curved his lips as he watched her. She had called it "sex" before, but this time she had said "make love." She was losing her wariness, though she still seemed to have no idea why he had married her. Did she think she was so totally without charm or appeal? Did she truly think he'd married her only because of Risa? He'd done his best to convince her that he was attracted to her, but the final argument would have to wait about five weeks longer.

Her thick lashes made dark fans on her cheeks, just as Risa's did. He wanted to lie down beside her and hold her while she slept. He'd known she was tired; since Risa's birth, Kathleen had been sleeping a great deal, as if she had been pushing herself far too hard for far too long. Her body was insisting on catching up on its healing rest now that she no longer had such a pressing need to do everything herself.

The telephone in the living room rang, but he'd had the foresight to unplug the phone by the bed, so Kathleen slept on undisturbed. Quickly he left the room, closing the door behind him, and picked up the other extension.

"Derek, is she asleep yet?" Sarah's warm voice held a certain amusement, as if she had known he would somehow have gotten Kathleen to take a nap by now.

He grinned. Sarah knew him even better than his mother, better than anyone else in the world, except perhaps Claire. Claire saw into people, but she was so quiet it was easy to underestimate her perception.

"She didn't think she needed a nap, but she went to sleep as soon as she lay down."

"Somehow, I never doubted it. Anyway, I've had an idea. Now that I've opened up the other store, I need to hire someone else. Do you think Kathleen would be interested? Erica is going to manage the new store, so I thought Kathleen could work with me, and she'd be able to have the baby with her."

Leave it to Sarah to notice that Kathleen needed a friend, as well as the measure of independence the job would give her while she adjusted to being his wife.

"She'll probably jump at it, but it'll be a couple of weeks before she's able to drive, and at least that long before Risa will be strong enough."

"Then I'll hold the job for her," Sarah said serenely.

"I'm going to remind you of this the next time

you accuse me of 'managing' people," he informed her, smiling.

"But hadn't you already thought of it?"

His smile grew. "Of course."

CHAPTER SIX

THE DAY THEY brought Risa home from the hospital, Kathleen could barely tolerate having the baby out of her sight for a moment. Risa was thirteen days old, and now weighed a grand total of five pounds and six ounces, which was still two ounces short of the five and a half pounds a baby normally had to weigh before Derek would allow it to be released from the neonatal unit, but, as he'd noted before, she was strong. Her cheeks had attained a newborn's plumpness, and she was nursing vigorously, with about four hours between each feeding.

Derek drove them home, then left the Cherokee with Kathleen so she would have a way of getting around if she needed anything, a gesture that eased a worry she hadn't known she had until he gave her the keys. The hospital was only a few blocks away, and the January day was mild, so he walked back.

She spent the day playing with Risa when the baby was awake, and watching her while she slept. Late that afternoon, Kathleen realized with a start that she hadn't given a thought to what she would prepare for dinner, and guilt filled her. Derek had been a saint, coddling her beyond all reason, letting her devote all her time to Risa, doing all the household chores himself, but Risa's homecoming marked a change in the status quo. It had been two weeks since Risa's birth, and Kathleen felt better than she had in years. She was rested, her appetite was better; there was no reason to let Derek continue to wait on her as if she was an invalid. He had given everything, and she had given nothing, not even her attention.

She rolled Risa's bassinet, which she and Derek had bought only the day before, into the kitchen so she could watch Risa while she prepared dinner. The baby slept peacefully, with the knuckles of one fist shoved into her mouth, undisturbed by the rattling of pots and pans. It was the first time Kathleen had cooked, so she had to hunt for everything, and it took her twice as long to do anything than it normally would have. She was relieved when Derek didn't come home at his usual time, since she was running behind schedule, but when half an hour had passed she became concerned. It wasn't like him to be late without calling her himself or having a nurse call to let her know that one of the babies needed him. As short a time as they had been married, she had already learned that about him. Derek was always considerate.

Derek was…incredible.

She wanted to give him something, even if it was

just a hot meal waiting for him when he came home. She looked at the steaming food, ready to be served, but he wasn't there. She could keep it warming on the stove, but it wouldn't be the same.

Then she heard his key in the door, and she was filled with relief. She hurried out of the kitchen to greet him, her face alight with pleasure.

"I was worried," she said in a rush, then was afraid he would think she was complaining, so she changed what she had been about to say. "Believe it or not, I actually cooked dinner. But I couldn't find anything, and it took me forever to do. I was afraid you'd be home before everything was finished, because I wanted to surprise you."

His eyes were warm as he put his arm around her shoulders and hugged her to him for a kiss. He kissed her a lot, sometimes with carefully restrained passion, and she had stopped being shocked by her own pleasure in his touch.

"I'm more than surprised, I'm downright grateful," he said, kissing her again. "I'm also starving. Where's Risa?"

"In the kitchen, where I could watch her sleep."

"I wondered if you'd spend the day hanging over her bassinet."

"Actually, yes."

His arm was around her waist as they walked into the kitchen. Risa was still asleep, so he didn't disturb her by picking her up. He set the table while

Kathleen served the food, then they ate leisurely, one of the few times they'd had a chance to do so. Kathleen knew she was a good cook, and it gave her a great deal of satisfaction to watch Derek eat with evident enjoyment.

When they had finished, he helped her clean up, then, as sort of an afterthought, took a set of car keys out of his pocket and gave them to her. She took them, frowning at him in puzzlement. "I already have keys to the Cherokee."

"These aren't for the Jeep," he explained calmly, going into the living room and sitting down to read the newspaper. "They're for your car. I picked it up on the way home this afternoon."

Her car? She didn't own a car, just the old truck. The truth burst in her mind like a sunrise, robbing her of breath. "I can't take a car from you," she said, her voice strained.

He looked up from the newspaper, his black brows rising in a question. "Is there a problem? If you don't want the car, I'll drive it, and you can have the Jeep. I can't continue walking to the hospital, so buying a car seemed like the logical thing to do."

She felt like screaming. He'd hemmed her in with logic. He was right, of course, but that only made her feel more helpless. She'd felt so proud of preparing dinner for him, the first time she'd contributed anything to their marriage, while he'd stopped on the way home and bought a *car* for her! She felt like an insatiable sponge, soaking up everything he had to give and demanding more just by her very existence, her presence in his life.

Licking her lips, she said, "I'm sorry. I'm just... stunned. No one ever bought...I don't know what to say."

He appeared to give it thought, but his eyes were twinkling. "I suppose you could do what anyone else would do—jump up and down, squeal, laugh, throw your arms around my neck and kiss me until I beg for mercy."

Her heart jumped wildly. He was as splendid as a pagan god, powerfully built and powerfully male; that wasn't a twinkle in his eyes, after all, but a hard, heated gleam, and he was looking at her the way men have looked at women since the beginning of time. Her mouth went suddenly dry, and she had to lick her lips again.

"Is that what you want me to do?" she whispered.

He carefully put the newspaper aside. "You can skip the jumping and squealing, if you want. I won't mind if you go straight to the kissing part."

She didn't remember moving, but somehow she found herself on his lap, her arms around his strong neck, her mouth under his. He had kissed her so often in the week they'd been married that she'd become used to it, expected it, enjoyed it. In a way his kisses reassured her that she would be able to have something to give, even if it were only physical ease. She couldn't even do that completely, at the present, but at least the potential was there. If he wanted her to kiss him, she was more than willing.

His arms closed around her, holding her to his strong chest as he deepened the kiss, his tongue moving to touch hers. Kathleen felt very brave and bold; she had no idea that her kisses were rather timid and untutored, or that he was both touched and highly aroused by her innocence. He kissed her slowly, thoroughly, teaching her how to use her tongue and how to accept his, holding himself under tight control lest he alarm her.

Finally she turned her head away, gasping for breath, and he smiled because she had forgotten to breathe. "Are you ready to beg for mercy?" she panted, color high in her face.

"I don't know anyone named Mercy," he muttered, turning her face back to his for another taste of her mouth. "Why would I beg for a woman I don't even know?"

Her chuckle was muted by his lips as he turned passion to teasing, kissing her all over her face with loud smacking noises. Then he hoisted her to her feet and got to his. "Wake up the tiny tyrant so I can show you which car is yours," he said, grinning.

Kathleen threw an anxious look at the sleeping baby. "Should we take her out in the cold?"

"Do you want to leave her here by herself? Unless you want to try the key in every car in the parking lot, you have to know which one is yours. It won't take a minute—just wrap her up and keep her head covered. It isn't that cold outside, anyway."

"Are you certain it won't hurt her?"

He gave her a very level look, and without another word she turned to get a jacket for herself and a blanket for Risa. She felt like kicking herself. Did he think she didn't trust him to know what would harm the baby and what wouldn't? He was a doctor, for heaven's sake! He'd taken care of her and Risa from the moment they'd met. She'd really made a mess of it again, kissing him as if she could eat him up one minute, then practically insulting him the next.

When she returned with the blanket, he'd already picked Risa up, waking her, and he was crooning to her. Risa watched him with a ridiculously serious expression, her tiny face intent as she stared up at him, her hands waving erratically. To Kathleen's surprise, the baby was working her rosebud mouth as if trying to mimic Derek's actions. She seemed totally fascinated by the man holding her.

"Here's the blanket."

He took it and deftly wrapped Risa in it, covering her head. The baby began fussing, and Derek chuckled. "We'd better hurry. She won't tolerate this for long. She wants to see what's going on."

They hurried down to the parking lot, and Derek led her to a white Oldsmobile Calais. Kathleen had to swallow her gasp. It was a new car, not a used one, as she'd expected. It was sleek and sporty looking, with a soft dove-gray interior and every optional convenience she could think of. Tears burned her eyes. "I...I don't know what to say," she whispered as she stared at it in shock.

"Say you love it, promise me that you'll always wear your seat belt, and we'll take the baby back inside before she works herself into a tantrum. She doesn't like this blanket over her face one bit." Risa's fussing was indeed rising in volume.

"I love it," she said, dazed.

He laughed and put his arm around her waist as the fussing bundle in his arms began to wail furiously. They hurried back inside, and he lifted the blanket to reveal Risa's red, tightly screwed-up face. "Stop that," he said gently, touching her cheek. She gave a few more wails, then hiccuped twice and settled down, once more intently staring up at his face.

He was perfect. Everything he did only compounded the imbalance in the deal she'd made with him. He not only took care of everything, gave her everything, but he was better at taking care of Risa. The parents of his tiny patients all thought he ranked right up there with angels, and all the nurses were in love with him. He could have had anyone, but instead he'd chosen to saddle himself with a...a *hick* who didn't know anything but how to work a ranch, and a child who wasn't his. Kathleen felt like a parasite.

If nothing else, she could begin to repay him for the car, but to do that she'd have to get a job.

She took a deep breath and broached the subject as soon as he'd laid Risa down. Kathleen didn't believe in putting things off. She'd learned the hard way that they didn't go away; it was better to meet trouble head-on. "I'm going to start looking for a job."

"If you feel well enough," he said absently as he tucked a light blanket around the baby. "You might want to call Sarah. She mentioned something about needing more help in one of her stores."

She'd been braced for objections, but his matter-of-fact acceptance made her wonder why she'd thought he wouldn't like the idea. Then she realized she had expected him to act as Larry would have; Larry hadn't wanted her to do anything except work like a slave on the ranch, and wait on him hand and foot. If she'd gone out and gotten a job, she might have been able to get out from under his thumb before he'd finished bleeding her dry. Derek wasn't like that. Derek wanted her to be happy.

It was an astounding revelation. Kathleen couldn't remember anyone ever going out of their way to give her any sort of happiness. Yet since Derek had appeared in her life, everything he'd done had been with her happiness and well-being in mind.

She thought about his suggestion, and she liked it. She wasn't trained to do anything except be a waitress, but she did know how to operate a cash register; working in a crafts store sounded interesting. She made up her mind to call Sarah Matthews the next day.

When they went to bed that night, Derek practically had to drag Kathleen out of the nursery. "Maybe I should sleep in here," she said worriedly. "What if she cries and I can't hear her?"

Sleeping in the same bed with her without touching her had been one of the worst tortures a man had ever devised for himself, but Derek wasn't about to give it up. Besides, he was ready to advance his plan a step, which wouldn't work if Kathleen wasn't in bed with him. He'd anticipated all her first-night-with-a-new-baby jitters, and set about soothing them. "I bought a baby-alarm system," he said, and placed a small black speaker by Risa's crib. "The other speaker will be by our bed. We'll be able to hear if she cries."

"But she needs to be kept warm—"

"We'll leave the heat turned up, but close the vents in our room." As he talked, he was leading her to the bedroom. He'd already closed the heat vents, and the room was noticeably cooler than the rest of the apartment. Anticipation made his heart beat faster. For over a week he'd let her get used to his presence in the bed; he even knew why she tolerated it. She thought she *owed* it to him. But now he was going to get her used to his touch as well as his presence, and he meant more than those kisses that were driving him wild. He wanted her so much he ached with it, and tonight he would take another step toward his goal.

She crawled into bed and pulled the covers up over her. Derek turned out the light, then dropped his pajama bottoms to the floor and, blissfully nude, got in beside her. He normally slept nude, but had worn the aggravating pajamas since their marriage, and it was a relief to shed them.

The cold room would do the rest. She would seek out his warmth during the night, and when she woke up, she would be in his arms. A smile crossed his face as he thought of it.

The baby alarm worked. A little after one, Kathleen woke at the first tentative wail. She felt deliciously warm, and groaned at the idea of getting up. She was so comfortable, with her head on Derek's shoulder and his arms around her so tightly—

Her eyes flew open, and she sat up in bed. "I'm sorry," she blurted.

He yawned sleepily. "For what?"

"I was all over you!"

"Hell, sweetheart, I enjoyed it! Would you listen to that little terror scream," he said in admiration, changing the subject. Yawning again, he reached out to turn on the lamp, then got out of bed. Kathleen's entire body jerked in shock. He was naked! Gloriously naked. Beautifully naked. Her mouth went dry, and her full breasts tightened until they began to ache.

He held out his hand to her. "Come on, sweetheart. Let's see about our daughter."

Still in shock, she put her hand in his as he gave her a slow, wicked smile that totally robbed her of breath.

CHAPTER SEVEN

THAT SMILE REMAINED in her mind the next morning as she drove carefully to Sarah Matthews's store, following the directions she'd gotten from Sarah only an hour before. Risa slept snugly in her car seat, having survived the first night in her crib, as well as being tended by her gorgeous, naked daddy. Kathleen had been too stunned to do anything but sit in the rocking chair and hold Risa to her breast. Derek had done everything else. And after Risa was asleep again, Kathleen had gone docilely back to bed again, and let him gather her close to his warm, muscular *naked* body…and enjoyed it.

Enjoyed seemed like too mild a description for the way her thoughts and emotions had rioted. Part of her had wanted to touch him, taste him, run her hands all over his magnificent body. Another part of her had panicked; deep in her mind she still hadn't recovered from the brutal, contemptuous way that Larry had humiliated her before walking out.

She didn't want to think about that; she shoved the memory from her mind, and found the blank space

it left promptly filled by Derek's sensual, knowing smile. *That was it!* Knowing! He'd known exactly how she had felt!

She found the cozy crafts store easily enough, despite her lack of total attention to where she was going. There was ample parking, but she carefully parked her spotless new car well away from everyone else, then gathered Risa and the ton of paraphernalia babies required into her arms and entered the store.

There were several customers browsing and chatting with Sarah, as well as each other, but when Kathleen came in a glowing smile lit Sarah's face, and she came right over to take the baby from her arms. "What a darling," she whispered, examining the sleeping infant. "She's beautiful. Missy and Jed will spoil her rotten, just like Derek spoiled them when they were little. I brought Jed's old playpen and set it up in the back, where I used to keep my kids, if you want to put all Risa's stuff back there."

Kathleen carried the bulging diaper bag into the back room, which was a section of the store stocked with doll supplies, as well as a cozy area with several rocking chairs, where Sarah's customers could sit and chat if they wanted. It was the most popular area of the store, and warmer than the front section. A sturdy playpen had been set up next to the rocking chairs, and Kathleen looked at it in bewilderment.

"You drove home to get the playpen after I called you this morning? Who watched the store?"

Sarah laughed, her warm green eyes twinkling. "Actually, I've had the playpen set up for several days. I called Derek the day you were married and told him I needed help here, if he thought you'd be interested."

"He didn't tell me until last night," Kathleen said, wondering if she should be angry at his manipulation, and also wondering if it would do any good.

"Of course not. I knew he'd wait until Risa was home and you were feeling better. But don't let the playpen pressure you into thinking you have to take the job if you don't want it."

Kathleen took a deep breath. "I'd like to take the job. I don't have any training for anything except being a waitress and doing ranch work, but I can work a cash register."

Sarah beamed at her. "Then it's settled. When can you start?"

Kathleen looked around the warm, homey store. This would be a good place to work, even though she hated the idea of leaving Risa during the day. She would have to find a day-care center or a babysitter nearby, so she could nurse the baby during lunch. She supposed Risa would have to get used to a bottle for supplemental feedings, though it made her want to cry to think about it. "I'll have to find someone to keep Risa before I can start," she said reluctantly.

Sarah blinked in surprise. "Why? My babies grew up in this store. That way I could keep them with me.

Just bring Risa with you. You'll have more helping
hands than you can count. Whenever you feel strong
enough to start work—"

"I'm strong enough now," Kathleen said. "After
working on a ranch my entire life, I'm as strong as
a packhorse."

"What does Derek think about this?" Sarah asked,
then laughed at herself. "Never mind. He wouldn't
have told you about the job if he didn't think you
were well enough to handle it. It isn't hard work—
the only physical labor is putting up stock, and Jed
usually manhandles the boxes for me."

Kathleen searched her memory for a picture of
Jed, because she knew he'd been at her wedding. "Is
Jed the tall, black-haired boy?"

"Yes. My baby's almost six feet tall. It's ridiculous
how fast they grow up. Enjoy every moment with
Risa, because her babyhood won't last long." Sarah
smiled down at the sleeping bundle in her arms, then
leaned over and gently deposited Risa in the playpen. "She's gorgeous. Derek must be insufferably
proud of her."

It hit Kathleen like a slap that everyone must think
Risa was truly Derek's daughter, which would explain why he had hustled Kathleen into such a hasty
marriage. Why wouldn't they think it? Risa's hair
was the same inky shade as Derek's, as well as her
own. She didn't know what to say, yet she knew she
had to say something. She couldn't let his friends

think he was the type of man who would abandon a
woman who was pregnant with his child, not when
he had been so good to her, given her so much. In
the end, she just blurted it out. "Risa isn't Derek's. I
mean, I'd never met him until the day she was born."

But Sarah only smiled her serene smile. "I know,
Derek told us. But she's his now, just like you are."

The idea of belonging to, or with, anyone was
alien to Kathleen, because she'd never known the
closeness. At least, she hadn't until Risa had been
born, and then she had felt an instant and over-
powering sense of possession. It was different with
Derek. He was a man...very much so. The image of
his bare, powerful body flashed into her mind, and
she felt herself grow warm. He had taken her over
completely, so in that respect she did belong to him.
The odd thing was that she had just sprung to his
defense, unwilling to let his friends think anything
bad about him. She had felt the need to protect him,
as if he belonged to her, and that sense of mutual
possession was confusing.

She pushed her thoughts away, concentrating on
learning about the shop with the same intensity she'd
learned how to be a waitress. As Sarah had said, it
wasn't hard work, for which Kathleen was grateful,
because she found that she did tire easily. For the
most part Risa slept contentedly, whimpering only
when she needed changing or was hungry, and occasionally looking around with vague, innocent eyes.

It seemed that all the customers knew Derek, and there was a lot of oohing and ahhing over the baby.

In the middle of the afternoon, when school was out, Sarah's teenagers came in, with Jed dwarfing his older sister in a protective manner. Missy, who was startlingly lovely, with her father's black eyes and black hair, nevertheless had Sarah's fragile bone structure. When she saw Kathleen, she rushed to her and hugged her as if they were long-lost friends, then breathlessly demanded to know where the baby was. Laughing, Kathleen pointed to the playpen, and Missy descended on Risa, who was just waking from another nap.

Jed watched his sister, and there was something fierce in his own black eyes. "She's crazy about little kids," he said in a rumbly voice, without any adolescent squeak. "She'll be pushing you and Derek out the door every night just so she can babysit." Then he turned and said, "Hi, Mom," as he enveloped Sarah in his muscled arms.

But there was a small frown in Sarah's eyes as she looked up at her son. "What's wrong? You're angry about something." He was too much like his father for her ever to mistake his moods.

"A pipsqueak punk has been hassling Miss," he said bluntly.

"There's nothing to it!" Missy insisted, approaching them with Risa cuddled to her shoulder. "He hasn't really said anything. He just keeps asking me out."

"Do you want to go?" Sarah asked calmly.

"No!" Missy's answer was too swift, denying her casual attitude. "I just don't want to make any big deal about it. I'd be too embarrassed."

"I'll talk to Rome," Sarah said.

"Oh, Mom!"

"I can handle it," Jed said, his voice deadly calm. He reached out and tickled Risa's chin, then deftly scooped her out of Missy's arms.

"Give her back!" Missy said, breathing fire.

They wandered into the back room, still arguing over who would get to hold the baby, and Sarah shook her head. "Teenagers. Just wait," she said with a smile for Kathleen. "Your turn will come."

"Jed's very protective, isn't he?"

"He's just like Rome, but he isn't old enough yet to know how to control all that intensity."

Ten minutes later Missy returned, having regained possession of Risa. Jed had settled down in the back room, watching the portable television and doing his homework at the same time. "Mom, please don't say anything to Dad about that guy," she began earnestly. "You know how Dad is. You almost couldn't talk him into letting me date, and I was *fifteen!*"

"What guy?" a deep voice asked calmly, and they all whirled to face the newcomer.

"Derek!" Missy said in relief, reaching to give

him a hug which he returned, cradling her head against his shoulder for a moment.

Kathleen couldn't say anything; she just stared at him with her tongue glued to the roof of her mouth. The light wind had ruffled his black hair, and with his naturally dark complexion it gave him a raffish look that almost literally stopped her heart. His broad shoulders strained the light jacket he wore, his only concession to the January weather.

Sarah was frowning at him. "Why didn't the bell ring when you came in?"

"Because I reached up and caught it," he answered calmly as he slid his arm around Kathleen's waist and drew her to him. His golden eyes went back to Missy. "What guy?"

"Some scuzzball keeps pestering me to go out with him," she explained. "Jed's gone all macho, and Mom is threatening to tell Dad, and if she does he'll *never* let me date anyone again."

Derek lifted his eyebrows. "Is this scuzzball dangerous?"

An uncertain look flitted over Missy's delicate features. "I don't know," she admitted in a small voice. "Do you think Dad should know?"

"Of course. Why would he blame you for something that isn't your fault? Unless he wants to blame you for being a traffic-stopper."

She blushed, then laughed. "All right. I guess he'll let me go to the prom…if I can get a date."

"No boyfriend?" Kathleen asked, having finally found her tongue. Talking to Missy seemed safe enough, though her attention was splintered by the heat of Derek's body against her side.

Missy shrugged. "No one special. They all seem so *young*." With that scathing denunciation of her peer group, she allowed Derek to take Risa from her and went to join Jed.

"You're off from work early." Kathleen finally managed to talk to him, since he had released her when he lifted the baby to his shoulder.

"I'm on call. We have a mother trying to go into labor three months early. If they can't get it stopped, I'll have to be there when the baby is born. I decided to take a break while I can, and see my women."

She felt a pang at the thought that she might not be sleeping with him that night, and even a little jealousy that it was Risa who was cuddled so lovingly on that broad shoulder. Well, he'd made it plain from the start that it was Risa he wanted. Why should she be jealous? Did she want Derek to demand more from her than she could give?

Maybe she just wanted him to demand *any*thing from her, so she would know *what* to give.

"What time do you leave work?" he asked as he checked his watch.

Kathleen looked at Sarah. They hadn't even talked about hours. It had been more like visiting with friends than working, anyway. "Go on," Sarah said, smiling. "You've been on your feet a lot today, and the kids are here to help. See you in the morning at nine. Wait, let me get a key for you." She fetched an extra key from the bottom of the cash register, and Kathleen put it in her purse.

Derek got the blanket and diaper bag from the playpen and wrapped Risa snugly in the blanket. Predictably, she began fussing when her face was covered, and he grinned. "We have to go," he told Sarah as he ushered Kathleen out the door. "Having her face covered makes her mad."

Quickly he carried the baby to the car and strapped her into her seat; she settled down as soon as he whisked the blanket from her face. Then he came around to Kathleen's side and bent down to kiss her. "Be careful on the way home," he said, then kissed her again. "I'll pick up dinner. What do you like? Chinese? Mexican?"

She'd never eaten Chinese food, but she liked tacos. "Mexican?"

He straightened. "I'll get the food and come straight home." Then he closed her door and walked to the Cherokee without looking back.

Kathleen licked her lips as she started the car, savoring the taste of his mouth. She could feel an unfamiliar tightening inside, and her breasts were aching. She glanced at Risa. "Aren't you hungry?"

A tiny fist waved jerkily back and forth as the

baby tried to find her mouth with it. She was monu-
mentally unconcerned with her mother's agitation.

Derek was less than half an hour behind her, but
they had scarcely sat down to the spicy meal when
his beeper went off. Without hesitation he went to
the phone and called the hospital. "All right. I'm on
my way."

He barely stopped to snag his jacket on the way
out. "Don't wait up for me," he called over his shoulder; then the door closed, and Kathleen sat there
with refried beans lumping in her mouth, suddenly
tasteless.

The hours passed slowly as she waited for him to
come home. Risa was fed and put to bed; then Kathleen tried to become interested in television. When
that failed, she tried to read. That was also a dismal
failure, and she was furious at herself. She was used
to being alone, and had never found it oppressive before. Had she become so dependent on him that she
couldn't function without his presence?

At last, disgusted, she went to bed, and her body
was tired enough that she went to sleep despite her
restless thoughts. When Risa's first hungry cries
woke her at one-thirty, the other side of the bed was
still empty.

But when she entered the nursery she jumped in
surprise, because Derek was sitting in the rocking
chair holding the baby while she cried, his hand rubbing her tiny back. There was a terrible emptiness

in his eyes that made her hurt, but she sensed that he got some comfort from holding Risa.

"The baby died," he said in a toneless voice. "I did everything I could, but he didn't make it. He wouldn't have had much of a chance even if he'd gone full term. His heart was hopelessly malformed. Damn it to hell and back, I still had to try."

She touched his shoulder. "I know," she whispered.

He looked down at the furious baby, then caught Kathleen's wrist and drew her down on his lap. Holding her against his chest, he unbuttoned her nightgown and bared her breast, then let her take Risa and guide the child's mouth to her nipple. The outraged wails stopped immediately. Derek looked down at the vigorously suckling infant and gathered both mother and child closer to his body, then leaned his head back and closed his eyes.

Kathleen let her head rest on his shoulder, her own eyes closing as she soaked up his warmth and nearness. He needed her. For the first time, he needed her. She knew that any warm body would have done for him right now, but the warm body was hers, and she'd be there as long as her touch gave him comfort. Or maybe it was Risa who gave him comfort, Risa whom he couldn't bear to release. She was a healthy, thriving baby now, gaining weight every day. He had seen death, and now he needed to see life, the precious life of a baby he'd helped into the world.

Kathleen had to bite her lip. Why hadn't he come to their bed? To her? Why didn't he need *her*?

CHAPTER EIGHT

FOUR WEEKS LATER, Kathleen could feel a secret smile tugging at her lips as she unlocked the front door and carried Risa inside to her crib. The baby grunted and waved her fists, then broke into a quick, open-mouthed smile as Kathleen tickled her chin. Even Risa was happy, but Kathleen thought her daughter was smiling at the world in general, while *she* had a very personal reason.

The obstetrician had given her a clean bill of health earlier in the day, and since then she hadn't been able to stop grinning. These past four weeks had been almost impossible to bear as she fretted the days away, impatient for the time when she could truly become Derek's wife. He was a healthy, virile man; she'd seen the evidence of it every day, because he had no modesty around her. She couldn't say that she'd gotten used to seeing him nude; her heart still jumped, her pulse still speeded up, she still grew very warm and distracted by all that muscled masculinity. She was even…fascinated.

Marital relations with Larry hadn't been a joy.

She had always felt used and even repulsed by his quick, callous handling; she hadn't been a person to him, but a convenience. Instinctively, she knew that making love with Derek would be different, and she wanted to experience it. She wanted to give him the physical ease and enjoyment of her body, a deeply personal gift from her to the man who had completely changed her life. Derek was the strongest, most loving and giving man she could imagine, but because he was so strong it sometimes seemed as if he didn't need anything from her, and being able to give him something in return had become an obsession with her. At last she could give him her body, and sexual fulfillment.

He knew of her appointment; he'd reminded her of it that morning. When he came home, he would ask her what the doctor had said. Then his golden eyes would take on that warm intensity she'd seen in them sometimes, and when they went to bed he would take her in his powerful arms, where she felt so safe and secure, and he would make her truly his wife, in fact as well as in name....

Risa's tiny hands batted against Kathleen's arm, jerking her from her exciting fantasy. "If I give you a bath and feed you now, will you be a good girl and sleep a long time tonight?" she whispered to her daughter, smiling down at her gorgeous offspring. How she was growing! She weighed eight pounds now, and was developing dimples and creases all over her wriggling little body. Since she had begun smiling, Missy and Jed were in a constant state of warfare to see who could get her to flash that adorable, smooth-gummed grin, but she smiled most often for Derek.

Kathleen checked her wristwatch. Derek had called the store while she'd been at the doctor's office and left a message with Sarah that he would be a few hours late, so she had time to get Risa settled for the night—she hoped—and prepare dinner before he'd be home. Would candles be too obvious, or would it be a discreet way of letting him know what the doctor's verdict had been? She'd never prepared a romantic dinner before, and she wondered if she would make a fool of herself. After all, Derek was a doctor; there were no physical mysteries for him, and how could there be romance without some mystery?

Her hands shook as she prepared Risa's bath. How could there be romance between them anyway? It was payment of a debt, part of the deal they'd made. He was probably expecting it. The only mystery involved was why she was letting herself get into such a lather over it.

Risa liked her bath and with the truly contrary nature of all children, chose that night to want to play. Kathleen didn't have the heart to hurry her, because she enjoyed seeing those little legs kick. How different things might have been if it hadn't been for Derek! She might never have known the joy of watching her child splash happily in the bathwater.

But finally the baby tired, and after she was dried and dressed she nursed hungrily, then fell asleep at Kathleen's breast. Smiling, Kathleen put her in the crib and covered her with a light blanket. Now it was time for her own bath, so she would be clean and sweet-smelling in case Derek came home in an impatient mood, ready to end his period of celibacy.

She bathed, then prepared dinner and left it warming in the oven until she heard Derek's key in the lock, then hurried to pour their drinks and serve the food while he hung up his coat and washed. Everything was ready when he joined her at the table.

As always, he drew her to him for a kiss; she had hoped he would deepen the kiss into passion, but instead he lifted the warm pressure of his mouth and looked around. "Is Risa already asleep?" He sounded disappointed.

"Yes, she went to sleep right after the bath." She felt disappointed, too. Why hadn't he kissed her longer, or asked immediately what the doctor had said? Oh, he had to know everything was okay, but she still would have liked for him to be a little eager.

Over dinner, he told her about the emergency that had kept him at the hospital. Just when she had decided that her visit to the doctor had slipped his mind and was wondering how to mention it, he asked casually, "Did the doctor release you from her care?"

She felt her heartbeat speed up. She cleared her throat, but her voice was still a little husky as she answered. "Yes. She said I'm back to normal, and in good health."

"Good."

That was it. He didn't mention it again, but acted as if it were any other evening. He didn't grab her and take her off to bed, and a sense of letdown kept her quiet as they read the newspaper and watched television. He was absorbed in a hockey game, which she didn't understand. Football and baseball were more her style. Finally she put down the newspaper she'd been reading and tried one more time. "I think I'll go to bed."

He checked his watch. "All right. I'm going to watch a little more of the game. I'll be there in half an hour."

She waited tensely in the dark, unable to relax. Evidently he didn't need her sexually as much as she'd been counting on. She pressed her hands over her eyes; had she been fooling herself all along? Maybe he had someone else to take care of his physical needs. As soon as the thought formed, she dismissed it. Derek. He had sworn fidelity in their marriage vows, and Derek Taliferro was a man who kept his word.

Finally she heard the shower running, and a few minutes later he entered the bedroom. She could feel the damp heat of his body as he slid between the sheets, and she turned on her side to face him.

"Derek?"

"Hmm?"

"Are you tired?"

"I'm tense more than tired." She could see him staring through the darkness at the ceiling. "It's hard to unwind after a touchy situation like we had this afternoon."

Kathleen moved closer to him, her hands going out to touch his chest. The crisp curls against her palm gave her a funny, warm feeling. Her head found the hollow of his shoulder, and the clean, masculine scent of his skin surrounded her. His arms went around her, the way they had every night for the past four weeks. It was going to be all right, she told herself, and waited.

But he didn't do anything other than hold her, and finally she decided he was waiting for her to give him the go-ahead. Clearing her throat, she whispered, "I... The doctor said it's okay for me to...you know. If you want to, that is," she added hastily.

Slowly Derek reached out and switched on the lamp, then lifted himself onto his elbow and looked down at her. There was a strange expression in his eyes, one she couldn't read. "What about you?" he asked in that even tone that sometimes gave her chills. "Do *you* want to 'you know'?"

"I want to please you." She could feel her throat

closing up under his steady gaze. "We made a deal…
and I owe you so much it's the least I—"

"You don't owe me a damn thing," he interrupted
in a harsh voice she barely recognized as his. Moving abruptly, he rolled away from her and got out of
bed, standing there glaring down at her with golden
eyes molten with fury. She had never seen Derek
angry before, she realized dimly through her shock,
and now he wasn't just angry, he was raging. Being
Derek, he controlled his rage, but it was there none-
theless.

"Before we got married, I told you we wouldn't
make love without caring and commitment. I never
said a damned word about keeping a deal or paying
a debt. Thanks, sweetheart, but I don't need charity." He grabbed a blanket and slammed out of the
bedroom, leaving Kathleen lying in bed staring at
the spot where he'd stood.

She shook her head, trying to deal with what had
just happened. How had it blown up in her face like
that? She had just been trying to give back some of
the tenderness he'd given her, but he hadn't wanted
her. She began to shake, lying there in the bed that
gradually became cool without his body to keep it
warm, but it wasn't just the temperature that chilled
her. His absence chilled her; she had come to rely
on him so much that now she felt lost without him.

She had been fooling herself all along. She didn't
have anything to give him, not even sex. He didn't

need her at all, despite his words about caring and commitment. She *did* care about him, and she was committed to making their marriage work, but he still didn't want her, not the way she wanted him to. But then, why should he? He was extraordinary in every way, while she was worse than ordinary; she had been, and still was, unwanted.

Her hands knotted into fists as she lay there, trying to control her convulsive shaking. Her parents hadn't wanted her; they had been middle-aged when she was born, and her presence had almost embarrassed them. They hadn't been demonstrative people, anyway, and they'd had no idea what to do with a curious, lively child. Gradually the child had learned not to make noise or trouble, but she had been so starved for love that she'd married the first man who had asked her, and gone from bad to worse, because Larry hadn't wanted her either. Larry had wanted to live off her and the ranch she'd inherited, and in the end he'd bled the ranch to death, then left her because she'd had nothing else to give him.

It looked as if she didn't have anything to give Derek, either, except Risa, but it was Risa he'd wanted, anyway.

DEREK LAY ON THE SOFA, his jaw clenched and his body burning as he stared through the darkness. Damn, he wanted her so much he hurt, but it was like being punched in the gut for her to tell him he could use her body because she "owed" him! All these weeks he'd done everything he could to pamper her and make her love him, but sometimes he felt as if he were butting his head against a stone wall. She accepted him, but that was it, and he wanted more than mere acceptance…so much more.

She watched him constantly, with wary green eyes, as if trying to gauge his mood and anticipate his needs, but it was more the attention of a servant trying to please than that of a wife. He didn't need a servant, but he desperately needed Kathleen to be his wife. He needed her to touch him with the fierce want and love he could sense were bottled up inside her, if she would only let them out. What had happened to her that she suppressed the affectionate side of her nature with everyone except Risa? He'd tried to tell her how much she meant to him without putting a lot of pressure on her, and he'd tried to show her, but still she held back from him.

Maybe he should take what she'd offered. Maybe emotional intimacy would follow physical intimacy. God knew his body craved the pleasure and release of lovemaking; at least he could have that. But she had told him, when he'd asked her to marry him, that things had happened to her, and she might never be able to accept lovemaking again; when he calmed down, he realized that she had come a long way to even be able to offer him the use of her body.

It just wasn't enough. He wanted to erase the shadows from her eyes, to watch her smile bloom for him. He wanted her slim body twisting beneath him in spasms of pleasure; he wanted to hear her chanting love words to him; he wanted her laughter and tenderness and trust. God, how he wanted her trust! But most of all, he wanted her love, with the desperate thirst of a man stranded in the desert.

Everything had always come so easily for him, including women. He'd scarcely reached his teens before older girls, and even women, had begun noticing him. It was probably poetic justice that he had fallen in love with a woman who protected her emotions behind a wall so high he couldn't find a way over it. He had always known what to do in any situation, how to get people to do what he wanted, but with Kathleen he was stymied. Wryly he admitted to himself that his emotions were probably clouding his normally clear insight, but he couldn't detach himself from the problem. He wanted her with a force and heat that obscured all other details.

He was so wrapped up in his rage and frustration that he didn't hear her enter the room. The first he knew of her presence was when her hand touched his shoulder briefly, then hurriedly withdrew, as if she were afraid to touch him. Startled, he turned his head to look at her as she knelt beside the sofa; the darkness hid her expression, but not the strain in her low voice.

"I'm sorry," she whispered. "I didn't mean to embarrass you. I know I'm not anything special, but I thought you might want to…" Her voice fumbled to a halt as she tried and failed to find the phrasing she wanted. Finally she gave up and simply continued. "I swear I won't put you in that position again. I'm not much good at it, anyway. Larry said I was lousy.…" Again her voice died away, and the pale oval of her face turned to the side as if she couldn't face him, even in the darkness.

It was the first time she'd mentioned her ex-husband voluntarily, and his name brought Derek up on his elbow, galvanized by this abrupt opportunity to learn what had happened between Kathleen and the man. "What happened?" His voice was full of raw, rough demand, and Kathleen was too vulnerable at the moment to deny it.

"He married me for the ranch, so he could live off it without having to work." Her words were almost prosaic, but her voice shook a little in betrayal of that false calm. "He didn't want me, either. I don't guess anyone ever has, not even my folks. But Larry used me whenever he had the urge and couldn't get to town. He said I might as well be some use, because even though I was lousy in bed, I was still better than nothing. Then finally he couldn't get any more money out of the ranch, and he filed for divorce so he could move on to something better. The last time I saw him, he…he used me again. I tried to stop him, but he was drunk and mean, and he hurt me. He said it was a goodbye present, because no man would ever be interested in me. He was right, wasn't he?"

Slowly, shakily, she rose to her feet and stood beside him in the darkness. "I just wanted to do something for you," she whispered. "You've done so much, given me so much, and I don't have anything to give you except that. I'd give you my life if you needed it. Anyway, I won't let loving you the way I do embarrass you again. I guess all you want from me is to be left alone."

Then she was gone, walking silently back into the bedroom, and Derek lay on his cold, lonely sofa, his heart pounding at what she'd said.

Now he knew what to do.

CHAPTER NINE

KATHLEEN HAD HAD years of practice in hiding her emotions behind a blank face, and that was what she did the next day at work. She talked to the customers as usual, played with Risa and chatted with Sarah, with whom she had developed a warm friendship. Being friends with Sarah wasn't difficult; the older woman was serene and truly kind. Within a few days Kathleen had easily been able to see why her children adored her and her big, fierce husband looked at her as if the entire world spun around her.

But Sarah was also keenly intuitive, and by lunchtime she was watching Kathleen in a thoughtful manner. Knowing those perceptive eyes were on her made Kathleen withdraw further inside her shell, because she couldn't let herself think about what a terrible mess she'd made of things.

She couldn't believe what she'd said. It horrified her that she had actually blurted out to him that she loved him, after he had made it so painfully plain that he wasn't interested in her even for sex. She hadn't meant to, but she had only just discovered it herself, and she'd still been reeling from the shock. The hardest thing she'd ever done had been to leave the bedroom that morning; she had steeled herself to face him, only to discover that he had already left for the hospital. Now she had to steel herself all over again, but her nerves were raw, and she knew she couldn't do it if she kept replaying the mortifying scene in her mind.

Sarah placed a stack of embroidery kits on the counter and looked Kathleen in the eye. "You can tell me it's not any of my business if you want," she said quietly, "but maybe it would help to talk about it. Has something happened? You've been so...*sad* all day long."

Only Sarah would have described Kathleen's mood as sad, but after a moment of surprise she realized that was exactly how she felt. She had ruined everything, and a choking sadness weighed on her shoulders, because she loved him so much and had nothing to give him, nothing he wanted. Old habits ran deep, and she had just opened her mouth to deny her mood when her throat closed. She had received nothing but kindness and friendship from Sarah; she couldn't lie to her. Tears stung her eyes, and she quickly looked away to hide them.

"Kathleen," Sarah murmured, reaching across the counter to take Kathleen's hands and fold them in hers. "Friends are for talking to—I don't know what I'd have done all these years without my friends.

Derek helped me through one of the hardest times of my life, even though he was just a boy then. I would do anything for him…and for you, if you'll only tell me what's wrong."

"I love him," Kathleen croaked, and the tears overflowed.

Sarah looked perplexed. "Of course you do. Why is that a problem?"

"He doesn't love me." Hastily she withdrew one of her hands and wiped her cheeks. "He only tolerates me."

Sarah's green eyes widened. "*Tolerates* you? He adores you!"

"You don't understand," Kathleen said, shaking her head in despair. "You think he married me because he loves me, but he doesn't. He only married me because of Risa, because it was the only way he could get her."

"Derek loves children," Sarah admitted. "He loves all children, but he doesn't marry all their mothers. He may have told you that for reasons of his own, and you may have believed it because it was something you wanted to believe, but *I* don't believe it for one minute. Surely you've noticed by now how he *manages* things. If something doesn't suit him, he works things around until it's just the way he wants it. He talked you into marrying him by using the only argument he thought you'd listen to, but Risa wasn't his main objective—you were."

"You wouldn't say that if you had seen him last night," Kathleen said in bitter hurt. She stared at Sarah, wondering if she should complete her humiliation by admitting everything, only to find that, once she had begun talking, it was more difficult to stop than to go on. "I told him that the doctor had released me—" She drew a deep breath. "I tried to get him to make love to me, and he b-b-blew up like a volcano. He was so angry it scared me."

Sarah's eyes were huge. "Derek? *Derek* lost his temper?"

She nodded miserably. "He doesn't want me, Sarah. He never has. He just wanted Risa. He's practically perfect. All the nurses at the hospital would lie down and let him walk on them if he wanted. He's strong and kind, and he'd done everything he could to take care of us. I owe him so much I can never begin to repay him. I just wanted to give him s-s-sex, if nothing else, but he doesn't even want that from me. Why should he? He can have any woman he wants."

Sarah folded her arms and gave Kathleen a long, level stare. "Exactly," she said forcefully.

Kathleen blinked. "What?"

"I agree with you. Derek can have any woman he wants. He chose you."

"But he *doesn't* want me!"

"In all the years I've known him, I've never seen or heard of Derek losing his temper. Until now,"

Sarah said. "If he lost his temper with you, it's because you touch him more deeply than anyone else has before. Few people ever cross Derek, but when they do, he never loses his temper or even raises his voice. He doesn't have to—one look from him can shrivel you. His control is phenomenal, but he doesn't have that control with you. You can hurt him, you can make him angry. Believe me, he loves you so much it might frighten you if you knew how he feels. That may be the reason he fed you that line about wanting to marry you so he could have Risa. Risa is adorable, but Derek could have any number of his own children, if children were what he wanted."

"Then why wouldn't he make love to me last night?" Kathleen cried.

"What did he say?"

"He said he didn't need my ch-ch-charity."

"Of course he doesn't. Of all the things Derek would want from you, that wouldn't even be on the list. He wouldn't want gratitude, either. What else did he say?"

Kathleen stopped, thinking, and suddenly it was as if a door opened. "He said something about caring and commitment, but he wasn't…I didn't think he meant…" Her voice trailed off, and she stared at Sarah.

Sarah gave a very unladylike snort. "Kathleen, you crawl into bed with him tonight and tell him you *love* him, not how grateful you are or how much you owe him. Believe me, Derek will take things from there. He must be slipping, or he'd have handled things better last night. But then, he's never been in love before, so his own emotions are in the way right now."

Sarah's absolute certainty lifted Kathleen out of the doldrums, and for the first time she began to hope. Was it true? Could he possibly love her? She had never been loved before, and it scared her to think that this strong, perfect, gorgeous man could feel the same way about her that she felt about him. She shivered at the thought of putting Sarah's plan into action, because she would be putting her heart, her entire life, on the line, and it would be more than she could bear if he rejected her again.

Her heart was pounding so violently as she drove home that afternoon that she felt sick, and she forced herself to breathe deeply. Risa began fussing, and she gave the child a harried look. "Please, not tonight," she begged in an undertone. "You were so good last night, let's try for an encore, all right?"

But Risa continued fussing, and gradually worked herself into a real fit. Kathleen was only a few blocks from the apartment house, so she kept driving, but her nerves frayed at the effort it took her to ignore her child's crying for even that short time. When she pulled into the parking lot and cut off the motor, she felt a painful sense of relief as she unbuckled Risa from her seat and lifted the baby to her shoulder.

"There, there," she crooned, patting the tiny back. "Mommy's here. Were you feeling lonesome?" Risa subsided to hiccups and an occasional wail as Kathleen gathered everything in her arms and trudged up to the apartment. She had a sinking feeling Risa wasn't going to have a good night.

Just as she reached the door, it opened and Derek stood there. "You're early," she said weakly.

She couldn't read his expression as he reached out to take the baby. "I heard her fussing as you came down the hall," he said, ignoring Kathleen's comment as he put the baby on one shoulder and relieved Kathleen of the diaper bag. "Why don't you take a bath and relax while I get her settled. Then we'll have a quiet dinner and talk."

She stepped into the apartment and blinked her eyes in astonishment. What was going on? There was a Christmas tree standing in the corner decorated with strands of tinsel and hand-painted ornaments, while the multicolored lights blinked serenely. There were piles of gift-wrapped boxes under the tree, and fresh pine boughs lent their scent to the air, while glowing white candles decorated the table. An album of Christmas music was on the stereo, sleigh bells dancing in her ears.

The apartment had been perfectly normal when she had left that morning. She put her hand to her cheek. "But this is February," she protested, her voice blank with astonishment.

"This is Christmas," Derek said firmly. "The month doesn't matter. Go on, take your shower."

Then they would talk. The thought both frightened and thrilled her, because she didn't know what to expect. He must have spent most of the day doing this, which meant he had someone covering for him at the hospital. And where had he found a Christmas tree in February? It was a real tree, not an artificial one, so he must have cut it down himself. And what was in those boxes under the tree? He couldn't possibly have found a tree out in the country somewhere, too. It just wasn't possible. Yet it was done.

Despite his instructions to relax, she hurried through her shower, unable to tolerate any delay. When she entered the nursery, Derek had finished bathing Risa and was dressing her. Risa had settled down and was waving her fists around while she gave the little half cooing, half squeaking noises she had recently learned to make. Kathleen waited until she was finished, then took the baby to nurse her. As she settled herself in the rocking chair she looked at Derek uncertainly, wondering if he intended to remain in the room. Evidently he did, because he propped himself against the wall, his warm, golden eyes on her. Slowly she undid her robe and bared her breast, putting Risa to it. The baby's hungry little mouth clamped down on her nipple with comical greed, and for a moment she forgot everything but the baby and this special closeness. Quiet filled the small room, except for the sounds Risa made as she nursed.

Kathleen kept her eyes down, cuddling the baby to her and rocking long after the tugging on her breast had ceased. Derek moved away from the wall, and at last she had to look at him as he leaned down and, with the gentle pressure of one finger, released her nipple from the baby's mouth. "She's asleep," he murmured, and put the baby in her crib. Then he turned back to Kathleen, hot need in his eyes as they moved over her bare chest, and she blushed as she quickly drew the robe around her again.

"Dinner," he said in a strained voice.

Afterward, she was never certain how she managed to eat, but Derek put a plate in front of her and told her to eat, and somehow she did. He waited until they had finished before taking her hand and leading her into the living room, where that impossible Christmas tree still blinked its cheerful lights. She looked at the nostalgic scene, and her throat was suddenly thick with tears. She could never remember truly celebrating Christmas before; it just hadn't been a part of her family's tradition. But she could remember looking at pictures of a family gathered around just such a tree, with love shining in everyone's faces as they laughed and opened gifts, and she could remember the painful longing she had felt for that kind of closeness.

She cleared her throat. "Where did you manage to find a tree?"

He gave her a mildly surprised look, as if wondering why she would think finding a Christmas tree would be difficult for him. "I have a friend who grows them," he explained in that calm manner of his.

"But...why?" Helplessly, she gestured at the entire room.

"Because I thought this was what we needed. Why should Christmas be restricted to one certain time, when we need it all the time? It's about giving, isn't it? Giving and loving."

Gently he pushed her down to the floor in front of the tree, then sat down beside her and reached for the closest present, a small box gaily wrapped in scarlet, with a trailing gold ribbon. He placed it in her lap, and Kathleen stared down at it through a veil of hot tears that suddenly obscured her vision. "You've already given me so much," she whispered. "Please, Derek, I don't want to take anything else. I can never begin to repay—"

"I don't want to hear another word about repaying me," he interrupted, putting his arm around her and drawing her close to his side. "Love doesn't need repaying, because nothing can match it except love, and that's all I've ever wanted from you."

Her breath caught, and she stared up at him with

liquid green eyes. "I love you so much it hurts," she said on a choked-back sob.

"Shhh, sweetheart," he murmured, kissing her forehead. "Don't cry. I love you and you love me. Why should that make you cry?"

"Because I'm not good at loving. How could you possibly love me? Even my parents didn't love me!"

"That's their loss. How could I *not* love you? The first time I saw you, there in that old truck with your arms folded around your stomach to protect your baby, staring at me with those frightened but unbeaten green eyes, I went down for the count. It took me a little while to realize what had happened, but when I put Risa in your arms and you looked at her with your face lit with so much love that it hurt to look at you, I knew. I wanted that love turned on me, too. Your love is so fierce and strong, sweetheart. It's concentrated from being bottled up inside you all those years. Not many people can love like that, and I wanted it all for myself."

"But you didn't know me!"

"I knew enough," he said quietly, looking at the tree, his eyes calm with a deep inner knowledge few people ever attained. "I know what I want. I want you, Kathleen, the real you. I don't want you tiptoeing around, afraid of doing something in a different way from how I would have done it. I want you to laugh with me, yell at me, throw things at me when I make you mad. I want the fire in you, as well as the love, and I think I'll lose my mind if you don't love me enough to give it to me. The last thing I've ever wanted is gratitude."

She turned the small box over and over in her hands. "If loving is giving, why haven't you let me give anything to you? I've felt so *useless*."

"You're not useless," he said fiercely. "My heart wouldn't beat without you. Does that sound useless?"

"No," she whispered.

He put one finger under her chin and tilted her face up, smiling down into her eyes. "I love you," he said. "Now you say the words back to me."

"I love you." Her heart was pounding again, but not because it was difficult to say the words; she barely noticed them. It was the words he'd said that set the bells to ringing. Then she realized bells really were ringing; the stereo was now playing a lilting song about Christmas bells. A smile tilted her lips as she looked at the twinkling lights. "Did you really do this just for me?"

"Umm, yes," he said, bending his head to nuzzle her ear and the curve of her jaw. "You gave me the most wonderful Christmas of my life. I got you and our pretty Christmas baby all at one time. I thought I should give you a Christmas in return, to show you how much you mean to me. Open your present."

With trembling fingers she removed the wrapping paper and opened the small box. An exquisite gold locket in the shape of a heart gleamed richly on its white satin bed. She picked it up, the delicate links of the chain sliding over her fingers like golden rain.

"Open it," Derek whispered. She used her nail to open it, and found that it wasn't just a simple two-sided locket. There was more than one layer to it. There was room for two pictures; then she lifted a finely wrought divider section and found places for two more. "Our picture will go in the first section," he said. "Risa's will go in the side opposite ours, and our future children will go in the second section."

She turned the locket over. On the back was engraved, *You already have my heart; this is just a symbol of it—Your loving husband, Derek.*

Tears blurred her eyes again as she clasped the locket in her hands and lifted it to her lips.

He put another, larger present in her lap. "Open this one," he urged gently.

There was a small white card uppermost in the box when she opened it. She had to wipe the tears from her eyes before she could read the inscription: *Even during the night, the sun is shining somewhere. Even during the coldest winter, somewhere there are bluebirds. This is my bluebird to you, sweetheart, so you'll always have your bluebird no matter how cold the winter.* Inside the box was a white enamel music box, with a small porcelain bluebird perched on top, its tiny head tilted upward as if ready to sing, the little black eyes bright and cheerful. When she lifted the top, the music box began to play a gay, tinkling tune that sounded like birdsong.

"Open this one," Derek said, putting another box in her lap and wiping her tears away with his hand.

He piled box after box in her lap, barely giving her time to see one present before making her open another. He gave her a bracelet with their names engraved on it, a thickly luxurious sweater, silk underwear that made her blush, bunny-rabbit house shoes that made her laugh, perfume, earrings, record albums and books, and finally a creamy satin-and-lace nightgown that made her breath catch with its seductive loveliness.

"That's for *my* enjoyment," he said in a deep voice, looking at her in a way that made her pulse speed up.

Daringly, she lifted her head, stopping with her lips only inches from his. "And for mine," she whispered, almost painfully eager to taste his mouth, to know the feel of his body on hers. She hadn't known love could feel like this, like a powerful river flooding her body with heat and sensation and incredible longing.

"And yours," he agreed, taking her mouth with slow, burning expertise. Her lips parted for him automatically, and his tongue did a love dance with hers. She whimpered, her hands going up to cling behind his neck as blood began to pound in her ears. She felt warm, so warm she couldn't stand it, and the world seemed to be tilting. Then she felt the carpet under her, and Derek over her. His powerful body crushed her against the floor, but it wasn't painful. His mouth never left hers as he opened her robe and spread it wide, his hands returning to stroke slowly over her bare curves.

Never in her imagination or her dreams had she thought loving could be as wildly ecstatic as Derek showed her it could. He was slow, enthralled by her silken flesh under his hands, the taste of her in his mouth, the restless pressure of her legs around his hips as she arched mindlessly against him, begging for something she didn't fully understand. Her innocence in that respect was as erotic to him as her full, love-stung lips or the entranced look in her green eyes. He took his time with her despite his own agonizing tension and need, soothing her whenever some new sensation startled her. Her rich, lovely breasts were his, her curving hips were his, her silken loins were his.

She cried out, her body surging against his as he finally entered her with exquisite care, making her his wife in flesh as well as heart. They loved each other there on the carpet, surrounded by the presents he'd given her and the strewn, gaily-colored paper that had wrapped them. The candles burned with their serene white flame, and the joyously colored lights on the tree cast their glow on the man and woman, twined together in the silent aftermath of love.

Derek got to his feet and lifted Kathleen in his muscled arms. "I love you," she whispered, lacing kisses across his throat.

Her naked body gleamed like ivory, with the lights casting transparent jewels across her skin. He looked down at her with an expression that both frightened and exalted her, the look of a strong man who loves so much that he's helpless before it. "My God, I love you," he said in a shaking voice, then glanced around the living room. "I meant to wait. I wanted you to wear the gown I bought you, and I wanted you to be comfortable in our bed."

"I'm comfortable wherever you are," she assured him with glowing eyes, and he cradled her tightly to him as he carried her to their room. Most of his presents to her remained on the living room floor, but two were clutched in his hands: the heart-shaped locket and the bluebird music box. The winter was cold, but not her heart. She would always have her bluebird and the memory of her first real Christmas to keep her warm while her bluebird sang her lover's song to her.

* * * * *

Stephanie Bond grew up in eastern Kentucky, but traveled to distant lands through Harlequin romance novels. Years later, the writing bug bit her, and once again she turned to romance. Her writing has allowed her to travel in person to distant lands to teach workshops and promote her novels. She's written more than forty projects for Harlequin, including a romantic mystery series called Body Movers. To learn more about Stephanie Bond and her novels, visit www.stephaniebond.com.

NAUGHTY OR NICE?

Stephanie Bond

CHAPTER ONE

THE STYLIST HELD A handful of dark hair high above Cindy Warren's head, the scissors poised only inches from her scalp. "Are you sure you want to do this, ma'am?"

Cindy bit her lower lip, wavering. Long hair was easy, uncomplicated. *And a security blanket,* her mind whispered.

Standing behind another salon chair a few feet away, Jerry cleared his throat meaningfully and pushed the fuzzy Santa hat he wore back on his bald head. An institution at the Chandelier House hotel, the elderly black barber gave trims to male guests, but declined to use his artistry on female heads. His implied subtle comment nettled her. Whose hair was it, anyway?

She looked up once again to the length of hair, then to the woman's name tag. "Tell me, Bea, how long have you been working in our salon?"

"Counting today? Hmmmm. Three—no, four days. I graduated from beauty school two weeks ago, ma'am."

Cindy digested the information as Jerry spun his seated customer around to face the action. "Well, I'm due for a change," she murmured, to no one in particular, sitting erect with new resolve. "Long, straight hair is ridiculous at my age. I need to either have it cut, or become a country music singer."

Jerry gave her a pointed stare. "Hum a few bars."

"What's wrong with long, straight hair?" Jerry's customer asked.

Cindy's gaze darted to the man's reflection and her breath caught in appreciation of his appallingly good looks. "Excuse me?" she squeaked, then warmed with embarrassment.

The visitor, a striking man with pale blue eyes and a prominent nose, sat tall in the chair, his long, trousered legs extending far below the gray cape Jerry had draped over his torso. His dark curly hair lay damp and close to his head, compliments of Jerry, and a mirror trimmed with glittery gold tinsel reflected his crooked smile. "I said, what's wrong with long, straight hair?"

Squashing a zing of sexual awareness, Cindy bristled. "I-it makes me look like a coed."

"Most women would be thrilled," the man offered with a shrug.

"Well, not this woman," Cindy said, growing increasingly annoyed with her unexpected—and unwanted—physical reaction to him.

Jerry leaned over the man's shoulder and said in a

conspiratorial voice, "She's trying to impress someone."

"Jerry," Cindy warned, narrowing her eyes.

The customer nodded knowingly at Jerry in the mirror. "Figures. Man?"

"Oh, yeah," Jerry drawled, pulling off the plastic cape to reveal the man's crisp white collarless dress shirt and burgundy leather suspenders.

"Jerry, that's enough!"

"Boyfriend?" the man asked Jerry.

"Nah," the barber said sadly, shaking the cape. "Ms. Cindy doesn't date much—works day and night."

"Really? Day *and* night." The man made a sympathetic sound. "Then who is she trying to impress?"

"Some corporate fellow," Jerry said, whipping out a brush and whisking it over the man's neck and broad shoulders.

"Jerry, I've never impressed anyone in my life!" Suddenly, she realized what she'd said. "I mean, I've never *tried* to impress anyone."

The old barber ignored her. "Headquarters is sending a hatchet man next week to check us out, and to check out Ms. Cindy, too, I reckon."

"Other than the obvious reason—" the man flicked his glance her way for a split second "—why would this fellow be checking out Ms. Cindy?"

"'Cause," Jerry said, nodding toward their topic of discussion, "she runs this whole show."

His customer looked impressed. "Is that so?"

"Yes," Cindy said, looking daggers at Jerry. "That's so."

"Ma'am?" prompted a shaky Bea.

"Don't do it." The man leaned forward, resting his elbows on the padded arms of the chair.

With ballooning irritation, Cindy scoffed and waved off the stranger's opinion. "If men had their way, every woman would have hair down to her knees."

The man steepled his fingers and glanced up at Jerry. "I would have said ankles. How about you, Jer?"

"Amen."

"Ma'am," Bea pleaded, "my arms are about to give out."

Cindy raised her chin. "Cut it. This will be my early Christmas present to myself."

"Punishment for being naughty?" the man asked Jerry.

"Punishment for being nice," Jerry amended.

Fuming, Cindy nodded curtly to the hesitant hairdresser. "Do it."

"Don't do it," the man said, his voice rich with impending doom.

"Whack it off," Cindy said more forcefully. "Layers all over. Make me a new woman."

The handsome man's eyes cut to Jerry. "Is there something wrong with the old woman?"

Jerry pursed his lips. "She's a little impulsive."

Cindy set her jaw. "Let's get this over with."

Bea swallowed audibly. "I'll leave the back shoulder length, ma'am." The woman closed her eyes.

Alarm suddenly gripped Cindy. "Wait!" she cried just as the shears made a slicing sound. Bea opened her eyes and stared.

The man winced, and Jerry grunted painfully when the hairdresser held up more than a foot of severed dark tresses. As the remnants fell back to her shoulders, Cindy tried to squash her own rising panic and painted on a shaky smile, encouraging the new stylist to continue.

Maybe, she thought, keeping her gaze down and dabbing at perspiration along her neck, this woman would stay longer than the seven days their previous hairdressers had averaged. Cindy had urged her staff members to give the salon their patronage, and felt compelled to take the lead. But twenty minutes later, when Bea stood back to absorb the full effect of her latest creation in the mirror, Cindy understood why none of her employees used the unproved stylists.

"Good Lord," Jerry muttered, shaking his head.

The man whistled low. "Too bad."

"You hate it, don't you?" Bea asked Cindy, her face crumbling.

"N-no," Cindy rushed to assure her. She lifted a hand, but couldn't bring herself to touch the choppy, lank layers that hugged her head like a long knit cap.

"It'll just take some getting used to, that's all." She inhaled and smiled brightly.

"Think he'll be impressed?" the man asked Jerry, doubt clear in his voice.

"If he can get past the hair," Jerry said, nodding.

"*Do* you two mind?" Cindy snapped, feeling a flush scald her cheeks. She tugged the cape off her shoulders and stood, brushing the sleeves of her blouse. Jerry, she could overlook. But this, this... arrogant guest was tap-dancing on her holiday-frazzled nerves.

The infuriating man stood as well, and in her haste to leave, Cindy slipped on a pile of her own hair and skidded across the marble floor, flailing her arms and legs like a windup toy. He halted her imminent fall with one large hand, his fingers curving around her arm. Cindy jerked upright to stare into his dancing blue eyes, then pulled away from his grasp. "Th-thank you," she murmured, her face burning.

"The haircut must have thrown off your balance," he observed with a half smile.

Feeling like a complete idiot, Cindy retrieved her green uniform jacket and withdrew a generous tip for the distraught Bea, then strode toward the exit. Her skin tingled with humiliation and her scalp felt drafty, but she refused to crumble. She simply had too much on her mind to dwell on the embarrassing episode with the attractive stranger—the upcoming review, going home for Christmas and now her hair.

Cindy squared her shoulders and lifted her chin. No matter. After all, the unsettling man was simply passing through. And Manny would know what to do with her hair.

"OH, MY," MANNY said when she walked within earshot of the concierge desk. "Cindy, *tell* me that's a wig."

Cindy smiled weakly at her blond friend. "It's a wig."

"Liar," he said smoothly, then emerged from behind his desk to touch her hair, a pained expression on his handsome face.

Hiring Manny Oliver as concierge over a year ago had been one of Cindy's greatest achievements in her four years managing the Chandelier House. Next to most of the oddball staff members she had inherited, Manny was a breath of fresh air: good-looking, polite, helpful and witty. A true friend, *and* he could cook. Cindy sighed. Why were all the good ones gay?

"Don't tell me," he said, stroking her head as if she were a pet. "You've been to see Bea the Butcher."

"You know about her?"

"I arranged a free dinner to console a lady she hacked yesterday."

Cindy felt like crying. "Now you tell me."

"You know I don't bother you with details. What were you *thinking* to cut your beautiful hair?"

"I was trying to drum up confidence in the salon among the staff."

"Now you're a walking billboard, all right."

She grimaced. "So can my hair be saved?"

He smiled. "Sure. There's this great little hat shop down on Knob Hill—"

"Manny!"

"Shh, I get off at one. I'll meet you in your suite," he promised. "If you get there first, plug in your curling iron."

Cindy frowned. "Curling iron?"

Manny pursed his lips and shook his head. "Never mind—I'll bring the tools."

She lowered her voice and scanned the lobby. "So, have you seen anyone who looks like they might be undercover?"

He leaned forward and whispered, "Not a trench coat in sight." When she smirked, he added, "What makes you think this Stanton fellow is going to come early to spy on us?"

"Because *I* would."

"It would be nice if we knew what he looked like."

"My guess is he's in his fifties, probably white—although I can't be sure—and walking funny because he's got his shorts in a knot." She leaned close. "And he might be in disguise. So be on the lookout for someone we'd least suspect to be on a corporate mission."

At that moment, Captain Kirk and Mr. Spock

look-alikes strolled by in full costume. Manny looked at Cindy. "Could you be more specific?"

"Okay," she relented. "Spotting a spy will be difficult in this hotel, but keep your eyes peeled. I'll see you at the staff meeting."

She cruised by the front desk and smiled at the dozen or so smartly suited reservations handlers, not missing their alarmed glances at her hair. Engineering workers were hanging garland and wreaths on the wall behind the reservations desk and at least a hundred overcoiffed females—guests who'd attended a cosmetics convention—waited in lines fashioned by velvet ropes to check out. Cindy slipped in behind Amy, the rooms director, and asked, "How's it going?"

"Fine," the brunette answered, then lifted a hand to her forehead. "Except for a raging headache."

Cindy tried to conjure up a bit of sympathy for the woman, but while Amy had proved to be very capable on the job, her tendency toward hypochondria remained legendary around the watercooler. "Must be the perfume," she offered in her most soothing tone, nodding toward the aromatic crowd.

Amy sighed noisily. "Don't worry—I'll survive. Once we get the makeup ladies out of here, we'll have a full two hours before the bulk of the Trekkies arrive."

"May the Force be with you," Cindy said solemnly.

Amy laughed. "Wrong flick, Cindy."

"I have thirty free minutes before the staff meeting. Any problems I can take off your hands?"

Amy gave her a grateful smile, then rummaged under the desk and came up with a clipboard. "Room 620 wants a better view, 916 wants a TV without the adult movie channel and room 1010 wants a smoking room with a king-sized bed."

"And do we have alternative rooms for them?"

Amy made check marks with her pencil as she moved down the list. "No, no and no."

"And 'no' means a personal visit," Cindy said wryly, taking the clipboard.

Grinning, Amy said, "Take it up with the GM—it's one of her policies."

"Touché."

"By the way." Amy squinted and tilted her head. "What happened to your hair?"

Cindy frowned. "I'll see you at the staff meeting."

Retracing her steps through the lobby, she noticed every detail. The gray marble floors were polished to a high sheen, the sitting areas populated with antique furniture and overstuffed couches were neat. Christmas was a scant two weeks away, and while everyone else in the world shopped and anticipated holiday gatherings, Cindy knew she and her staff had many grueling hours ahead of them during their busiest time of the year.

Top that with headquarters' announcement they

were sending a man from a third-party downsizing firm to look over her shoulder for the next couple of weeks... And not just any man—Cindy shivered—but a highly touted, much-feared hatchet man named Stanton. Her intercompany contacts informed her he was ruthless, and the fact that he was coming at all did not bode well for the future of the Chandelier House. No uptight corporate stiff would appreciate the nutty flavor of her eccentric staff.

Avoiding the crowded elevator corridor, she headed toward the sweeping three-story staircase in the front of the lobby. The climb up the dark-gold-carpeted stairs gave her an impressive view of her front operation.

The hotel's signature item, an enormous sparkling chandelier, presided over the lobby. She gave the dazzling piece a fond wink in memory of her grandfather, thinking of his stories of the hotel in its heyday, then turned her attention to the pulsing activity below. Every employee seemed occupied, from the valets to the bellmen to the lobby maids. Greenery, garlands and lights, thanks to engineering, were slowly enveloping the lobby walls and fixtures. Jaunty Christmas Muzak kept everyone moving and lifted Cindy's spirits as well.

A new beginning lay just around the corner. A clean slate. A promising year for the Chandelier House, a better relationship with her mother, maybe even a man in her life.

Cindy smirked. Why settle for one Christmas miracle?

At the top of the stairs, she paused to catch her breath, then caught an elevator to the sixth floor. An owlish-looking middle-aged man answered her knock to room 620. Wearing suit slacks, dress shirt and tie, he held a pad of paper under his arm and, oddly, the room's antique desk lamp in one hand. Cindy raised an eyebrow, then quietly introduced herself and explained that a room with a better view of the city was available, but it was a suite, and therefore, considerably more expensive.

The man frowned behind thick glasses and complained loudly, but Cindy remained calm, her eyes meaningfully glued to the lamp. In the end he huffily claimed the room to be adequate and slammed the door. Cindy shook her head, then jotted a reminder to send him a complimentary prune Danish the following morning. The man was obviously constipated.

The robed couple in room 916 cleared up a misunderstanding—they weren't complaining about having access to the adult channel, they were complaining because they thought the channel should be free. No, Cindy explained, but an evening of pay-per-view was still relatively cheap entertainment in San Francisco.

She was two for three approaching room 1010, thankful the complaints were small compared to what her staff normally dealt with. Wrinkling her nose at the ancient orange carpet bearing a nauseating floral pattern, she pledged to put the case forcefully to headquarters about the need for new hallway floor coverings, then lifted her hand and rapped lightly on the door.

Within seconds, the handsome stranger from the hair salon stood before her, minus his dress shoes. His imposing masculinity washed over Cindy and his smile revealed white teeth and slight crow's-feet at the corners of his ice-blue eyes. Late thirties, she decided. "We meet again," he said pleasantly.

"Um, yes," Cindy murmured, resisting the urge to pull her jacket up over her head. She checked the clipboard. "Er, Mr. Quinn?"

"Eric Quinn," he said, extending his hand.

She returned his firm and friendly shake. "I'm Cindy Warren, Mr. Quinn, I—"

"—run this whole show…I remember."

She flushed. "I'm the general manager, and I came to discuss your request for another room."

He crossed his arms and leaned against the doorjamb, smiling lazily. "Do you personally oversee every guest request, Ms. Warren?"

"No, I—"

"Then I'm flattered."

He was an extremely handsome man, Cindy decided as she struggled to regain control of the situation. And very full of himself. "No need, Mr. Quinn," she replied coolly. "My reservations staff is swamped at the moment, so I'm pitching in. If you're interested, we have a smoking room available, but it doesn't have a king-sized bed."

Mr. Quinn frowned and stroked his chin with his left hand.

No ring, she noticed, then chastised herself. The absence of a ring didn't mean the man was available. And despite her mother's increasingly urgent pleas for her to find a nice man and settle down, even if he *was* available, Cindy wasn't in the market for a relationship with a guest…who rubbed her the wrong way…at the most professionally chaotic and emotionally vulnerable time of the year.

Mr. Quinn shook his head ruefully. "No, a smaller bed will never do. I can afford to go without cigarettes more than I can afford to go without sleep. I'm a big man," he added unnecessarily.

To her horror, Cindy involuntarily glanced over his figure again, then felt a heat rash scale her neck. She fidgeted with the clipboard, clacking the metal clip faster and faster as her pulse rate climbed.

He shrugged. "I guess I'll stay put since I need a big, roomy bed."

Cindy's hand slipped and the metal clip snapped down on her fingers, sending pain exploding through her hand. "Yeeeeooooow!"

Mr. Quinn grabbed the clipboard and released her pinched fingers in the time it took for Cindy to process the distress signals from her brain.

"You're bleeding," he uttered, clasping her fingers.

"It's nothing," she gasped, bewildered that such a minor injury could produce so much blood—and agony—and wondering what it was about this man that made her behave like the Fourth Stooge.

"Come in and wash your hands," he said, tugging gently at her arm.

"Uh, no." Cindy knew there was a good reason to turn him down, but the rationale escaped her for a few seconds.

"But you need to stop the bleeding."

Suddenly Cindy's brain resumed functioning— oh, yeah, she *lived* here. "I have my own suite," she explained hurriedly.

"Be reasonable, Ms. Warren. You'll ruin your clothes." His mouth curved into a wry smile. "Not to mention this, er, lovely carpet."

She relented with a laugh, gritting her teeth against the pain. "Maybe I will borrow a wet wash-cloth, if you don't mind."

He stepped back and swept his arm inside the room. "This is your hotel. I'll wait here."

"I'll just be a moment," she murmured. As he held open the door, she slid past him, their bodies so close she could see the threads on the buttons of his starched white shirt. The proximity set what hair she had left on end.

Keeping her eyes averted from Mr. Quinn's personal belongings, she stepped over his barge-sized dress shoes in the doorway of the bathroom, squashing down her instantaneous thought of the anatomical implications. She also ignored the masculine scents of soap and aftershave as she turned on the cold-water faucet and grabbed a washcloth.

Glancing into the mirror was a mistake—her hair looked straight out of the seventies and her makeup needed more than a touch-up. Cindy groaned, then gasped when the water hit her fingers. *What an idiot I am.*

She applied pressure with a white washcloth and looked toward the bedroom. The door he held open cast light into the room from the hallway, sending his long shadow across the carpet. No doubt he was belly-laughing at what must seem like her talent for self-destruction.

Cindy removed the washcloth, relieved the bleeding had slowed.

"You'll find a couple of bandages in my toiletry bag," he called out, and for the first time she noticed a slight Southern accent. "It's on the back of the door. Help yourself."

She hesitated to go through his personal belongings, but then told herself she was being ridiculous over a couple of lousy bandages. Cindy stepped back and closed the bathroom door, immediately smelling the soft leather of Mr. Quinn's black toiletry bag. Her hand stopped in midair at the sight of pale blue silk pajama pants barely visible behind the large hanging bag. A picture of the handsome Mr. Quinn in his lounge wear zoomed to mind and the urge to run overwhelmed her.

With jerky hands, she unzipped the left side of the toiletry bag, but to her dismay, a barrage of small foil packets rained down on her sensible pumps. Condoms. At least a dozen in all varieties—colored, textured, flavored.

Oh, good Lord. Cindy dropped to her knees and snatched up the condoms, then stood and crammed them back into the pocket, knocking down Mr. Quinn's pajama pants in the process. *Dammit.* She yanked up the flimsy pants, remembering too late the cuts on her hand. And silk was nothing if not absorbent. Cindy watched in abject horror as the pale fabric soaked up her blood. She dropped the garment as if it were on fire.

"Are you all right in there?" he called.

Cindy nearly swallowed her tongue. "Y-yes."

"Did you find what you were looking for?"

Her heart thrashing, Cindy tore open the right zippered pocket of the toiletry bag and fished out the bandages amongst shaving cream, shampoo and toothpaste. "Got them!" she called. Quickly she rewashed her fingers and slapped on the bandages despite the tremor of her hands. Finally, she turned and carefully picked up the silk pants to assess the damage.

One clear red imprint of her hand embellished the backside, as if she'd grabbed the man's tush.

Cindy closed her eyes, her mind reeling. Why did things like this happen to her?

"Is everything okay in there?"

She leaned on the sink for support. *Should I tell the man I found his stash of rubbers and fondled his pajamas?* Then Cindy straightened. She could have the pants cleaned, then slip them back inside his room before tonight—Mr. Quinn would never know. Considerably cheered, she wadded the pants into a ball and shoved them down the back of her skirt. Thankfully, her jacket covered the lump.

Cindy took a deep breath and emerged from the bathroom, nearly faltering when she had to sidle past him again to reach the hall. "Thank you," she said, as she retrieved the clipboard.

"No problem."

At the sight of his devilish grin, Cindy remembered the man's sexual preparedness and told herself he was a lady-killer to be avoided. Recalling her original errand, Cindy cleared her throat. "And I'm sorry about the room, Mr. Quinn. Of course you're welcome to smoke in the hotel lounge."

He shrugged. "Perhaps I'll take this opportunity to rid myself of a nasty vice."

Backing away on wobbly legs, Cindy nodded

curtly. "Well, good luck." Then she turned and fled, horrifically aware of the man's pants jammed in her pantyhose.

ERIC STEPPED INTO THE HALL and watched her hurry away. He was at a loss to explain why he'd felt so compelled to tease the woman. In scant days Cindy Warren would see him in an entirely different light, and laying a friendly foundation wouldn't hurt, he reasoned. He ignored the fact that such a gesture had never seemed necessary in past assignments. Perhaps the thought of her cutting her lovely hair to impress the hatchet man had made the difference.

From the reports concerning the Chandelier House, he had known the general manager was a woman, but nothing had prepared him for her youth or her beauty. Yet after observing her in the salon for only a short time, he understood why Cindy Warren held the top position in the grande dame hotel. She had fire in her beautiful green eyes and a firm set to her chin. And even with the haircut from hell, she was still pretty damn cute.

Eric stepped back into his room, pushing the stiff leather suspenders over his shoulders to fall loosely past his waist. Crossing to the antique desk where he'd abandoned a stack of paperwork, he reclaimed the surprisingly comfortable chair.

Using a pen with the hotel's name on it, he jotted down notes about the room he'd received as an incognito business traveler. His head pivoted as he surveyed the space.

Although the wood furnishings were far from new, the bed, armoire and desk were charming and smelled pleasantly of lemon furniture polish. The bed linens were a restful combination of taupe checks and plaids, and the worn areas in the carpet had been cleverly concealed by attractive wool rugs. The electrical outlets worked and the spacious bathroom smelled fresh and sunny, although the Sweet Tarts on the pillow struck him as slightly odd.

He scribbled a few more notations, then stopped and dragged his hand over his face, picturing the determined set of Cindy Warren's shoulders. Frustrated by the attraction he felt for her, he reminded himself of the danger of getting too involved with someone who might suffer from his assignment.

Craving a cigarette, he expelled a noisy breath, then reached for the phone and dialed out. After a few seconds, a familiar voice came on the line.

"Lancaster here."

"Bill, this is Stanton. I just wanted to let you know I'm on-site."

"Great. How's the preliminary—is the place as nutty as we've been told?"

Eric fingered the package of Sweet Tarts. "Too early to tell."

"Well, I spoke to our liaison from Harmon today. If you discover in the next few days that the Chandelier House doesn't fit the future profile for a corporate property, we won't even send in the rest of the team."

Eric frowned. "I'm good, but that hardly seems fair."

"Sounds like Harmon wants to get rid of this property."

"If the numbers are that bad, why don't they just dump it?"

"Because the numbers aren't that bad. And some old cow on the board of directors has a soft spot for the place, so they need justification. We're it."

Eric leaned back in his chair. "Look, Bill, I came here to do a job and I'm not turning in a phony report. Plan on sending the team as scheduled. My reputation aside, there are people here to consider."

His associate snorted. "People? I'm sorry, I thought I was talking to Eric Stanton. Are the holidays making you soft?"

Cindy Warren's green-gray eyes flashed through his mind. "No—I guess I'm just tired."

"Have you met the GM?"

"Yeah." *Oh, yeah.*

"Is she onto you yet?"

Eric pinched the bridge of his nose. "Nope, she's not onto me yet." *But she's already under my skin.*

CHAPTER TWO

CINDY TRIED TO ERASE Eric Quinn's image from her mind as she approached the executive meeting room. If ever there was a time not to be distracted by an attractive guest, it was now, when the fate of her staff depended on her. Worry niggled the back of her mind. Working in the close confines of the hotel, coworkers rapidly became like family, and she felt responsible for their future.

In the two years since Harmon Hospitality had purchased the Chandelier House, she and her staff had received countless memos from the home office mandating changes that would force their beloved hotel to fit into a corporate mold. So far, she had resisted. Her employees had no concept of a corporate direction—at any given time, most of them had no idea which direction was *up.* Yet somehow jobs were done and guests were delighted enough to return time after time.

"Good morning, everyone," she said, flashing a cheerful smile around the room as she walked to the head of the long table. Six directors and a handful of assorted managers chorused greetings and exchanged barbs while vying for a choice doughnut from the boxes being passed around.

The meeting room reeked of the mingling brews gurgling from appliances in the corner: regular coffee, cappuccino, sassafras tea and something scarlet dripping from the juicer. Cindy wrinkled her nose and refilled her cup with black coffee.

"New haircut, Cindy?" Joel Cutter, the food and beverage director, covered a smile by biting into a powdered doughnut.

Amidst the good-natured chuckling, Cindy threw him her most withering look, which didn't faze him. A valued employee and personal friend, Joel oversaw the restaurant, the lounge and catering. Hot coffee sloshed over the edge of her happy-face mug as she set it on the table. She tucked herself into an upholstered chair, ignoring the unsettling lump at her back. "Pass the doughnuts. And thanks for the opening, Joel. We'll begin with the hair salon. Amy?"

All eyes turned to the wincing rooms director, who was shaking white pills from one of the four bottles sitting on the table in front of her. She downed them with a drink of the scarlet liquid. "If it wasn't for Jerry, I'd say turn the place into an ice-cream parlor. I talked the new stylist into staying through tomorrow, but after that, we'll be short-handed again." Amy smiled sheepishly. "Jerry said she hasn't stopped crying since you left, boss." The room erupted into more laughter.

Cindy waved to quiet the melee. "Ha-ha, very funny. Seriously, what seems to be the problem with keeping a qualified stylist?"

Amy leaned forward. "Most hairdressers I've interviewed want to keep their skills sharp in areas other than simple cuts, like perming and coloring. In my opinion, we need to offer a full range of services."

Nodding, Cindy made a few notes on a yellow legal pad. "Fine."

Amy angled her head. "And it would help if Jerry—"

"—would agree to wait on female customers," Cindy finished for her. "I know. But Jerry's good at what he does, and we can't afford to lose him. He's a legend."

"Much like your new hairdo," Joel mumbled into his napkin, prompting more laughter.

Ignoring him, she shifted her gaze to Samantha Riggs, director of sales. "How's business, Sam?"

"Never better," Sam replied, completely at ease in full Klingon war regalia, including the lumpy forehead mask. "If the Trekkies are happy with the way we handle the regional conference, we're bound to get the business of the Droids and the Fantasms." She adjusted her chain-metal sash for emphasis.

Cindy hoped her smile wasn't as shaky as it felt.

Although the buying power and loyalty of the role-playing groups was strong, she'd heard the hotel was getting quite a reputation at headquarters as well—as the Final Frontier.

Sam counted off on her black-tipped fingernails as she spoke. "The crystal readers will be here at the end of the week, the vampires are arriving at midnight on Saturday and the adult toy trade show starts next Monday."

Panic seized Cindy. "Adult toys next Monday?"

"Isn't that corporate fellow arriving next Monday?" Joel asked casually, reaching for a honey cruller.

Cindy nodded, trying to mask her alarm. She didn't mind hosting the X-rated trade show, but the timing couldn't have been any worse.

"Let's hope he has a sense of humor," Amy chirped.

"And a sex life," Manny interjected.

"Don't worry," Joel said, "Cindy has cornered the market on celibacy."

"You're a laugh a minute, Joel," Cindy said dryly, ignoring the burst of applause. Joel and his wife were constantly trying to fix her up, but their matchmaking attempts had produced one disaster after another. "Sam, let's keep the trade show as low-profile as possible, okay?"

Sam nodded convincingly. "You want low-profile, Cindy—you got low-profile."

"Said the woman in the Klingon costume," Manny pointed out.

"Hey, whatever makes the customer happy," Sam said smoothly.

Cindy looked to William Belk, director of engineering, a burly fellow who rarely spoke. Smiling broadly, she asked, "William, how goes the search for the perfect lobby Christmas tree?"

He glanced around uneasily, twisting his cap in his big hands. "The nursery is still looking."

Cindy's stomach pitched. "We're running out of days in the month of December," she said with mustered good humor. "I'd like to see the tree up and decorated before our visitors arrive next Monday."

"Uh, yeah."

She smiled tightly and wrote herself a note to follow up with the nursery. After discussing a few administrative details with the comptroller and the human resources manager, she glanced at Joel and lifted one corner of her mouth. "Would you like to close out the meeting, or is my hair too distracting?"

"I'll try to be strong," Joel responded fiercely, then added, "Farrah."

Cindy rolled her eyes heavenward. "Start with banquets."

"Booked to 90 percent through New Year's."

She blinked. "Great. The restaurant?"

He pushed a newspaper article toward her. "The *Chronicle* gave us a mediocre review."

"That beats the flogging they gave us last spring," she said. "Anything else?"

"I doubt I'm the only one wondering about this axman, Stanton."

Cindy glanced around the room, which had suddenly grown so quiet she could hear her hair moaning. After a deep breath, she rested her elbows on the table. "The corporate review was next on the agenda, but I'm glad you brought it up, Joel." She wet her lips. "As most of you know, a third-party firm has been hired to study select properties under the corporate umbrella." She smiled. "And we're one of the lucky ones—the Chandelier House is going to be treated to the works."

Cindy counted on fingers that hadn't seen a manicure in months. "An audit of our accounting procedures, our reservations process, sales, customer service—if we do it, it's going to be scrutinized."

Manny cleared his throat. "Is there a reason we're being studied so closely?"

Cindy clasped her hands in front of her. "The inspection might be related to the fact that I've resisted efforts to change the way the hotel does business."

"And that you have breasts," Amy muttered.

"I have no reason to believe this has anything to do with me being a woman," Cindy said with sincerity, then grinned and pointed her thumb toward the slight curves beneath her jacket. "Besides, your point is debatable."

Laughter eased the tension in the room.

"They want to turn us into a cookie-cutter corporate operation," Joel supplied.

Cindy weighed her words. "It would seem that headquarters would like for us to conform more to a corporate profile, yes." She forced optimism into her voice, then swept her gaze around the room. "A Mr. Stanton is scheduled to arrive next Monday with an examination team. But I wouldn't be surprised if he arrives a few days early to check us out. Let me know if you notice anyone suspicious."

"Should we be worried?" Amy asked, massaging her temples. "I think I'm getting a migraine."

"We should all be *aware*," Cindy corrected gently. "Aware that everything we do will be under a microscope. As soon as Mr. Stanton arrives, I'll call an executive committee meeting and make the proper introductions." She conjured up an encouraging smile. "Now, if there's nothing else—"

"Whoa," Joel said, raising his hand. "Don't forget about the Christmas party tomorrow night."

Cindy nearly groaned. Nothing could have been further from her mind. "How could we forget?" she croaked.

"With cutbacks on the horizon, should we bring a bag lunch?" Sam asked.

Everyone laughed, but Cindy shook her head emphatically.

"Forget the lunch," Joel said, "but feel free to bring a date for Cindy."

Amid the laughter, Cindy narrowed her eyes at Joel. "*You* are treading on thin ice." She smacked her hand on the table. "This meeting is adjourned."

As everyone filed out of the room, Joel fell in step beside her and she poked him in the shoulder. "What makes you so sure I'm not bringing a date? It just so happens that I might."

Joel's look of incredulity made her wish she actually *did* have a date. And the flash of Eric Quinn's face in her mind exasperated her further. "You don't have a date," Joel scoffed. "Name one eligible bachelor in this town you haven't neutered with indifference. Your name is on the bathroom wall—for a hard time, call Cindy Warren."

"You flatter me."

"Cindy, if you bring a date tomorrow night—" He looked toward the ceiling. "I'll cover for you all day Wednesday."

She straightened. Since her home consisted of a small suite near the top of the hotel, excursions outside the walls—especially for an entire day—were rare. This could be her last chance to go Christmas shopping before the hotel descended into seasonal chaos. "You'd cover my office calls?"

"Yep."

Her last chance to buy a few casual clothes before she headed home to Virginia on Christmas Eve. "My pager?"

"Sure thing." Then he grinned. "Of course, if you come stag, I get your parking spot for a month."

And hadn't the lock on her garment bag jammed the last time she'd traveled to L.A. overnight on business? She definitely needed new luggage. "And all I have to do is produce a man?"

"He has to be straight," Amy qualified, walking on the other side.

"Right," Joel agreed sternly. "I expect to see definite heterosexual groping before the night's over."

Cindy put her hand over her heart. "I'm wounded—you two honestly think I can't find a date?"

"Right," they said in unison.

She squinted at Joel. "You're on, buster."

Joel rubbed his hands together and squeezed his eyes shut. "VIP parking—I can hardly wait."

"Well, *I* can't wait to meet this mystery man," Amy said over her shoulder as she followed Joel toward the stairs.

Cindy stopped and stared after her friends, dread surging in her stomach. "Neither can I."

ERIC SPENT THE NEXT couple of hours touring various areas of the hotel as unobtrusively as possible, occasionally ducking into alcoves to scribble on index cards. If employees stopped to offer assistance, he either manufactured requests for directions or said he was waiting for someone.

The covert stage of his job had always been his least favorite. Eric didn't have a problem with pointing out deficiencies in an operation, but he much preferred doing it face-to-face with the staff.

He spotted Cindy Warren twice as she practically jogged from one task to another, but he stayed out of her line of vision despite his urge to talk to her again. He typically made his most valuable observations early in the review process and he liked as much done as possible in the first couple of days, since he never knew if or when his cover would be blown. After that, the sucking-up factor set in—an ego trip for some consultants, but merely a hindrance to productivity in his opinion.

After he'd exhausted his many checklists, he made his way to the concierge desk, where a pleasant-looking blond man offered him a professional smile.

"Good afternoon, sir. How can I help you?"

Eric sized him up in seconds—he knew from the man's demeanor he was an asset to Cindy Warren. "I'm looking for a dinner recommendation."

"Any particular type of cuisine, sir?"

"Maybe a good steak."

"Unless you want to see the city, our chef grills a great rib eye."

Eric inclined his head, silently applauding the

man's response. "Sounds good. I'll try it. How's the lounge?"

"Great drinks, but not much action on Monday night."

Shaking his head slightly, Eric laughed. "Fine with me."

The concierge extended his hand. "I'm Manny Oliver."

Eric clasped his hand in a firm grip. "Quinn. Eric Quinn."

"Glad you chose the Chandelier House for your trip, Mr. Quinn. Let me know if there's anything I can do to make your stay more enjoyable."

At that moment, Eric caught sight of Cindy across the lobby. He hadn't realized he was staring until Manny's cool voice reached him. "That's our general manager, Cindy Warren."

Eric tried to appear casual. "We met briefly in the salon this morning. I was quite impressed with her, um, professionalism." *And her legs.* Eric watched her move alongside a barrel-chested man, gesturing from floor to ceiling in the curve of the magnificent staircase.

"She's first-rate," the man agreed. "The Chandelier House is lucky to have her."

"She seems young for so much responsibility," Eric said, fishing.

"Early thirties," Manny offered.

"Is she single?" The words came out before Eric

could stop them, and he wasn't sure who was more surprised, himself or the concierge.

Manny straightened, his defenses up, and Eric wondered if the man had romantic feelings for his boss. "Ms. Warren is unmarried," he said tightly.

Mentally kicking himself, Eric simply nodded. "Thank you for the meal recommendation, Mr. Oliver." He withdrew a bill from his wallet, but before he could extend it, Manny stopped him with the slightest lift of his hand. "Don't mention it, Mr. Quinn. It's my job to take care of *everyone* in the hotel."

Manny's friendly smile didn't mask the glimmer of warning in his clear blue eyes.

"I'm sure you're good at your job," Eric said lightly.

"The best," Manny assured him as another guest approached his station. "Enjoy that steak, Mr. Quinn."

Unable to resist another peek in her direction, Eric was treated to an inadvertent display of lower thigh as Cindy stretched her arm high to make a point to the man, presumably in preparation for installing more seasonal decorations.

Feeling Manny's stare boring into his back, Eric dragged his gaze away from Cindy Warren. Checking his watch and finding he had plenty of time for a drink before dinner, he moved in the direction of the lounge, trying to shake off the undeniable surge of attraction he felt for the general manager. The nostalgia of the season must be getting to him, he decided. Making him sappy. Or horny. Or both.

The name "Sammy's" stretched over the entrance to the lounge, one of the few areas in the hotel Eric had not yet staked out. He walked down two steps and into the low-lit interior, fully expecting the lounge to resemble the hundreds of other generic hotel bars he'd visited during his fifteen-year stint in the business. Instead, he was pleasantly surprised to find a motif of antique musical instruments. An old upright piano sat abandoned in a far corner. The strains of Burl Ives played over unseen speakers, evoking memories of past Christmases. A bittersweet thought; family gatherings hadn't been the same since his mother's death.

The place was practically deserted, with only a handful of customers dotting the perimeter of the room. A knot of Trekkies indulged in a down-to-earth pitcher of beer.

But to his pleasure, Jerry the barber sat on one of the upholstered stools, still wearing the Santa hat. He chatted with a thick-armed bartender and smoked a sweet-smelling cigar.

"Weeeeell, if it isn't Mr. Quinn." Jerry grinned and nodded to the stool next to him. "Have a seat. Tony'll get you a drink."

Eric slid onto the stool and rested his elbows on the smooth curved edge of the bar. "Bourbon and water," he directed Tony with a nod. "Taking a break, Jer?" He patted his shirt pocket for a cigarette, then remembered he had left them in the room.

The older man nodded and took a long drag of his cigar. "I'm through for the day—got tired of that woman caterwauling."

"Excuse me?"

Jerry used the cigar as a pointer while he talked. "That woman who whacked off Ms. Cindy's hair—she's been bawling all day."

"It wasn't her fault," Eric said with a laugh. "We warned your boss."

"You know Cindy?" Tony glared as he slid Eric's drink toward him.

Another besotted employee, Eric surmised. "Not really," he said lightly.

Tony sized him up silently, flexing his massive chest beneath his skintight dress shirt. The red jingle bell suspenders did little to soften the man's looks. Finally Tony walked down the bar to help another customer.

"Don't mind him," Jerry said with another puff. "He's Ms. Cindy's self-appointed bodyguard."

"He looks dangerous."

Jerry glanced around, then leaned toward him. "Just between me and you, he did a stint at San Quentin."

Eric glanced up from his drink in alarm. "For what?"

"Never asked," the man admitted. "But he's fine as long as he stays on his medication. A bit protective of the boss lady, though."

"Ms. Warren is a popular woman," Eric observed.

"She's a *good* woman," Jerry amended. "But stubborn." He shook his head. "Stubborn as the day is long."

"She's not a good manager?"

"She's the best. But a big company bought this place a couple of years ago and has been trying to change it ever since. Ms. Cindy is wearing herself out digging in her heels."

Eric kept his voice light. "There's always room for improved efficiency."

"People don't come to the Chandelier House for efficiency, Mr. Quinn. You can go down the street and get a bigger room with a better view for less money."

"So why come here at all?"

The man laughed and nodded toward the Trekkies. "We're oddballs, Mr. Quinn, and we cater to oddballs. It's a profitable niche, but Ms. Cindy can't get anyone up the ladder to listen to her."

"She confides in you?"

"Nope." Jerry grinned. "But I know this hotel—been here thirty years, and I know women—been married three times."

"The last one is a dubious credential," Eric noted, taking another drink from his glass.

"Women are the most blessed gift the good Lord put on this earth," the old man said with a ring of satisfaction. "Ever been to the altar, son?"

A short laugh escaped Eric. "No."

Jerry nodded knowingly. "But Ms. Cindy's interesting, isn't she? An attractive woman."

Eric frowned, alarmed that his interest was apparently so easy to spot. He needed to find a way to spend time with Cindy Warren, but he didn't want it interpreted as a come-on. "I barely know her."

Jerry sucked deeply on the cigar, then blew out the smoke in little puffs. "Oh, yeah, you like her all right."

Feeling warm with a mixture of annoyance and embarrassment, Eric finished his drink. "No comment."

"Mmm-hmm. Got it bad." He laughed, a low, hoarse rumble. "How long you planning to stay in San Francisco?"

A bit rankled, Eric shrugged. "My business will be over in a few days, but I'm thinking about hanging around through New Year's. Maybe visit the wine country."

Jerry studied the burning end of his cigar. "Spending Christmas alone, are you? No family?"

Eric considered lying, then decided the truth was just as simple. "My father and I aren't very close since my mother's passing a few years ago. My younger sister will be with him for the holidays."

"You and your sister don't get along either?" Instead of judgmental, Jerry sounded only curious.

"No, that's not it. Alicia is quite a bit younger than I am, and she has her own family."

The barber looked sympathetic. "Still, kinfolk should stick together, especially at this time of year."

Eric shifted on the stool, struck by a pang of longing for Christmases of his childhood. Popcorn garlands on a live tree, homemade cream candy and his father playing the piano. But Gomas Stanton had grown taciturn after his wife died, until finally Eric couldn't bear to spend holidays at home, God help him.

If this holiday turned out like the last few, Eric would call his father on Christmas Eve, only to be subjected to a diatribe about how Eric's work contributed to the fall of American capitalism. A master glassblower who had worked in a union factory for thirty-three years, his father believed a man's contribution to the world came from a hard day's work to produce a tangible good, something that could be bought and sold and owned. Eric's chosen field, business consulting, was a mystery to him. *"People like you are doing away with mom-and-pop enterprises—the kind of businesses and people who built this country,"* his father had once said. And then there was the music, always the music.

The more Eric thought about it, the better Christmas right here on the West Coast sounded. Especially if he could manage to maintain an amicable relation with one Cindy Warren. Some GMs stayed close to their hotels for Christmas. Perhaps they could ring in the New Year together. He smiled wryly. If the accident-prone woman lived that long.

"Course, you'll feel different about Christmas when you settle down with a lady," Jerry pressed on, blowing a slow stream of smoke straight up in the air. "Love's got a way of makin' holidays special, yessir."

Eric laughed. "There's no danger of me falling in love, my man, Christmas or no."

The man squinted at him. "Famous last words. I saw you two this morning, bouncing off each other like a couple of magnets turned the wrong way. I'm old, but I ain't blind."

Shaking his head, Eric set his glass on the counter and pushed away from the bar. "You're imagining things, Jer." He stood and gave the man a curt nod. "But thanks for the company anyway."

"You'd better watch your step around her," Jerry warned without looking up.

"Don't worry," Eric said dryly. "I'm not going to give Tony a reason to violate parole."

Jerry laughed. "Mr. Quinn, don't you know a pretty woman is ten times more dangerous than a hardened criminal?" He took a last puff on his cigar, then set it down with finality. "You're a goner, son. Merry Christmas."

CHAPTER THREE

"So, WHO'S THE LUCKY GUY?" Manny asked as he rolled a section of Cindy's hair with a fat curling iron.

Concentrating on his technique for later reference, she glanced at him in the mirror of her dressing table. "Lucky guy?"

"Amy told me you had a hot date for the party tomorrow night—who is he?"

"Is nothing sacred in this hotel?"

"I think we still have a bottle of holy water from a baptismal lying around somewhere."

She sighed. "I don't have a date…yet."

"I can make a few calls."

"He has to be straight."

Indignant, Manny scoffed. "I know some straight guys—two, in fact." Then he frowned. "Oh, but they're married, and one is Joel."

Cindy sniffed. "I smell smoke."

Manny jumped and released the lock of hair, which fell limply back in place, perhaps straighter than before. "No harm done," he assured her, then clucked. "Your hair is thin."

"Thanks." She lifted her bandaged hand. "Would you like to pour alcohol on my cuts, too?"

"What the heck did you do to your hand, anyway?"

Cindy hesitated. "I'll tell you later. Maybe. Fix my hair—and hurry."

"The hairdresser should have known better than to give you all these layers," he grumbled.

"I told her to."

"Then she should have exercised her right to a professional veto."

"Maybe *you* should be our new stylist."

"Cindy, contrary to popular belief, all gay men cannot cut hair and we don't have track lighting in our refrigerators."

"So tell me again why I'm submitting to your ministrations."

Manny shrugged. "I'm simply trying to make the best of this tragedy." He released another dark lock of hair that stubbornly refused to curl. "But I'm failing miserably—your hair won't even *bend*."

"Never mind." She groaned and held up her hands in defeat. "I'll borrow a nun's habit."

"You jest, but I think there's one in the lost and found."

"What am I going to do? My mother will have a stroke when I go home for Christmas."

He scoffed. "You'll be there for what—three days? You'll live and so will she."

"I'm glad you're coming home with me," Cindy said earnestly. "She'll believe you if you tell her my haircut is in style."

"Oh, no. I'm going home with you for baked ham and pecan pie, not to play referee for Joan and Christina Crawford."

"We're not that bad," she retorted, laughing. "Just the normal mother-daughter, tug-of-war relationship. She'll think you and I are sleeping together, you know."

His forehead wrinkled. "Is that a compliment?"

"Yes!" She punched him. "And thanks in advance for saving me from the usual harangue about settling down."

"So, what's up with that?" he asked, fluffing and spraying her hair.

"My mother?"

"No—you not settling down. Got a bad suit in the old relationship closet?"

Cindy gnawed on the inside of her cheek for a few seconds, pondering the sixty-four-thousand-dollar question. "I can't recall any particularly traumatic experiences. On the other hand, I can't recall any particularly noteworthy ones either." She shrugged. "I've never met a man who appreciates the more *unusual* things in life. You know, a guy who uses words like 'happenstance' and 'supercalifragilistic-expialidocious.'"

Manny stared.

"Okay, maybe I'm expecting too much."

But he merely shook his head, tucked her hair behind her ears, and studied the effect. "Nope. Don't settle, because if you're like most of my friends—male *and* female—falling in love will be an agonizing event with a man who represents everything you hate."

She laughed. "Don't hold back."

"I'm serious. Oh, yeah, *now* they're giddy with newlyweditis, but right here is the shoulder most of them cried on during the courtship." He tapped his collarbone. "And frankly, I'm not sure it was worth the trouble."

Cindy held up one hand. "You're preaching to the choir. But I am in desperate need of a day off, so I've got to find a date for the party even if I have to hire a man."

He nodded. "Now that's the ticket—retail romance." Exhaling noisily, he shook his head at her reflection. "Sorry, Cindy, that's the best I can do. I must say, though, without all that hair, your eyes really come alive."

She stared at the bottom layers hanging limply around her shoulders, the top layers hugging her ears. "Thanks, but I simply can't go around looking like this." Cindy told herself she was *not* trying to look good in case she bumped into the man from room 1010 again.

"Just go back to the salon tomorrow and take the

advice of the stylist. Their instincts are usually correct." He gave her a pointed look. "They mess up by trying to satisfy the armchair experts."

"It looks like I slept with panty hose on my head," she mumbled.

"Control top," he agreed.

She stood with resignation. "I have to get back to work—believe it or not, I have more pressing issues at hand than my coiffure." Like the wad of silk at her back that she still hadn't had time to take care of.

"Don't forget to work in some time today for man-hunting."

"With this hair, I'll need an Uzi to bag a date."

"Where's that nice Chanel scarf Mommy dearest sent for your birthday?"

"The yellow one?" Cindy walked over to a bureau and withdrew the filmy strip of silk. "Here. Why?"

"Wrap it around your throat and let the ends hang down your back." He smiled apologetically. "It'll draw attention away from your hair."

She made a face, then followed his advice, checking the result in the mirror. As usual, he was right.

Manny slowly wound the cord of the curling iron. "Cindy," he said, his voice unusually serious. "You're worried about this Stanton man coming, aren't you?"

She caught his gaze, then nodded. "Among other things."

He sighed. "Just when I was starting to like this crazy place."

"We're not out of a job yet," she assured him. "But I won't lie to you, Manny—we're a company stepchild and I suspect Harmon is looking to prune the family tree."

"This scrutiny could be a good thing," he pointed out. "Maybe Stanton's people will see the potential of the old gal and headquarters will throw some improvement funds our way."

"As long as those funds don't dictate changing what makes the Chandelier House unique." She forced a smile. "Just who are you calling an old gal, anyway?"

Manny smiled, his good humor returned. "By the way, since you're on the make, there was a guy in the lobby this morning who looked like he wouldn't mind having you in his Christmas stocking."

She frowned. "Me?"

"Uh-huh. Guy named Quinn."

Cindy's pulse kicked up. "Eric Quinn?"

"You've already met him?"

Anxious to get it over with, she reached around, stuck her hand down the back of her skirt, and whipped out the pajama pants. "Sort of."

Manny's eyes bulged. "You siren, you."

"It's not what you think."

"I think those are the man's pants."

"Okay, it is what you think, but I didn't get them the way you think."

He crossed his arms. "I guess you expect me to believe you stole them?"

Cindy bit her lower lip.

His jaw dropped. "You *stole* them?"

She collapsed into a chair. "I don't believe this day."

Manny sat too. "Now you're starting to worry me."

"*I'm* starting to worry me. Every time I see Eric Quinn, I end up doing something stupid."

"Cindy, I'm dying here—what's up with the silk drawers?"

Just thinking about the incident made the backs of her knees perspire. "I went to his room to handle a simple request. Next thing I know, I've cut myself on a freaking clipboard and I'm in his bathroom washing up."

He made a rolling motion with his hand. "Get to the good part already."

"His pajamas were hanging on the back of the door. They fell, I picked them up." She turned the pants around to show him the handprint.

Manny frowned. "So you offered to get them cleaned?"

"Not exactly." She buried her head in her hands. "I was afraid he'd think I was some kind of pervert stroking his pajamas, so I took them."

Her friend pursed his lips. "You run this entire

hotel, and that was the best plan you could come up with?"

Cindy lifted her head. "It sounded good at the time!"

He took the wrinkled pants by the waistband, then peered closer at the stain, tsk-tsking. "I hate to tell you this, Cindy, but your chances of getting blood out of nonwashable silk are zippo."

She moaned. "Now what?"

"Beckwith's," Manny declared, scrutinizing the label. "It's a men's boutique in Pacific Heights that carries this brand."

Cindy brightened. "Really?"

"Yeah. The man has expensive taste."

She reached for her purse. "Manny, I don't suppose you would—"

"Run to Beckwith's and see if they have a duplicate?"

Steepling her hands, she said, "I'm officially begging you."

Manny pressed his lips together and adopted a dreamy expression. "Well, I have a few errands to run first, but there *is* this tie in their window I've had my eye on."

"It's yours!" she exclaimed, handing over her gold credit card. "But I need those pajama pants before dinner."

"Now there's a sentence you don't hear every day."

"And—" She lifted a finger in warning. "Not a word of this outside these walls."

His mouth twitched. "Didn't you know that concierge is French for 'keeper of dirty little secrets'?" He stuffed the pants into the toiletry bag, along with the curling iron. "By the way, Amy said to stop by the front desk—she might have a line on our undercover Mr. Stanton."

Cindy perked up. "No kidding?"

"She wouldn't tell me a thing. She said she'd only talk to you."

They rode the elevator to the lobby together, then separated after Manny promised to page her as soon as he returned "with the goods." Cindy started feeling shaky again as she approached the front desk— she'd hoped that at least the tree would be installed and all the holiday decorations completed before Stanton arrived.

Amy stood with her head back, placing drops in her eyes.

"Allergies?" Cindy asked.

Blinking rapidly, Amy nodded toward the wall behind her. "I think it's the evergreen wreaths."

"Christmas is a lousy time of the year to be allergic to evergreen," Cindy noted.

"It's almost as bad as Valentine's Day."

"Are you allergic to chocolate, too?"

The rooms director frowned. "No, penicillin."

Cindy squinted. "How does penicillin— Never mind." She leaned close and lowered her voice. "Manny said you might have spotted Stanton posing as a guest?"

"I think so." Amy reached into her jacket pocket and withdrew a slip of paper. "Here's his room number—you might want to check it out yourself."

After reading the scribbling, Cindy gasped. "I spoke to this man about a room change this morning. Why do you suspect he's Stanton?"

Amy sniffed, then dabbed at her eyes with a tissue. "Besides the name similarity and the fact that he's alone, he's been all over the hotel asking questions about the furniture and making notes. Plus—" she lowered her voice "—he's booked in his room through Christmas Eve and instead of using a credit card, he paid cash for his room deposit."

Cindy nodded, the implications of the man's identity spinning in her head. "Sounds like he could be our man. I think I'll drop by his room again to say hello."

"Um, boss." Amy leaned over the counter and glanced at Cindy's sensible navy skirt. "If you're going to pay him a visit, show some leg, would you?"

Her mouth fell open. "Amy! Do you honestly think I'd resort to feminine wiles to influence the man's decision?"

Amy looked at her for a full minute.

Cindy sighed, looked around, then opened her jacket to roll down the waistband of her skirt. "How much leg?"

CINDY SMILED BRIGHTLY as the door swung open to reveal the man still dressed in slacks, shirt and loosened tie. "Hello again, Mr. Stark."

Holding the same pad of paper as earlier, the graying man's eyes swam behind wavy lenses. "Yes?"

"I'm Cindy Warren, the general manager. I spoke to you this morning about changing rooms?"

"Oh, right," he said tartly. "I don't want a better view now since I'm already settled in."

"Fine," she said quickly, deciding not to mention they had already booked the room she'd offered him earlier. "I wanted to express our regret once again, and let you know if there's anything we can do to make your stay more enjoyable, don't hesitate to contact me or someone on my staff."

"A couple of free meals would be nice," he said bluntly.

She cleared her throat mildly. "I've already arranged for a complimentary breakfast to be delivered in the morning, sir."

He glanced over the top of his glasses. "More than coffee and a doughnut, I hope?"

She bit her tongue. "Yes, sir. Enjoy your stay."

After the door closed behind her, none too gently, she backed away and frowned. If that sour man had their fate in his hands, they were all in trouble. Waiting for the elevator, she got an unwanted view of her hair in the mirrored doors and groaned. When she remembered her foolish bet with Joel, she groaned again. The doors opened and she stepped inside, lost in thought.

"Hello," a deep voice said.

She glanced up to find Eric Quinn smiling at her. For a few seconds, she could only absorb his good looks. She noticed a high dimple on his left cheek she'd missed before. He had changed into gray sweatpants, a loose white T-shirt and athletic shoes. She prayed he hadn't yet missed his jammies.

"Uh-oh," he said. "Problems?"

"No," she assured him hurriedly, then smiled. "Well, no more than usual."

"No more injuries, I hope."

Her cheeks warmed. "No, no more injuries." She cleared her throat, searching for a new topic. "How is your stay so far, Mr. Quinn?"

"Productive," he said smoothly, glancing at her shortened skirt, his gaze lingering on her legs before making eye contact again. "And I'm Eric."

Oh, those eyes. Her fingers tingled slightly—the clipboard had probably severed a few nerves. She scrutinized the numbers panel, trying to remember where she'd been headed. "What's your line of work...Eric?"

"Sales."

"What kind of sales?" she asked, for the sake of conversation.

"Oh, trinkets and...things."

She puzzled at his vagueness, then remembered the adult toy show the following week. "Are you here in preparation for the trade show next week?"

He shifted uneasily. "As a matter of fact, I *am* preparing for next week."

Which explained the condom smorgasbord in his toiletry bag. She nodded and averted her gaze, hoping she hadn't turned as pink as she felt. She was liberal, she was hip. She'd even gone to a men's nude dancing club once with Manny. So why should the thought of this man selling dildos and fringed pasties unnerve her?

"Are you going to the basement, too?" he asked, nodding to the only lit button.

"Er, no," she said, stabbing the button for the lobby. The door slid open almost immediately, and she practically fell out in her haste to flee.

Cindy didn't look back as the doors closed, but was brought up short by a sudden yank to her neck. She stumbled backward and swung around, horrified at the sight of her scarf caught in the elevator door and being dragged down the shaft. She stood frozen as the bit of silk whipped off her neck with a swish and disappeared into the floor.

Thankful she hadn't knotted the noose, Cindy

closed her eyes and hit the palm of her hand against her forehead.

"Was it him?"

At the sound of Amy's voice, Cindy turned to find her employee walking toward the elevator, scratching her arms.

"Rash," Amy explained. "Do you think Stark is the man we're looking for?"

Nodding, Cindy murmured, "Could be. He's a bit contrary."

The rooms director's forehead creased. "Maybe he's not a leg man." Then she grinned. "Or maybe he's a man's man—perhaps we should have sent Manny."

Cindy shook her head, smiling wryly. "Just let the staff know they need to be on their toes around our grumpy Mr. Stark."

Amy snapped her fingers. "Why don't you invite him to the Christmas party tomorrow night?"

She stared. "Are you insane?"

"Why not? Show him a good time."

"Let him see the staff at their most drunken, uninhibited selves?"

"Oh." Amy frowned. "You have a point, but you also need a date."

"Well, it won't be the man who has come to make mincemeat out of us," she insisted. "Besides, I don't mind playing nicey-nicey, but I certainly don't want the staff thinking I'm kissing up to this man to save my own job."

"You're right," Amy said, scratching at her neck. "I'd better get back to the desk."

"See you later." Sighing, Cindy jogged down the stairs to the basement in the unlikely event her scarf had escaped the moving parts of the shaft and had somehow floated out intact onto the floor. Nothing. Her mother's gift was probably wrapped around some critical gear, damaging the working parts of the elevator even as she stood wringing her hands.

She glanced at her watch. Three o'clock—Manny should be back within the next hour. Then she'd easily be able to replace the pajamas while Eric Quinn worked out in the health club, a vision that conjured up a sweat on her own body. Cindy called engineering again about a Christmas tree, but the nursery had not yet located a candidate.

She dropped by the crowded Trekkie trade show and skimmed the many rows of tables to make sure the spring show's bestseller, a stun gun capable of administering a dizzying shock, was nowhere to be found. The public swarmed over the trading card tables. Costumes and masks were also enjoying a brisk trade. All in all, the show had successfully attracted a sizable family crowd.

Cindy fast-forwarded to next week's adult toy show. Picturing Eric Quinn surrounded by erotic paraphernalia was enough to convince her to skip that particular exhibition.

At seven o'clock, still without a word from Manny, Cindy decided to have dinner while she waited. She descended the service stairs to the restaurant and walked through the kitchen to say hello to the staff. After a few minutes of small talk with the chef, she chose a bad table near the rest rooms and slipped off her shoes. *What a day.*

"Surely you don't intend to eat alone," Eric Quinn said behind her.

She turned to see him seated at a table a few feet away, half hidden by a silk tree. Her pulse picked up. "I don't mind."

"It's kind of silly for both of us to dine alone, don't you think?" His voice was empty of innuendo. "May I join you, Ms. Warren?"

Say yes, she told herself. He was simply a nice sex-toy salesman, looking for light dinner conversation. Besides, this way she'd be able to keep track of him until Manny paged her. "Please." He stood and carried his wineglass to her table, then gave her a tired little smile. She nodded toward the vacant chair across from her. "And call me Cindy."

"All right, Cindy." He had changed into casual brown slacks and a pale blue button-down. He settled into the chair with athletic grace, his movements triggering an awareness in her limbs.

"What do you recommend?" he asked.

A married girlfriend had once diagrammed a position she'd always wanted to try on a napkin. "The rib eye," Cindy said, her heart thumping wildly. *Not that she hadn't had her chances with men.*

He nodded. "Rib eye is what the concierge suggested."

"You talked to Manny?" *It was just that none of those guys she dated had particularly lit her fire.*

"Yeah—seems like a nice fellow."

"He's my right-hand man." *Oh, the restaurateur from Oakland showed the spark of a promise, but she'd been mired in hotel problems at the time and... oh, well.*

"Good help is hard to find," he agreed.

"Especially in the hospitality industry." *But this man—this man was one big mass of flammable substance.*

"Cindy, before we go any further," he said, his eyes merry, "there's something we need to discuss."

A sense of doom flooded her. He knew about the pajamas. He'd discovered them missing and deduced that she'd taken them. "Wh-what do you mean?" she asked, reaching for her water glass.

His smile sent a chill up her spine. "I mean a certain piece of clothing."

She gulped down a mouthful of water, choking in her haste, her mind racing. "Oh, that. Well, I can explain—"

"It's not necessary," he said, shaking his head,

his smile never wavering. "You were a little embarrassed—I understand."

"Um, yes, I was, but—"

"Actually, I think your little mishaps are funny."

Irritated, Cindy squirmed. "I'm glad, but—"

"And I hope you don't mind that I consulted the cleaners around the corner," he said, reaching inside his jacket.

"Well, as a matter of fact," she said, "I've already made arrangements for a replacement, so you don't have to worry about the bloodstain." Then she stopped. Cleaners? He knew the pants were gone, but how would he know about a stain?

He frowned as he withdrew a small paper bag. "Bloodstain? You were injured when your scarf came off?"

"My scarf?" she croaked.

"Yes, your scarf." Laughing, he withdrew her yellow Chanel scarf, folded neatly. "What did you think I was talking about?"

"I thought you were talking about…my scarf, of course," she replied lamely. "The cuts on my hand—I was afraid I had gotten blood on my scarf when I tried to grab it."

"I was able to pull it inside the elevator," he explained. "But the silk was soiled, so I thought I'd have it cleaned for you." He smiled again. "I had to drop off a few shirts anyway—I hope you don't think it was too forward."

Not when I have your PJs. "Not at all," she said. "Thank you. This was a gift from my mother."

"Ah. And where is she?"

"Virginia. Along with my father and older brother."

He blinked. "Really? I'm from Virginia, too."

Her surprise was interrupted by the sound of her beeper. "I'm sorry, I'm still on call." She glanced at the number, then withdrew a small radio from her pocket and punched a button. "Yes, Amy?"

"Sorry to bother you, Cindy, but our special guest in room 620 is complaining about the room temperature."

Suspecting Mr. Stark was still testing them, Cindy asked, "Too hot or too cold?"

"Too hot."

"Check the air-conditioning personally, Amy. And take a fan with you just in case."

"Sure thing, Cindy."

She stowed the radio and smiled at Eric. "Where were we? Oh, yes—what part of Virginia?"

"Near Manassas."

"Ah. I grew up farther south on Interstate 95, near Fredericksburg."

"I've been to Fredericksburg too many times to count," he acknowledged. "Small world."

A waiter took their order and they agreed to split a carafe of white wine. Cindy relaxed somewhat, but wished Manny would hurry up and call. The wine arrived and Eric filled her glass, then his.

"Do you go back often to visit?" she asked.

Something flashed over his face. Regret? He shook his head. "My sister and I are close, but my father doesn't exactly approve of my, um, line of work."

She nodded sympathetically, but she could see his father's side, too. That your son sold sex toys wasn't exactly something to brag about. But she had to admit, the combination of Eric's good looks, the dim lights and the good wine made his occupation seem kind of...titillating.

"Do you like your job?" he asked.

She opened her mouth to say yes, but her beeper went off and they both laughed. "Excuse me," she said. Within a few seconds, she had Amy on the line again.

"Cindy, now he's complaining about the noise next door."

"What noise next door?"

"I walked up, but I didn't hear a thing."

"Walk up again."

Amy sighed. "He's kind of hateful."

"I know, but hang in there." She put away the phone. "Yes, I like my job most of the time. Working with the public has its frustrating moments."

They chatted until appetizers arrived, and Cindy found herself warming up to Eric Quinn, despite his somewhat questionable vocation. Once their fingers brushed when they reached for the wine, and Cindy felt a definite spark of sexual energy. From the slightly hooded look of his eyes, she knew Eric felt it too.

What perfect Christmas-party date material— gorgeous, gentlemanly and temporary. "Eric, I was wondering—" Her beeper sounded again, and she groaned, then laughed.

When she pushed the button, Manny's voice came on the line. "Cindy, I have what you asked for—meet me at the concierge desk."

Her heart lifted. The sooner the pajama pants incident was taken care of, the better. "I'll be there in two minutes." Then she smiled at Eric. "This shouldn't take long. I hope you don't mind waiting alone for our meals to arrive."

"Not at all," he said politely, standing when she did.

"I'll take this opportunity to put on my scarf," she said, scooping up the handful of silk. She wanted to look her best if she ever scrounged up the nerve to invite him to the Christmas party.

"Beware of attack elevators." His flirty grin sent a bolt of desire through her midsection that hastened her steps.

Eric watched her leave the restaurant. The woman was such an enigma, an irresistible mix of beauty and strength and vulnerability. And the chemistry between them was undeniable.

He drained his glass of wine. Ethically, he shouldn't become involved with her physically, at least not until after the conclusion of the study. He frowned, feeling unsettled, then glanced at his watch. He probably had time to return to his room and make a quick call to Lancaster before Cindy came back. Perhaps talking about the study would reinforce his resolve to maintain a respectable distance from the fetching general manager.

After flagging the waiter on the way out to let him know they'd both be returning, Eric strode toward the elevator.

CHAPTER FOUR

"WHY ARE YOU MAKING ME go with you?" Manny demanded, trotting down the hall behind Cindy toward Eric Quinn's room.

"For a ninety-five-dollar tie," she retorted, "the least you can do is stand lookout."

"Compared to the pajama pants, the tie was a bargain."

Cindy stopped and her friend nearly barreled into her. "How much were the pants?"

Manny winced. "Three hundred and fifty."

Her knees weakened. "Dollars?"

"What can I say? I told you the man has expensive taste. What does he do for a living, anyway?"

Cindy resumed walking. "He's a salesman," she answered evasively. *And apparently, sex sells.* She stopped in front of door 1010, then draped the Chanel scarf over her shoulder to free her hands. After looking both ways, she inserted a master key into the lock.

"I could get fired for this," Manny said, his voice stern.

"I'll put in a good word for you with your boss." The door clicked open. "Give me the pants and cover me."

He handed her a small bag with handles. "What if Quinn shows up?"

Heat climbed to Cindy's ears. "He's in the dining room…waiting for me."

"Ho ho ho. Dinner?"

"Don't start."

"And what if he ambles up here while you're gone?"

Cindy sighed. "I don't know—sing or something. Work with me, Manny. There's no section in the handbook on breaking into a guest's room!" Her heart thumping like a snare drum, she pushed open the door and stepped inside, where she moved quickly to the bathroom and flipped on the light. With shaking hands she withdrew both the old and the new pants. She had to give Manny credit—they were identical, all right, except the new pair looked a little too…well, new. Quickly she removed the alarming price tag, then gently twisted the garment to add a few wrinkles. With considerable trepidation, she lifted the old pair and inhaled the scent of the velvety pale blue fabric, detecting the trace of a vaguely familiar cologne.

She glanced toward the toiletry bag, then unzipped the non-condom-carrying side before she had a chance to change her mind. Cindy rummaged for cologne, smiling unexpectedly when her fingers curved around an unpretentious bottle of English Leather. Eric Quinn wore three-hundred-and-fifty-dollar silk pajamas, and used seven-dollars-a-bottle cologne? Intriguing. She squirted her father's standby fragrance into the air, then held the new pants beneath the falling mist. Satisfied, she carefully hung the pajama bottoms behind Eric's toiletry bag and checked her watch. Six minutes—not bad.

She stuffed the old pants into the paper bag and started to leave the bathroom when she heard an odd racket in the hall. Was someone belting out "Santa Claus Is Coming to Town"? Then Cindy bit down hard on her tongue—Manny's warning!

Nearly tripping over her feet, she dived for the light switch. Manny stopped singing and began conversing loudly with someone outside the door. *Please, let it be housekeeping.* Panic paralyzed her limbs as she heard a key being inserted into the lock. Manny's words were indecipherable, but his tone had elevated considerably.

In the darkness of the bathroom, Cindy could see the whites of her eyes shining back in the mirror. There was nowhere to go but…she gulped and leapt into the tub in one motion, then jerked the curtain closed in another. Feeling faint, she shrank in the corner, visualizing her career going down the drain beneath her feet.

The door opened and Manny's shaky voice reached her. "Just a little holiday entertainment, sir."

The low rumble of Eric Quinn's laugh sounded, sending sheer mortification through her body. "I didn't realize I was on the concierge level, Mr. Oliver."

Manny cleared his throat. "Could I adjust your room thermostat, sir?"

"Uh, no thanks."

"Fill your ice bucket?"

"It's full, thanks."

"Check your towels?"

"I'm fine. Excuse me, I need to make a phone call, then get back to the dining room."

"Of course, sir."

Cindy allowed herself a tiny surge of hope—maybe he wouldn't be here long.

She heard him move through the bedroom and pick up the phone. He wouldn't be able to see the door if she left very quietly. But she hesitated—what if he hung up quickly and caught her leaving? Deciding to stay put, Cindy made herself as small as possible.

She could hear his murmured voice on the phone. Cindy wondered about the person he was calling. A girlfriend? A wife? A frown pulled at her mouth. Then she pushed aside the silly response—neither the presence nor the absence of a woman in Eric Quinn's bed made any difference in her life.

What life? I'm cowering in the bathroom of a guest whose pants I stole. She broke out in a fresh sweat at the sound of Eric putting down the handset. His footsteps came closer, then to her horror, he stepped into the bathroom. Her heart lodged in her constricted throat as fluorescent light bathed the room. She clamped her hand over her mouth, biting back a gasp. What was he going to do?

Remove something from his toiletry bag, from the telltale sound of a zipper. A condom? Indignation lifted her chin. Did the man think he was going to get lucky with her? Water splashed in the sink, and Eric Quinn proceeded to…brush his teeth with the fervor of a dentist.

She felt a sliver of disappointment, but apparently Eric was in a grand mood because when the water stopped, he began whistling under his breath. Cindy strained to make out the tune and pressed her lips together when she recognized "Santa Claus Is Coming to Town."

…gonna find out who's naughty or nice…

She frowned wryly, thankful she no longer believed in Santa Claus, because she'd never been so naughty.

He tapped his toothbrush on the counter, then returned it to his bag. Her heart stopped when he folded a towel over the shower curtain rod, rattling the plastic liner. Faintly silhouetted in the harsh light, his tall figure seemed even more imposing. Would he fling back the curtain and find her squatting in his bathtub? Just when she thought she might pass out, the room went dark and he left the bathroom. Seconds later, he exited the room and Cindy's body went limp with relief.

She sat on the edge of the tub for a full two minutes, then climbed out and crept to the main door, her muscles taut. After checking the peephole and finding the coast clear, she sucked in a breath, opened the door and stepped into the corridor.

"Well, it's about time!" Manny whispered harshly behind her.

Cindy jumped. "You scared the schnitzel out of me!"

"I was going out of my mind—what the devil happened in there?"

Heading down the hall, she lifted the paper bag. "I switched the pants."

"Did he see you?" he asked, exasperated.

"No." She stopped in front of the elevator and stabbed the button, then sheepishly turned to face her friend. "I hid in the bathtub."

He shook his head slowly. "Unbelievable."

"No," she corrected, shaking her finger, "un*repeat*able."

Manny grinned. "Wonder what a good black-mailer pulls down these days?"

"I have to get back to dinner with Mr. Quinn." Her chest heaved as if she'd been running a marathon.

She held up the bag. "Would you mind disposing of these for me?"

"Okay. So how's it going?"

She frowned. "What do you mean?"

"Supping with the quintessential Mr. Quinn."

Cindy pressed the button again. "Dinner with Eric Quinn was simply a ploy to keep tabs on him until you returned."

"No footsie under the table?"

She scoffed. "Of course not." In the elevator, Cindy selected the basement button and Manny chose the lobby. With a tissue from her jacket pocket, she dabbed at the perspiration on her forehead.

"If I didn't know better," Manny said, his voice singsongy, "I would think you're starting to like this guy."

"Except you know better," she reminded him as the doors opened to the lobby.

"See you tomorrow." He stepped into the corridor, then turned. "And don't forget to tell Mr. Quinn the Christmas party tomorrow night is black tie."

Cindy opened her mouth to protest, but the doors slid closed on Manny's knowing smirk.

Feeling completely exhausted, she exited at the basement and hurried back to the restaurant. Eric Quinn sat at the table with his hands wrapped around his wineglass, but he stood when she approached the table.

Manufacturing a smile, she lowered herself into

her seat, hoping to get through the meal without another embarrassing disaster. "Sorry for the delay." Someone had lit a votive candle in the table centerpiece, and the light from the flickering flame threw the planes of his chiseled face into relief. Either Eric had grown handsomer during her absence, or her own glass of wine was kicking in.

His eyes crinkled with a smile. "No trouble, I hope?"

"Um, no."

The waiter arrived with their entrees under domed lids, but Cindy had lost her appetite. Instead she found herself studying Eric for some sign of sleaziness, some manifestation of peddling provocative products for a living that would give her a reason to avoid his company. But she saw only a darkly gorgeous, thoroughly masculine man politely waiting for her to begin eating.

Eric gazed across the table at the ruffled Cindy Warren, trying to figure out how he could spend time with the beauty without arousing her suspicion—or his libido. "Where were we?" he asked as he raked the grilled onions off the top of his steak—not that he expected to be kissing anyone tonight.

"Virginia," she said, tucking a strand of dark hair behind her ear.

Even with the hacked haircut, the woman was stunning. Classically beautiful with large eyes, high apple cheeks and skin as flawless as glass. "Ah, yes," he said, already wanting to change the subject. Thinking about his argumentative father gave him indigestion.

"Do you still live near Manassas?"

He sliced into the rib eye, shaking his head. "No, I'm on the road quite a bit. I maintain condos here and there."

"Will you be traveling back for the holidays?"

First Jerry and now Cindy. Eric wondered if his cover had been blown and if the employees were trying to cozy up to him. "Probably not," he answered as casually as possible. "I believe you were about to ask me a question before you left the table?"

Cindy reached for her wine. "Whatever it was has slipped my mind." She fidgeted, then asked, "Is this your first time staying at the Chandelier House?"

"Yes, although I'm in the Bay area several times a year on business." When she averted her eyes, Eric wondered again if she knew why he was here. If so, there wasn't anything he could do about it now except play along. "This is a very charming place."

"Thanks. The hotel was built in the twenties, suffered through two substantial earthquakes, plus countless tremors. She's been repaired, added on to, torn down and built up again. And still, she perseveres."

Noting the affection in her voice, he said, "You speak of her more like an acquaintance than a structure."

"The Chandelier House is something of a family friend," she said wistfully. "My maternal grandfather was one of the original owners."

Surprise infused him. He hadn't been informed of Cindy Warren's personal connection. "That's remarkable. So it's no accident that you're here—" he smiled "—and running the whole show."

"Yes and no," she said between picking at the salmon on her plate. "My grandfather sold his interest in the Chandelier House years before I was born." A smile lit her face. "My mother says I take after him, although I hardly remember him at all." She sipped her wine. "Anyway, I studied hotel management in college and worked in a couple of small, independent hotels before stumbling onto this opening a few years ago."

He played dumb. "So the Chandelier House is independently owned?"

"When I came here, it was. But about two years ago a company in Detroit bought it and, thankfully, allowed me to stay on as general manager."

"A vote of confidence for you, I'd say."

She shrugged. "I'm not bragging, but the Chandelier House is a special place, with special employees. It takes a certain kind of person to appreciate the, um, atmosphere."

On cue, a crew of Vulcans filed by, in full costume. Cindy smiled. "It's never dull." He refilled her glass from the carafe, but she stopped him at the half-full mark. "I'm still on call for another hour," she said, an adorable blush on her cheeks.

"So," he said, nodding toward the Trekkies, "are they your typical clientele?"

"Oh, no. Our typical clientele is much weirder than that."

"Really?"

She took another deep drink of wine and nodded. "The snake handlers were the scariest, I think."

Eric blinked. "Snake handlers?"

"And surprisingly, the tattoo artists were the most courteous."

"Hmm."

"And last year the vampires ran up an incredible bar tab, so we're looking forward to having them return in the spring."

He leaned forward. "Vampires, did you say?"

"Oh, don't worry—the whole staff gets tetanus boosters ahead of time."

Eric's jaw went slack. "That's good."

"And, um, your people will be arriving shortly."

So, she had somehow discovered who he was. Relieved, but unreasonably disappointed at the same time, he nodded slowly. "I hope you understand why I had to be discreet."

She averted her gaze. "Yes, I can see why."

"People tend to treat you differently once they know the truth."

A smile curved her mouth and her eyelids drooped

sexily. "Well, I have to admit had I not had the opportunity to get to know you, Eric, I might have been one of those people."

"I'm glad to see my line of work won't interfere with our, um…friendship."

Another wine-induced smile. "I'm an open-minded woman."

Eric's body leapt in response. Alarms went off in his ears. Was she going to come on to him in hopes of favorable treatment? "I'd rather not talk about work at all," he said, "because I hate mixing business with pleasure."

"Fine with me," she said agreeably, then turned back to her plate with more gusto.

Eric watched her with no small amount of surprise. He had worried the moment of revelation would be confrontational, or tense at the very least, but obviously he'd been wrong. If anything, Cindy seemed more at ease—happy even—that his reason for being at the Chandelier House was out in the open. He relaxed back into his chair and lifted his glass to his mouth, studying the woman before him.

She wasn't wearing the yellow scarf, but realizing how embarrassed she'd been over the elevator incident, he decided not to say anything. Eric did, however, wonder if she had any idea this was the most enjoyable meal he'd had in months.

Cindy pushed aside her plate, her eyes shining and

her lips wet with wine. Suddenly she leaned forward and confided, "I have a confession to make."

Lifting his eyebrows, he said, "Okay, but I feel compelled to warn you I'm not a priest."

She laughed, making a bubbly little sound, then hiccuped and clapped her hand over her mouth. "Excuse me," she gasped.

Eric laughed, delighted at her lack of inhibition. He pushed his own plate aside and split the remaining measure of wine between their two glasses. "So what's this confession?"

She drank deeply, then toyed with the stem. "Actually," she said, her voice tentative, "I *was* planning to ask you something earlier."

"Good evening, Cindy." A suited man walked up to the table holding two full-bellied glasses and a small beribboned bottle.

Straightening, Cindy said, "Joel. This is Eric Quinn, one of our guests. Mr. Quinn, this is Joel Cutter, our food and beverage director."

At least she was planning on keeping his identity a secret for a while longer, Eric noted. Cutter set the glasses on the table and extended a hand.

"Sorry to interrupt," the man said smoothly, "but since you're finished with your meal, I thought you might like to try a cinnamon liqueur I ordered in for the holidays."

"Sure," Cindy agreed. "Eric?"

"Sounds interesting."

Cutter poured an inch of reddish liquid into the fat goblets. "Enjoy," he said, then moved away. Cindy studied the liqueur thoughtfully, holding on to the edge of the table as if trying to orient herself. Maybe she'd had too much wine.

"Shall we drink a toast?" Eric asked, lifting his glass.

"I'm not sure," she said carefully.

"Just a taste," he said, respecting her restraint.

"Okay." She smiled, wrapping her hand around her own glass. "To Christmas."

"To Christmas," he agreed, clinking his glass to hers over the candle, then added, "May we both get what we want."

Cindy's smile faltered and her glass fell, struck the candle, then bounced across the table. The white tablecloth absorbed a second's worth of liqueur before the flame caught, setting the table ablaze. Eric reached over the flame and pushed Cindy away, catching his sleeve on fire in the process. Screams sounded across the dining room. Someone yelled for a fire extinguisher, but Eric yanked the edge of the tablecloth and folded it over his arm, smothering the fire instantly.

Hovering six feet away, Cindy stared at the smoking tablecloth.

"Are you all right?" Eric clasped her elbow and gently turned her toward him.

Mortified, she blinked his concerned face into focus. "I set you on fire."

"No, you didn't—it was an accident." He held up his arm, displaying a smoke-blackened but intact shirtsleeve. "See?" He unbuttoned the cuff and rolled back the fabric. "No damage."

She still stared, astounded at her own carelessness. First the man's pajamas, now his shirt…and very nearly his arm!

"Cindy!" Joel jogged toward them. "What happened?"

"Everything's okay," Eric said. "The liqueur spilled and the candle—"

"Joel," Cindy cut in, finally finding her voice. "I'm sorry for causing a disturbance. If you'll send someone to clean up this mess, I'll sign for Mr. Quinn's dinner and see him to the first-aid station."

"That's not necessary," Eric assured her, but she gave him her best don't-argue-with-me look. He relented with a nod and an eye-locking smile that made her knees grow even weaker.

Cindy signed the meal receipt with a shaky hand, still marveling over her own stupidity. "Look, Cindy," Joel whispered over her shoulder. "Don't worry about the mess—I'm just glad you weren't hurt." He smiled sheepishly. "And I know this isn't the best time, but I'm looking for a volunteer to be Santa for the party tomorrow night."

She glanced up with a laugh. "You want me to be Santa Claus?"

"Well," her friend squirmed, "I thought it would be good for morale if everyone saw you in the holiday spirit, you know, with the review coming up and all."

She sighed. "Okay, bring the suit to the party—I'll duck out and change when it's time to give out gifts."

"Swell, and don't worry—the suit is flame-retardant."

"You're a real gas."

As Joel walked away, Cindy glanced at Eric who stood a few feet away reassuring everyone he was all right. Even if she could get up the nerve to ask Eric to the Christmas party, the man would be nuts to go—she was liable to kill him!

He joined her and they walked out together, Cindy blushing with humiliation. "I strike again," she said finally.

"It wasn't your fault," he repeated gently.

Cindy punched the elevator call button. Her body was a quaking mass of fear, embarrassment, exhilaration and confusion. When the doors opened, she chanced a glance at Eric, noticing a smoky streak marking his left cheek. Pulling a tissue from her jacket pocket, she turned toward him and reached high, then stopped in midmotion as their gazes met.

Cindy swallowed. "There's a...here." She handed

him the tissue and gestured to the black mark, then stepped away from him.

Out of the corner of her eye, she saw him stretch his neck toward the stainless panel, then swipe at the mark. "Think we'd better choose a floor?"

Completely bereft of dignity, Cindy lifted her hand, then stopped. Choose a floor? Was he dropping a hint that he'd like to spend the night with her? Her finger started to shake, and the ten button lit suddenly. His floor.

"And for you?" he asked.

"F-fifteen," she squeaked, feeling ridiculous. He wasn't dropping a hint about spending the night with her. He was probably going to call his insurance agent—or his lawyer.

"Unless you'd like to come in for a nightcap," he said, checking his watch, then offering an unreadable smile. "And you never did get around to asking me that question."

Panic washed over her. The way things were going, she'd probably go back to Eric's room and the roof would collapse, or he'd be electrocuted, or heaven only knew what else. But the man must be desperate if he was willing to entertain a firebug. Unless he was looking for someone to tie to the bed while he demonstrated S&M toys from sample cases. "No!"

"Okay. Thank you for a wonderful dinner."

Cindy smiled wryly. "Despite the crash and burn?"

He revealed white teeth in a broad smile. "Despite the crash and burn."

His eyes were so riveting. "I had fun, too."

The elevator dinged and the doors opened to his floor. "Perhaps our paths will cross again tomorrow."

Her throat ran dry. "Perhaps."

When the doors closed, Cindy leaned against the wall heavily and looked at the ceiling. *Please let this day end.* First the bad haircut, then cutting her hand, the pajama-pant mess, the scarf thing—

She straightened. Where was her yellow scarf? She closed her eyes, her mind rewinding. She remembered taking it when she left the table and she recalled tossing it over her shoulder just before she'd...

Her eyes popped open. Eric's room! Somehow, she'd lost her scarf in his room, probably in the bathroom—or in the *bathtub*. If he found her scarf, he'd know she'd been in his room, and when. Choking back hysteria, Cindy darted out of the elevator as soon as the doors opened, and fled toward the stairs.

CHAPTER FIVE

CINDY ZOOMED DOWN the five flights of stairs in record time, twisting her ankle twice. Thank goodness Eric's room was at the far end of the building—with luck she could catch him before he went in. She sprinted down the hall, turned the corner and saw him standing in front of his door, inserting his key.

"Eric!"

He turned, his gaze questioning.

She jogged toward him, then slowed, suddenly realizing how out of breath she'd become.

"Cindy, is everything okay?"

Her chest heaved while she searched for an explanation. "I…I…want to…buy you…another shirt!"

His face creased in amusement. "You ran all the way back here to tell me you want to buy me another shirt? I assure you it isn't necessary. I'm not overly attached to my clothing."

A fact she wished she'd been privy to three hundred and fifty dollars ago.

"I insist. If I can borrow…a piece of scratch paper…I'll write down the brand…and your size."

He shrugged good-naturedly. "Okay, if it will make you feel better. But how about just taking the shirt?"

She massaged the stitch in her side and nodded.

"Give me a minute to change."

Panic gripped her again—she had to get in his room. "Um, Eric!"

He turned back, the hint of a smile still hovering. "Yes?"

"About that question I was going to ask."

"Yes?"

Desperate, she looked both directions, then lowered her voice. "Well, it's kind of personal."

"In that case, please come in."

As expected, he unlocked the door and gestured for her to precede him into the room. Her heart pounded at the compromising situation in which she'd managed to land herself—again. She scanned the carpet in the entranceway for her scarf, but found nothing. The darn thing had to be in the bathroom.

"Would you like a drink?" he asked.

"Um, no, I have to go to the bathroom," she blurted. Then she added, "to freshen up."

He blinked. "Be my guest."

She fled to the bathroom and closed the door behind her. Cindy glanced at her reflection, then closed her eyes. Bizarre hair and even more bizarre behavior. What must he think of her? She hurriedly searched the room, then found her scarf—surprise,

surprise—in the bathtub. After tying the scrap of yellow silk around her neck in a secure knot, she fluffed her hair, brushed her teeth with her finger, then washed her hands.

When she could stall no longer, Cindy opened the door. With a deep, calming breath, she walked down the short hall to the opening into Eric's bedroom. She wasn't sure what to expect—candles, Eric reclining on the bed in a smoking jacket?—but she felt vague disappointment to find every light blazing, from the corner lamps to the night-light in the electrical outlet, and Eric standing across the room looking out the window.

Gazing at the illuminated city of San Francisco, even more spectacular than usual due to added holiday lights, Eric mulled the unfolding situation. Of all the women in the world, why did he have to be attracted to one who not only ran a hotel, but a hotel he had been sent to terminate? And even though she said she was open-minded about the conflicts that could arise, Eric wasn't as comfortable. In fact, he was beginning to wonder if he was drawn to the woman simply because he knew deep down that she wasn't accessible. Or if she was drawn to him out of some conscious or unconscious desire to influence his decision in the coming weeks? He'd been approached before by comely employees who were under the microscope of a corporate review.

He heard a movement and turned his head to

see her standing in the entrance to his room, looking nothing like a woman hell-bent on seducing or
being seduced. As a matter of fact, she looked a little scared.

"Nice view," he said, nodding toward the vista.

"Mmm-hmm. If you have a chance before you
leave, go up to the roof at night. Just phone the concierge desk and they'll buzz you through the security door."

"I'll do that. You put your scarf on," he noted
with approval.

"Um, yes, I did." She fussed with the ends. "Well,
Eric, if you'll give me your shirt, I'll be on my way."

Maybe she'd lost her nerve, or maybe she was
waiting for him to make the first move. His body
screamed yes, peel off her uniform and find out if she
loved with as much energy as she lived. But a sexual
encounter had never taken priority over doing a job
to the best of his ability, so he simply unbuttoned his
shirt quickly, smiling when she turned to scrutinize
an unremarkable painting on the wall. Shrugging out
of the ruined shirt, Eric walked toward her, glad for
his father's advice to always wear a T-shirt under-
neath a dress shirt. "Here you go."

Visibly relieved to see his torso covered, she
reached for the garment. "I'll get a replacement as
soon as possible."

He inclined his head, realizing the futility of arguing. Their fingers brushed and desire surged through his chest. "Cindy."

She felt it too, the chemistry. He could tell by the confusion in her green-gray eyes. "Yes?"

He imagined himself pulling her against his chest, capturing her mouth with his, and then to his astonishment, he realized he wasn't imagining it. He tasted her breath, her lips, her tongue. Her hands curled, then splayed against his sides, her breath escaping in little sighs. Eric drank the wine that lingered in the depths of her mouth while resisting the urge to fill his hands with her body. Instead, he smoothed back her hair and tilted her face to allow him greater access. His body swelled with longing to crush her closer, but the fierce response was uncommon enough to deliver a dose of reality. Eric lifted his head and released her, attempting to check his raspy breathing.

She took a half step back, biting her swollen lips.

"I didn't mean for that to happen," he said lamely, bending to retrieve the shirt lying at their feet. "But since I've been fighting my attraction to you all day, I can't truthfully say I'm sorry."

"Fighting?" she asked softly. "Are you married?"

He shook his head, laughing. "Oh, no, I'm not married, or engaged." Then he sobered and ran his hand through his hair. "But I still have reservations about us becoming, er, involved, because of my job."

Cindy retrieved the shirt from his hand and studied the blackened sleeve for a few seconds, then she lifted her gaze. "I can get past it if you can."

Eric caught his breath at the sensation her words evoked. He'd never lacked for female company, but he couldn't remember being more satisfied to realize a woman found him attractive. So, while his mind warned that he was about to embark on a path of potential destruction, his mouth said, "Perhaps we could have dinner tomorrow night."

She laughed—not quite the answer he'd hoped for.

"Eric, the question I've been trying to ask you all evening is whether you'd like to escort me to our employee Christmas party tomorrow night."

Ridiculously pleased, he remained wary. "Have you told your employees why I'm here? I'd hate to get nasty rumors started about the boss."

She angled her head at him. "Right now I don't see a need to share this kind of information with my subordinates."

"And if it comes up?"

Cindy shrugged. "Tell the truth and let everyone deal with it."

The party, he reasoned, would be a great chance to see her interact with her staff informally—not to mention an opportunity to see how money was spent on after-hours activities. "Sounds great. Black tie?"

She nodded. "Donte's tuxedo shop is just a couple of blocks over, but I insist on paying for it. It's the least I can do." She moved toward the door and he followed.

"Well, thank you anyway, but I travel with my own tux."

She stopped, her hand on the doorknob. "Oh."

"What time is the party?"

"Eight o'clock until midnight in the lounge."

He smiled, despite the warnings going off in his head. "I'll knock on your door at fifteen of."

"A BODY WAVE?" Cindy asked, staring in the mirror. "Are you sure?"

"Sure as shootin'," Camelia, the new hairdresser, said, her animated nod sending her high ponytail whirling around like a ceiling fan. "There are only two ways to add volume to thin, straight hair like yours. One is to layer it, and it looks like you've already been down that road. Number two is a perm. You're a prime candidate for Miss Fern's Permanent Wave with Aloe, fifteen to eighteen minutes, I'd guess."

Cindy brightened. "It'll take less than twenty minutes?"

"Heck, it'll take me an hour to roll this mess, but after that, it'll be a breeze."

Cindy glanced over at Jerry who was shaving a gentleman in the other chair, but the barber kept his head down. "But what will it look like?" she asked the hairdresser.

"Nice and full," Camelia assured her. "Big, loose curls—it'll be darling, just you wait and see."

"I've always wanted curly hair," Cindy admitted, then smiled. "And I have a party to go to tonight, so I want my hair to look nice."

"They won't be looking at anyone else," the lady assured her. "Let's get started."

Cindy suffered through agonizing tugging on her hair as the zealous Camelia rolled the small sections tight enough to draw up the corners of her mouth.

She studied her hollowed eyes in the mirror, trying to recall when she had looked worse. The sleepless night she'd had after yesterday's numerous fiascos was reflected plainly on her face. Not to mention the thoughts of Eric Quinn that had haunted her all night.

She'd risen with that sick feeling in her stomach she first experienced during puberty when the cutest boy in school winked at her in algebra class. The stress of wondering what to do next paralyzed her. Oh, during high school she'd managed to shuffle a few steps further, and in college she'd stumbled over the edge, but the nagging refrain—"Is this *it?*"—always came back to haunt her.

Much as she lusted after Eric Quinn, she had the vague sensation she was setting herself up for a huge letdown. Even though she hated to admit it, his line of work *did* bother her, the eroticism notwithstanding. Her mother's head, of course, would explode before her very eyes if she found out. And Christmas was the worst time of the year for launching a new relationship.

"Almost ready for the solution," Camelia sang. Cindy endured the eye-stinging pain of the last too-tight curler, and smiled as Camelia squirted the pungent-smelling liquid across the helmet of rollers. "We'll let it soak in and I'll check the curl in a few minutes."

The peal of Cindy's beeper sounded and she punched a button on her radio. "This is Cindy."

"Hey, it's Amy—can you come up to the lobby?"

Cindy glanced in the mirror. "I'm a little indisposed at the moment. Is this an emergency?"

The rooms director's voice floated to her in a scratchy whisper. "That annoying Mr. Stark is here swearing there's a rat in his room. He insists on seeing the general manager."

Cindy rolled her eyes heavenward. "Take him to the break room and get him a cup of coffee—decaffeinated. I'll be right there." She turned and smiled apologetically at the hairdresser. "Can you wrap a towel around my head or something? I'm needed in the lobby."

Camelia frowned, unfolding a bright green towel. "You can't be gone too long, now, you hear?"

"Ten minutes, tops," Cindy promised.

She trotted to the lobby, one hand on the towel and her eyes on her feet, hoping to get through unnoticed.

A split second later, she collided with a large body and landed on her rump, sliding three feet on the marble floor before coming to a halt. She instantly recognized the feet and bit back a curse. At least the towel remained intact, but she couldn't imagine how silly she looked to Eric—this time.

"Good morning," he said, the laughter clear in his voice.

"Morning," she mumbled, refusing to look up.

"Are you all right?"

She nodded, causing the curlers to rattle beneath the towel.

"I'm sorry, Cindy, I didn't see you coming, although now I can't imagine why."

"Everyone's a comedian."

He squatted down and angled his head until their eyes were on a level plane. "Would you like a hand?"

The man was just plain gorgeous. "A round of applause is exactly what I had in mind," she said miserably.

Eric laughed and her sick stomach flipped over. "Here." He reached for her hand and she reluctantly accepted his warm grasp, allowing herself to be pulled to her feet. Devastating in gray slacks and a plum dress shirt, he surveyed her turban. "Is this a West Coast thing?"

"I was interrupted in the salon," she explained, thinking the green towel was the perfect complement to her undoubtedly scarlet face.

"Then I guess I'd better let you go," he said merrily. "We're still on for tonight?"

"You mean you still want to?" she asked wryly.

"See you then, swami."

Well, at least the man had seen her at her worst—she hoped. Cindy rushed to the break room to find Amy fussing over a scowling Mr. Stark. She stepped forward, wondering how many times her name already appeared on his reports. "Mr. Stark, I'm Cindy Warren, the general manager."

"We've met twice before, Ms. Warren," he said with agitation. "I'm not senile."

She swallowed a retort while Amy escaped without a backward glance. "My apologies, Mr. Stark. Of course you aren't. Amy told me you saw a, um, rodent in your room?"

"It was a rat." He straightened his conservative burgundy tie. "What's wrong with your head?"

Her cheeks warmed. "I was in the salon, sir."

The man's bushy gray eyebrows rose. "You were having your hair done while on duty?"

Cindy squirmed. "I'm almost always on duty, sir. I rarely leave the hotel, so I work in personal services when I can."

"You look like the rest of those fruitcakes walking around here in costume. What kind of freak show are you running?"

She bit the inside of her cheek to calm herself. He was testing her again. "I'm sorry if any of our guests make you uncomfortable, sir, but I assure you, their role-playing is a harmless hobby." She inhaled deeply. "Now, about the, um, animal you saw in your room. I'll send someone from maintenance immediately, and I apologize profusely for the incident."

His chin jutted out. "I think I'm entitled to some kind of compensation for my ordeal."

Cindy maintained her friendly smile. "I agree, Mr. Stark. I'll instruct the front desk to deduct one night's stay from your bill. I hope this incident doesn't ruin your visit with us."

He harrumphed and, jamming a hat on his head, strode toward the door. "The prune Danish this morning already did that."

Cindy winced as she realized she'd forgotten to change his breakfast order. Then, remembering her hair, she sprinted back to the salon, where Camelia stood tapping her foot. "You're ten minutes late."

Cindy dropped into the chair. "Is my hair ruined?"

"Let me check—the curl isn't permanent until I put on the neutralizer."

The woman unrolled a curler and to Cindy's delight, the lock of hair sprang back to her head in a spirally curl. She threw Jerry a triumphant smirk in the mirror. He simply shook his head.

Camelia frowned. "The curl's a little tight."

But to Cindy, who'd never had curly hair, there was no such thing. "I love it!"

"Okay," the woman said, breaking open the bottle of neutralizing solution. "Curly it is."

WHEN SHE OPENED THE DOOR, Manny only stared. "Oh…my…God."

Her worst fears were confirmed. "It's horrible, isn't it?"

He reached to touch it, then pulled back. "It's like that awful wig Jan Brady wore when she wanted to be different."

"Except it's orange!"

He looked sympathetic. "It does appear that the permanent leached the color a bit."

She burst into tears. "What am I going to do?"

Manny put his arm around her and walked her toward the dressing table. "There, there, it's not that bad. What happened?"

"I got a perm," she wailed. "Then I had to handle a problem and the solution stayed on too long."

"What did Jerry say?"

"He isn't speaking to me." She dropped onto the padded stool and tearfully glanced in the mirror at her friend standing behind her.

He reached into her brassy, stiff hair tentatively. "Good grief, Jimmy Hoffa could be in here." His nose wrinkled. "And pew."

"I didn't know it was going to smell so bad, either," she moaned.

"Better stay away from open flames tonight, or you'll spontaneously combust."

She sniffed. "I take it you heard about the little incident in the restaurant last night."

"I caught it on Joel-SPAN this morning."

"I toasted Eric Quinn's shirt."

He tsk-tsked. "Cindy, I know you want to see this guy naked, but don't you think destroying his wardrobe one garment at a time is a little too obvious?"

She scoffed. "Who says I want to see him naked?"

"Okay, maybe I'm projecting, but you do seem to lose control when he's around."

She stuck out her lower lip. "You're supposed to make me feel better."

He gestured wildly to her eight-inch-high hair. "You're not giving me much to work with here."

Cindy brightened a smidgen. "Well, at least I have a date for the Christmas party." Then her shoulders drooped. "Of course that was before the perm."

"Ah, but *after* the fire," Manny pointed out. "So at least we know he doesn't scare easily. Just in case, better wear the Donna Karan."

"You think? The slit's a little high."

"With this hair, you'd better rip it another six inches."

"Is there any hope?"

He clucked and tried to get his hands around the mass. "You can gel it for a wet look this evening, but for now we'll have to strap it down. Where's your scarf?"

Cindy opened the top drawer and handed him the Chanel scarf. "Remind me to tell you *that* story later. Look at this mess—as if I didn't have enough to worry about today."

"Problems?"

"Did you hear that Mr. Stark-Stanton reported a rat in his room?"

"Any truth to it?"

"Maintenance found some half-eaten food under the heat register, but no rat."

"He could have planted the vittles."

"Exactly. I'm getting tired of these little tests." She sighed. "And engineering said the nursery bumped us down on the list for Christmas trees. At this rate, we might get one by New Year's."

Manny jammed his hands on his hips. "Can I use your phone, dear?"

She pointed into the bedroom. "The handset isn't working in here, but try the one on my nightstand."

"Back in a jiff."

While he was gone, Cindy wrapped her scarf around her head in different configurations. After a few minutes, she admitted defeat and considered wearing the scarf as a veil so that no one would recognize her.

Manny returned with a satisfied look on his face. "The tree will be here in an hour."

Cindy gaped. "How did you do that?"

Shrugging, he said, "Connections. I simply called the nursery, dropped a few names and told them if they didn't deliver a fabulous tree today, I'd sic the gay Mafia on them." He snapped his long fingers. "They'd never get flowers wholesale in this town again."

She grinned. "Manny, where would I be without you?"

He emitted a long-suffering grunt. "In *Glamour* magazine with a black strip across your eyes and a big 'Don't' by your picture." Smoothing her hair back from her face, he fastened the mop into a fat ponytail, then reached for the scarf. "So tell me about this Quinn fellow who has you whipped into such a lather."

Injecting as much innocence into her voice as possible, she said, "He's a salesman."

"So you said. What kind?"

"Hmm?"

He sighed, exasperated. "What kind of salesman?"

Cindy decided to confess, since Manny would find out anyway. She cleared her throat. "Adult entertainment articles."

His hands stopped. "Sex toys?"

She squirmed. "You make it sound so tawdry."

"If the stiletto boot fits, wear it."

"Well, somebody's got to sell the stuff."

He held up both hands. "Hey, I'm grateful, but that doesn't mean I trust him with my best friend."

She smiled and elbowed his thigh. "You're just a big old softy."

"Keep it to yourself, would you? I have an image to uphold." He leaned down. "So do you think you could get me some free samples?"

"I have a box of stuff under the bed that Sam gave me to preview for the trade show—you're welcome to sift through it."

"I'm there."

ERIC STEPPED THROUGH the door of Sammy's and claimed a seat at the bar. A tent sign by an ashtray announced the bar would be closed to guests after eight to accommodate a private Christmas party. The piano bench was stacked high with decorations. He extracted a cigarette from his pocket, suddenly realizing he'd begun smoking about the time he'd become too busy to play the piano.

He ordered a Canadian beer from a glowering Tony and lit his cigarette, frowning after the first drag. He really needed to quit—the damn things didn't even taste good anymore.

"Those things'll kill you." A middle-aged suited man with thick glasses slid onto a stool next to him and plopped a limp fedora on the bar. "Got an extra?"

Eric slid the pack of cigarettes toward him. "Help yourself."

The man ordered a Scotch from Tony, then lit a cigarette. "Thanks. Reginald Stark."

"Eric Quinn."

"Glad to know you." He glanced around, taking note of the group of Trekkies glued to the TV set in the corner. Frowning, he leaned close. "I think you and I are the only people in this hotel who aren't in costume."

Eric laughed. "I'm here strictly for business. You?"

Stark shrugged. "I'm an antiques dealer, here on a shopping trip. I always stay in older hotels and keep my eyes open." He took a drag on his cigarette and exhaled sloppily in Eric's direction. "Sometimes I get lucky and stumble across things the hotel is ready to throw out or sell for next to nothing."

"And have you found any good stuff here?"

"Nah," the man said. "Oh, the furniture is great, but not what I'm looking for at the moment." He laughed, a dry hacking sound. "This place is kind of pricey, but I've discovered that if you complain enough, you can usually get some freebies."

Eric experienced a pang of sympathy for the staff who had to deal with people like Mr. Stark, day in and day out.

The irksome man expelled a cloud of smoke, glanced side to side, then murmured, "You got any money, Quinn?"

Eric reached for his wallet. "I can spot you a ten if you need to cover your tab."

"No, man. I mean do you have any *real* money? I have an investment opportunity."

Eric shook his head. "I'm not interested in the latest multilevel marketing scheme."

Tobacco fumes hung thick around the graying man's head. "It's not like that. I happen to know where there's a fortune in plain sight, waiting for someone to jump on it."

What a con man. Eric put out his own cigarette.

"You don't believe me? Okay, I'll tell you because you look like a man of honor." Stark glanced around surreptitiously again. "It's the chandelier."

Eric frowned. "The chandelier?"

"Yeah, that huge one in the lobby."

"I remember," he said. "What about it?"

"Worth a fortune, that's what." The man reached into his pocket and withdrew a ragged page torn from a book. "See for yourself."

His curiosity piqued, Eric studied the page which featured an aged black-and-white photo of a chandelier, with a small amount of text beneath. "French lead crystal. This says that three chandeliers were produced, but only two are accounted for."

Stark nodded, then pointed toward the lobby. "I think the third one is hanging right in plain sight."

Dubious, Eric said, "The chandelier in this photo looks different."

"From what I can tell, there's a piece missing in the center, but the rest of it's the same."

"But this page says it's worth over seven hundred thousand dollars."

"That's from an old book," the man said, puffing on the cigarette. "Probably worth a cool million now."

Eric's heart rate picked up. "And you're telling me that no one knows about this?"

"I don't think so."

Eric squinted, trying to remember the hotel's balance sheet. To his recollection, the fixtures category hadn't seemed inordinately large, but it was something to look into.

"The way I see it, if you've got, say, five hundred Gs, we can make the hotel an offer."

He blinked. "If *I* have five hundred Gs?"

"Sure. I have a party interested in buying it, but I need up-front purchase money. I'll split whatever we clear with you."

The man was a total scam. Eric shook his head and handed back the dog-eared page. "Sorry, buddy. I'm not biting."

Stark stuffed the paper into his pocket, then drained his drink. "Your loss, pal." Slapping a bill on the bar, the man stood and snuffed out the cigarette. "Thanks for the smoke, anyway. See you around."

Eric watched as the man left, wondering if he'd actually find someone dumb enough to give him five hundred thousand dollars. Still marveling over the man's gall, he signaled Tony and was settling his own tab when the guy who'd given them the Christmas liqueur at the restaurant sauntered over, extending a hand. "Joel Cutter. We met last night. Quinn, isn't it?"

Eric nodded and shook his hand. "No crises today?"

Cutter grinned. "The day's not over yet. I hear you're coming to the party with Cindy."

Eric cut his gaze to Tony the bartender, who was frowning at the news. "Strictly as friends," he assured them both, pushing aside the memory of their kiss. Thankfully, a ringing phone distracted Tony.

"Cindy's a great gal," Joel said warmly. "She certainly loves this place—to the point of neglecting her personal life, if you know what I mean."

Eric nodded pleasantly, wondering if Joel was singing his boss's praises because he knew Eric's true identity. He hated second-guessing those around him, but speculating about ulterior motives was part of his job.

"Joel!" Tony hung up the phone and reached behind him to untie his waist apron. "Problem in the lobby—Cindy needs all available staff, pronto."

"Is Stanton here?"

Joel's question caused Eric to jerk his head involuntarily. So Cindy hadn't yet told them who he was.

And it sounded as though the staff expected his arrival to be traumatic.

"It's not Stanton," Tony said, bringing his stout, muscular body from behind the bar. "The Christmas tree just arrived, and the delivery men have it wedged in the front entrance."

Joel glanced at Eric. "What did I tell you about the day not being over?"

Eric pushed away from the bar. "Think you'll need an extra hand?"

"Come on." Joel trotted toward the door. "If not, we can always use an eyewitness."

CHAPTER SIX

CINDY MASSAGED THE ACHE at the base of her neck, not quite sure if the pain stemmed from the hairdresser's brutal rolling job, her skinned-back ponytail, or the stress of seeing a twenty-five-foot Christmas tree wedged in the double-door entrance of the hotel.

Beneath the massive shimmering chandelier, chaos reigned in the lobby. Guests snapped pictures, some posing in front of the spectacle. Employees stood around with their hands in their pockets, gazing first at the giant blue spruce, then at her, expectantly.

The top half of the tree lay inside the lobby, the bottom half sprawled across the sidewalk plus one lane of the busy street in front of the hotel. Manny stood outside, his long arms waving wildly as he gave the delivery crew a tongue-lashing. Cindy had sent a woman from security out to direct traffic around the tree trunk—and to make sure Manny didn't kill anyone.

"Ms. Warren, how am I supposed to leave this place?"

Cindy closed her eyes and groaned inwardly, then turned to face an impatient Mr. Stark. "I apologize for the inconvenience, sir. There is a side exit past the elevators."

"I decided I'd better go out and buy a rat trap," he said contrarily.

Thankfully, Cindy spotted Amy hovering in the background, a white filtering mask over her allergic nose and mouth. She signaled her rooms director, who came forward with something less than a spring in her step. "Amy, please arrange for a complimentary cab to meet Mr. Stark at the side entrance and take him wherever he needs to go."

The man's bushy-browed frown lessened, but only slightly. Amy led him away, explaining that he might be part of a growing medical phenomenon known as Christmasitis—people who are grumpy around the holidays who, in fact, are experiencing physiological sensitivity to Christmas trees, angel-hair...

"What happened?"

Joel skidded to a halt beside Cindy, followed by Tony, Samantha in a yellow, caped uniform, and to her consternation, Eric. Oh, well, she wouldn't want him to wait more than a few hours before seeing her in yet another jam. Cindy sighed. "The plastic netting around the tree split open when they had it halfway through the door, and now with the branches fully extended, they can't budge the thing."

Joel stared at her. "I meant what happened to your hair."

Resisting the urge to pinch him, she snarled, "I had it done."

Sam squinted. "It looks kind of...orangey."

"It's the glare of the fluorescent lights," Cindy said through clenched teeth.

"Your head has a real nice shape," Tony offered.

She smiled tightly. "Thanks, Tony."

"Do you have a plan?" Eric asked, his expression amused.

"I was considering shaving my head and borrowing one of Sam's costumes."

"I was talking about the tree," he said, the corners of his mouth twitching.

"Oh. No." She glanced around the group. "But the floor is officially open for suggestions."

Her staff assumed identical blank expressions. Eric walked closer to the tree, stroking his jaw with his thumb. Hugging her clipboard, she followed him, self-consciously smoothing a hand over her wiry hair. "What do you think?"

After a few seconds, he gave her a half smile. "I'd call the maintenance department and see if they can remove the panels around the door to widen the opening."

"Great idea," she agreed. "I already called, and they can't."

His smile flattened. "Oh. Well, you could cut the tree in two and use just the top."

"But then we'd be left with a mighty short Christmas tree for this mighty big lobby."

He shrugged. "It's just a tree. It'll be up for what—three weeks. Then it will wind up being mulch in somebody's yard."

Cindy blinked at his unexpected Scrooginess, evidence of a definite chasm within his family. The sad realization made her own comments about dealing with her mother seem petty, triggering a stab of remorse. She made a mental note to call home later.

Her expression must have betrayed some of her thoughts, because Eric straightened and laughed softly. "Of course, that's only my opinion."

She wagged her finger as if he were a child. "You need a big dose of Christmas spirit." Turning, she addressed Joel. "Round up every pair of gloves you can find. Sam, drag Manny in here, would you?"

"What are we going to do?" Tony asked.

Looking back to the tree, Cindy lifted her chin. "Let's try to hold down the branches one by one and push it inside. Even if we break a few, we'll still be better off than if we cut the tree in two."

She slid a smile toward Eric and paused, mesmerized by his incredible ice-blue gaze. This man turned all her peaceful, orbiting atoms into crazed, overcharged ions. Cindy swallowed. Tomorrow she would write an apology note to her high school science teacher for saying she'd never use that stuff.

Joel returned with a bundle of work gloves and passed them around. The self-appointed team leader, Manny waved his arms for silence, then pulled on his gloves as precisely as a surgeon. "Okay, everybody, we can get through this if we work together. Remember to use your legs, not your back. I know you'll feel like you want to push, but wait until I say."

Many employees and several guests pitched in, stepping into the branches and grabbing hold. Eric positioned himself amongst the tangle of towering limbs opposite Cindy, by chance or design, she wasn't sure. From her vantage point, she could see the lower part of his face, see him smile and his lips move as he spoke to a young man next to him. And in that instant, surrounded by cool air swirling in through the open doors, Cindy decided that Eric Quinn would be an easy man to fall for.

She quelled a little thrill of anticipation by wrapping her fingers around a sturdy branch the width of a soda can...not that she was looking for a phallic substitute. She sighed—might as well drop a note to her psychology teacher too.

Amy handed Manny an extra filter mask. He pulled it over his mouth, then squatted by the door, wrapping his hands around a branch. "Okay, take a deep breath and push on three. One...two...three!" With the nursery workers pushing from the outside and everyone else pushing from the inside, the tree inched through the doorway.

"Easy now," Manny yelled. "Easy, don't let her turn."

Cindy kept her gaze averted from Eric as she threw her weight behind her section of trunk, but she was so aware of him she could scarcely concentrate. In less than six hours, she would be spending the evening on the arm of the sexiest man she'd met in ages. And he had a great sense of humor, good taste in clothes, a decent job.

Okay, maybe *decent* wasn't the right word. Stable. After all, what could be more stable than a career in sex?

"One last push!" Manny yelled. "Here she comes!"

With a collective grunt, they shoved one more time and the tree whooshed through the door and into the lobby, sliding easily across the marble floor. Cheers and applause broke out, and relief washed over Cindy—the tree would be set up by the time cranky Mr. Stark-Stanton returned.

Laughing, Eric pulled off his gloves. "Why do I feel like passing out cigars?"

Cindy decided he really should laugh more often. Her heart danced a crazy little jig. Despite the uproar around them, she felt strangely secluded with this man who had affected her so in such an alarmingly short period of time. She seized on a neutral subject. "Speaking of which, how goes the decision to quit smoking?"

"I'm okay as long as I keep my hands busy," he said with the barest smile.

Cindy swallowed. So much for neutral. Over his shoulder she noted the arrival of the two tree decorators. Feeling flirtatious, she lowered her voice. "What if I told you I had something to keep your hands and your mouth busy at the same time?"

He looked around them. "I'd say we're in public."

"Okay." She shrugged. "The tree decorators are here, so I'd better get back to work."

"Hey." He laughed, grasping her arm as she half-heartedly started to leave. "All right, I'm curious."

Cindy angled her head at him. "You also have a very dirty mind." She reached into her pocket, pulled out a pack of Sweet Tarts, then handed it to him with a grin. "Ta-da! The quitting smoker's secret weapon. Use it wisely, grasshopper." Cindy sobered slightly, then said, "If our paths don't cross again, I'll see you tonight. Thanks for helping with the Christmas tree."

He nodded slowly. "Thanks for the dose of Christmas spirit."

Fingering the package of candy, Eric watched her cross the lobby and greet two men, obviously gay. They embraced Cindy, then touched her hair with concern. He smiled—she'd been harboring a permanent under that towel this morning. Actually, he found the reddish highlights in her hair attractive.

In fact, he couldn't imagine anything she might do to herself that would diminish her beauty.

Eric maintained a calm exterior while his insides thrashed with sensory overload. He couldn't rationalize the urge he felt to keep her within eyeshot—hell, he could barely *acknowledge* the urge, much less explain it. Away from Cindy, the arguments against spending time with her stacked up neatly, but in her proximity, those arguments tumbled with alarming ease.

Workers were building scaffolding and tying ropes up and down the massive trunk in preparation for hoisting the evergreen next to the magnificent staircase. Eric's gaze traveled to the dazzling chandelier hanging high above everyone, thinking for the first time how much his father would appreciate the craftsmanship of the glass. Perhaps he would send him a postcard of the chandelier with a quick note to let him know his son was thinking about him. Mysteriously buoyant, Eric made his way back through the lobby.

THE REST OF CINDY'S AFTERNOON passed in a merciful blur. She spot-checked the installation of the towering spruce, then left the somewhat flaky decorators to their own devices after they promised her "a masterpiece" by morning.

She also arranged for Mr. Stark to enjoy a night out at the theater, gratis. At least the play would keep the man occupied while the employees drifted in and out of the Christmas party. She swung by Sammy's to make sure preparations were under way. Joel waved to her from the other side of the room and gave her a thumbs-up. Jerry stood on a ladder where the piano used to sit, hanging an armful of lights.

Cindy walked over, struck by affection for the elderly man who always pitched in, in any area of the hotel. "Are you still mad at me?" she asked, looking up at him.

Without glancing down, he grunted. "It's your head of hair to ruin, I reckon."

She sighed. "Okay, okay, I should have left well enough alone. It'll grow out."

"No, it'll *fall* out."

"Maybe," she conceded. "But I have it on good authority that my head has a nice shape."

At last he laughed and sat down on top of the stepladder, shaking his head. "You look like you got your head caught in a rusty commode and you're still able to charm the birds out of the trees."

She shot him a wry smile. "So glad we've made up. Where's the piano?"

"They moved it around the corner to the Asteroid Room to get it out of the way. Hey, I found a sprig of artificial mistletoe—do you think I should put it up?"

She shook her head. "Just last week I received a memo prohibiting mistletoe at company Christmas parties."

"Never listened to 'em before."

"I think I'd better this time," she said. "Nix the mistletoe."

He climbed down the ladder slowly. "Afraid you'll be caught under it, are you?"

"No!"

He grinned. "Afraid you won't be?"

"I won't dignify that question with a response."

"Bringing that Quinn lad, aren't you?"

"Jerry, he's hardly a lad." Then she narrowed her eyes. "Besides, how did you know?"

"Camelia told me when I walked into the salon this morning."

"But I didn't even *meet* her until she gave me this dreadful perm!"

He shrugged. "She said Stan, the shoeshine man, told her."

Cindy shook her head. "Unbelievable." She threw up her hands, defeated. "Well, at least she's working out."

The old man grimaced.

"She's not working out?"

"You keep scarin' them off with your hair disasters."

Cindy looked up at the ceiling. "Now what are we going to do for a hairdresser?" She cut her gaze to Jerry, then smiled sweetly. "You know, Jerry, if you'd agree to wait on female customers, your tips would probably skyrocket."

He held up one brown, weathered hand. "Oh, no. Men, give 'em a few snips here and there, clip the eyebrows, mustache and the occasional bushy ear, and they're happy. Women? No, thanks."

"I guess I need to call personnel to arrange for another temp."

Jerry glanced at his watch. "You'd better pick up the pace if you're going to get all duded up for the party."

She pretended to be hurt. "How long do you think I need?"

He gave her a rare one-armed hug. "Build in some time to relax, okay? Try to forget about this old hotel and have a good time tonight with your young man." Then he held up the mistletoe and grinned, revealing large, perfect teeth. "And I'll try to find someplace appropriate for this."

Cindy punched him playfully. "You're determined to get me into trouble. I'll see you tonight."

But Jerry's words stirred up the anticipation she'd suppressed all afternoon. She tied up a few administrative loose ends, distracted to the point of craning for a glimpse of Eric as she moved through the hotel.

At six o'clock, she returned to her suite and grabbed an apple. Then, sinking onto her bed, she wistfully dialed her parents' number. Janine Warren answered on the first ring.

"Hi, Mom. How's everything— Nothing's wrong, Mom. In fact, I'm going to a party tonight and I had

a few minutes— Hmm? Yes, I have a date. He's a
very nice man who happens to be a guest— What?
Of course he's not married. Yes, he told me—huh?
Eric Quinn. No, with a *Q,* not a *K.* Guess what?...
No...No...No. He's from Virginia, can you believe—
Manassas...Manassas...Ma-nass-as. Right. Virginia.
Right. So how's everything? He's a salesman. What
kind? A successful salesman, Mom. So how's everything? Right, Christmas Eve. No, Mom, Manny
is just a friend, he doesn't care that I— As a matter
of fact, they *have* met. Oh, look at the time! I have
to get ready for the party. I will. Okay, I will. Say
hello to Daddy for me. Love you, too. Bye-bye...
okay, bye-bye...okay, bye-bye."

Cindy replaced the handset with a sigh, then bit
a chunk out of the apple. "I'll know I'm grown up
when my mother lets me finish an entire sentence,"
she mumbled. But she had to admit it was comforting
to know her mother still fretted over her. She would
probably be the same kind of mother. Cindy stopped
in midchew—mother? It was definitely time to stop
thinking and get ready for the party.

Her stomach was so full of butterflies, it fairly
flapped. She undressed slowly, then turned on the
shower and let the water run over her fingers until
it warmed.

With trepidation, she unfastened her hair, not
surprised when the coarse, reddish mass instantly
vaulted toward the ceiling. Manny had instructed

her to wash her hair twice to diffuse some of the curl and most of the odor. Resigned, she stepped under the water and lathered the rat's nest carefully, unused to the shortened length and springy texture. After dousing her hair with thick conditioner, she soaped her body, then went for the big shave—both the bottoms *and* tops of her legs.

She rinsed, then wrapped her hair in a towel. The flashlight from her nightstand was required to locate her special-occasion matching body lotion and perfume in the depths of her vanity cabinet. After slathering her slight curves with moisturizer and stepping into a robe, she finally dredged up the nerve to remove the towel from her head.

The tight curls clung to her head haphazardly, brassy in color even when wet. Cindy moaned and reached for the cosmetic bag Manny had given her with various picks, gels and a little black thing that looked like a tiny hammock. She smoothed out his page of written instructions and drew a calming breath.

Thirty minutes later she had managed to pull out most of the tangles with a wide pick, but by then the mass stood around her head like some kind of exotic hat. She worked the gel through her wild tresses, then slicked it back into a low ponytail according to Manny's drawing. The little hammock, she discovered, was called a snood, a fancy name for a ponytail net. She fastened the snood in place, then turned sideways to critique her handiwork in the mirror and smiled. It didn't look half-bad.

She turned back to the vanity mirror and frowned. Her face was another story. She hadn't arched her eyebrows in ages and next to her perm-lightened hair, they looked darker and more severe than usual. "Glam up the eyes," Manny had told her. She fished tweezers and an eyelash curler from a cluttered drawer, then pulled her magnifying mirror closer. With grimacing plucks, she thinned her wayward eyebrows, begrudgingly acknowledging her greenish eyes were her best feature.

Carefully, she positioned the eyelash curler to tackle her long straight lashes, and squeezed the handle. The phone in her bedroom rang, startling her, and her hand jerked. She gasped as searing pain zipped across her eyelid, then jumped up to answer the phone, covering her stinging eye with the heel of her hand.

"Hello?"

"Cindy, this is Manny. You have a delivery—shall I bring it up?"

"What kind of delivery?" She wiped at the involuntary tears running down her cheek.

"Let it be a surprise."

Glancing down at the eyelash curler, she frowned at the number of lashes stuck to the little rubber pad, then froze. "Yes, Manny, bring it up." Cindy slammed down the phone, dread washing over her

as she stumbled back to the vanity table. She pressed
her face close to the mirror, then gasped. Funny—
she'd never realized how much eyelashes, or the lack
of them, contributed to the overall balance of a person's face. The top of her left eye was nearly bald
in places.

She groaned, then threw up her hands. She'd
simply have to call Eric and cancel. Obligation dic-
tated that she attend the party, but she couldn't face
him with only half her lashes on one eye. Then she
chewed her bottom lip—maybe it wasn't so noticeable. A knock at her door interrupted her panicked
scrutiny.

Cindy secured the sash around her robe and
jogged to the door. After a quick check of the peephole, she swung open the door to find Manny sporting a smashing black tux with a silver cummerbund
and bow tie, and holding a small vase of exquisite
flowers with a card tucked among the blooms. She
smiled. "What on earth?"

"I didn't check the card, but I suspect they're from
your dashing date." He handed her the vase and followed her inside the room. "Hey, your hair looks
great."

"You sound surprised," she said, setting down the
fragrant mixture of white roses and lilies. "By the
way, love the tux."

"Thanks. Was I right?"

Cindy read the card, a zing of pure pleasure coursing through her at Eric's neat handwriting. *Thank you in advance for an engaging evening. Eric.*

"Well, is his note naughty, or nice?"

Scoffing at his implication, Cindy said, "Nice, of course."

He made a face, then he leaned forward, squinting. "Cindy, your eye." His jaw dropped. "What happened to your eyelashes?"

She sighed. "So much for it not being noticeable."

"Let me guess—eyelash curler?"

Cindy nodded miserably.

"A dangerous tool in the hands of a nervous woman," he observed.

"I'm not nervous."

He gave her a pointed look.

"Okay, I'm a little nervous—my hand jerked when the phone rang. What am I going to do?"

"They'll grow back."

"I mean about tonight!"

He tilted his head to one side. "Got any falsies?"

She frowned. "Are we still talking about eyelashes?"

"Yes."

"Then no."

He turned and strode back toward the door. "Put on the rest of your makeup—everything but the eye stuff. I'll be right back."

After he left, Cindy buried her nose in the flowers, then dropped onto the stool at her vanity. *An engaging evening.* He didn't seem the type to copy words from some generic book at the flower shop. Eric was a sincere and forthcoming man. After all, he obviously suspected his vocation might turn her off, yet he'd been up front with her.

Cindy smoothed foundation over her skin, then applied blush and rummaged for the brightest red lipstick in her makeup case. As Cindy drew on the rich color, she remembered in vivid clarity the pressure of Eric's lips against hers the previous night. She closed her eyes and relived the taste of him, the sensation of his hands holding her face…a shudder traveled her shoulders and she knew the hair on her neck would have stood straight up were it not plastered down.

She had to admit, the man captivated her at a time when she'd have bet she couldn't be distracted from the goings-on within the hotel. The presence of the notorious Mr. Stark-Stanton hadn't consumed her the way she'd feared, although she would continue to do her best to placate the difficult man.

Keeping a near-bald eye on the clock, she stepped into the fitted long black gown. Cindy checked the top half of her dress in her vanity mirror, then climbed on her bed to check the bottom half. "Someday I'll invest in a full-length mirror," she mumbled, jumping down to slide her feet into suede pumps.

She slicked clear polish on her short nails, which had dried by the time Manny knocked on the door again. He strode in and whipped a package of false eyelashes out of a bag.

"I don't have time to put on false eyelashes," she said in exasperation. "Eric will be here in fifteen minutes!"

Manny, slightly out of breath, lifted his hands high. "Okay, if you want to get nose to nose with this guy with nothing to bat at him as he unlocks the door to his room—"

"You don't think he'll ask me to go back to his room," she gasped, then added, "do you?"

He laughed and gestured toward the vase. "*Hello?* Do these flowers say 'I'll settle for a goodnight kiss' to you? No. More like 'I want to devour you, my pet.'..." He plucked a white rose from the vase, clenched it between his teeth, and wagged his eyebrows.

"Do you honestly think so?" She nibbled on a freshly painted nail.

Manny pursed his lips and nodded, then broke off the rose and motioned for her to turn around.

"So," she said sheepishly as he inserted the flower in her hair, "how long does it take to put on falsies?"

"Sit down and give me five," he said, ripping open the package and pulling out a tiny bottle of something clear. "Your dress is fab, by the way."

"Thanks." She eyed the flimsy semicircle of lashes warily. "I've never worn these things before."

"You'll get used to them in no time."

Cindy gave him a questioning look.

"So I've been told," he added.

She flinched throughout, but true to his word, Manny quickly patched the gap in her lashes quite convincingly. She tested the subtly heavier eyelid with a few blinks, then grinned and pulled him down for a quick peck on his cheek. "Thank you." A knock sounded at the door, sending her heart into her throat.

"I'll stall Mr. Quinn for a few minutes while you finish your eye makeup," Manny assured her. "And don't forget your glass earrings."

Her hands started shaking. "I'm a nervous wreck," she said. "Any last-minute advice?"

Her friend gave her a wry smile. "Try not to destroy any more of the man's clothing tonight when you undress him."

CHAPTER SEVEN

ERIC FELT LIKE A TEENAGER picking up his date for the prom. He had to acknowledge, however, that his anxiety about developing an attraction to Cindy Warren had increased tenfold since the tree incident in the lobby. The woman moved him…it was an unsettling sensation.

During the afternoon, he'd stumbled onto more disturbing aspects of the hotel operation. On the two floors with the most conference-room space, there were three bathrooms marked Men, Women and Other. Scary. And instead of the conference rooms bearing regal names, they were dubbed the "Phenomenon Room" and the "Dimension Chamber."

A quick look at the balance sheet had revealed the chandelier was booked at a legitimate-sounding twenty-eight thousand dollars. So why had he penned on the postcard to his father: *Dad, wondering if you can help me dig up information about the chandelier in this photo—possibly French, nineteen-twenties? I'll call you soon.* And why did he feel as if every

minute spent with Cindy Warren would suck him
deeper into a quagmire of right and wrong?

The door opened and his anxiety turned to puzzlement. Manny, not Cindy, stood in the doorway.
"Hello," he ventured.

The blond man smiled tightly. "Cindy will be
ready in a couple of minutes. Come on in."

Bemused, Eric followed him down a short hallway to a surprisingly spacious sitting room taste-
fully decorated in a celestial motif of blues and golds.

"Have a seat," Manny invited, making no move
to sit himself.

"Thanks, I'll stand," Eric replied, once again wondering if the concierge was smitten with his boss.
Closer scrutiny revealed a red lipstick mark on the
man's cheek, eliciting an unreasonable stab of jealousy in Eric. Did Cindy have romantic feelings for
her employee? It didn't seem likely considering the
way she'd responded to his kiss last night, but what if
she was just trying to butter him up after all? Questions chewed at Eric, renewing his resolve to resist
her charms, especially in light of the troubling revelations about how business was conducted at the
Chandelier House.

Manny glanced over Eric's tux and pursed his
lips. "Nice threads."

"Thanks," Eric said with a nod. "Yours, too." The
subject of clothing reminded Eric of the bizarre incident he'd been meaning to report, but he hadn't

wanted to bother Cindy. He lowered his voice. "Listen, Mr. Oliver—"

"I'm ready."

Cindy floated down the hallway toward them, her beauty taking Eric's breath away. The black dress covered her gleaming shoulders and neckline modestly, but hugged her curves, confirming his earlier suspicions of what lay beneath the plain green and navy uniform she wore—a shapely bust, trim waist, flaring hips. A mid-thigh slit revealed a long, lean leg encased in shimmering black stockings. Eric's body hardened, reminding him again of a high-school date.

Their gazes locked and his tongue grew thicker. Translucent, faceted earrings hung from her small ears like huge raindrops. With her hair skimmed back from her face, her lovely features were brought into relief. Her green-gray eyes shone luminously, set off by thick dark lashes. She winked, surprising him, and he smiled in return. Her bee-stung red lips curved into a shy smile. Eric couldn't take his eyes off her, and his tongue refused to budge. She, too, seemed hesitant to speak.

"Cindy received your flowers," Manny injected. "She loves white roses, don't you, boss?"

Cindy nodded, but didn't otherwise acknowledge the presence of her concierge. Eric spotted her pulse jumping at the side of her slender neck.

Manny cleared his throat. "Well, I guess I'll be

leaving you two chatty kids alone. Don't mind me, I'll show myself out."

Eric heard the shuffle of the man's footsteps, and the click of the door closing behind him. After a few seconds of heavy silence, he murmured, "Hi."

One side of her mouth went up. "Hi, yourself."

"You look…great."

The other side of her mouth joined the first. "That's the look I was aiming for."

He swallowed. "I like your—" *body* "—earrings."

She touched one lobe, setting the glasslike bauble into sparkling motion. "Thank you. The flowers are beautiful." She turned her head slightly to show him the rose in her hair. "And thank you for the nice card."

"You're very welcome."

"I guess we'd better get to the party."

Eric moved toward the door, his steps faltering when she turned to retrieve an evening bag from the breakfast bar. He devoured the sight of her bare back, imagining the sensation of running his hands down the indentation of her spine. Promising himself some unimaginable treat in the morning for resisting her tonight, Eric opened the door and kept his eyes averted as she preceded him into the corridor. As if sharing his awkward awareness, she moved down the hall beside him, staring straight ahead.

Since Cindy, too, seemed quieter than usual, Eric decided the long ride down the elevator might be a good time to casually broach at least one topic niggling at him. "Cindy, when we were moving the tree this morning, I was noticing that amazing chandelier—is it valuable?"

She raised her lovely shoulders in a slight shrug. "The chandelier holds sentimental value to everyone who works here, I suppose."

"So it's not a particularly historic piece?" he pressed gently.

"I guess the chandelier is an antique, even though it's a reproduction."

"A reproduction?"

Cindy nodded. "I was told the original crystal fixture came from France. Allegedly, three were delivered to the States in the twenties—one to our hotel, one to a hotel in Chicago and the other to a department store in Beverly Hills." She smiled sadly as the doors slid open to the lobby. "But during the Second World War, all three chandeliers were replaced with glass replicas, and the originals donated to help the war effort." She smiled and led the way toward Sammy's. "Sorry to burst your bubble, Mr. Quinn."

She was teasing him by using the name under which he'd registered. He played along—after all, she probably didn't want to slip and use the name Stanton in front of her employees. "It still makes for an interesting story." He extended his arm to her as they reached the entrance to the bar, already alive with moving bodies and Christmas music. "What happened to 'Eric'?"

She smiled as she tucked her arm inside his. "Shall we, Eric?"

They walked down the two steps at the entrance, and heads turned. More than one set of eyebrows rose, telling Eric they were not used to seeing their boss on the arm of a man, or at least not on the arm of a stranger. He scanned the room for Manny, and as he suspected, the blond man, unaccompanied, had already captured them in his unwavering gaze.

The room glowed with strand upon strand of Christmas lights. A DJ sat on the elevated stage, surrounded by stacks of music selections. Tall speakers were currently blaring "Jingle Bell Rock." He estimated two hundred people in sparkling dresses and fancy suits studded the room.

Cindy was soon swept up in a circle of employees, meeting spouses and shaking hands, introducing him simply as Eric Quinn. He asked what she wanted to drink, then excused himself and approached the bar. Jerry, dashing in a charcoal-gray suit and red tie, occupied a stool in the middle. Eric shouldered in next to him, then shouted their drink orders to Tony who was managing the open bar.

"Did you come alone, Jerry?"

The old man nodding, smiling. "Yep."

"I thought you were married."

"I said I'd *been* married," the barber corrected,

then his mouth split into a wide grin. "I'm between wives right now."

"Ah."

"Do you and Ms. Cindy have big plans tomorrow?"

Confused, Eric frowned. "Tomorrow?"

Jerry nodded his graying head. "Since you're the reason she has the day off and all, I figured you'd be spending it together."

Eric laughed. "Excuse me?"

"She didn't tell you? Joel Cutter bet Cindy she couldn't get a date for the party and if she did, he'd cover for her tomorrow." Jerry slapped him on the back. "She must have wanted that day off mighty bad, son."

Piqued, Eric frowned. Cindy had invited him as part of a wager?

"Ah, don't get all down in the mouth about it, son. I'm sure she likes you a bit, too."

Producing his best casual shrug, Eric said, "We're just two people at a party having a good time. No big deal." He collected the mixed drinks and headed back to Cindy. Approaching her, Eric experienced another pull of sexual longing. She was a beauty, all right. And smart. And sexy.

And off-limits, he reminded himself, swallowing a mouthful of cold rum and cola to cool his warming libido. And although at times he would have sworn he detected a glimmer of interest in her eyes, per-

haps her invitation to the party had more to do with
the silly bet than with influencing the man who held
her livelihood in his hands. The thought cheered him.
Then he frowned—either explanation ruled out the
possibility that she was just plain interested.

When Cindy lifted her head to see Eric thread-
ing his way back to her, she acknowledged a thrill
of excitement. He handed her a Fuzzy Navel and
winked, warming her with his intense gaze. She
sipped her drink, a feeling of bonelessness overtak-
ing her. Given the chance, she just might seize the
moment and spend one night of abandon with this
gorgeous man.

"Hey," he said, leaning close, his eyes dancing.
"What's this I hear about a bet?"

Heat suffused her cheeks. "B-bet?"

His mouth twitched. "Yeah, word has it that my
going rate is a day off with pay."

Tingling with embarrassment, Cindy pressed her
lips together. "It was just a harmless bet between
friends."

"And what was the wager?"

"If I won, Joel would cover for me tomorrow."

He pursed his lips. "And if you lost?"

She sighed. "Joel would get my parking spot for
a month."

"And I thought you actually liked me."

"Oh, I do—" She flushed. "I mean, believe it or
not, I actually forgot about the bet."

He grinned. "In that case, I'm sure Joel will be glad to hear—"

"Wait!" she cried, laughing. "I need the day off tomorrow."

"In that case," he said, capturing her hand and leading her toward the center of the vacant dance floor, "let's dance and discuss *my* compensation."

Her heart thudded at the touch of his hand against hers. "I'm not a very good dancer," she protested.

"Just follow my lead," he said smoothly, spinning her into a slow waltz to "I'll Be Home for Christmas." Other couples joined them.

Supremely conscious of his hand at her waist, grazing the bare skin on her back, Cindy kept as much distance between herself and Eric as possible, stiffly following his footwork.

"Relax," he said, drawing her closer. "This is supposed to be fun."

"I think it's the song," she quipped.

"Does it make you sad?"

"'Stressed' is a better word. My mother can be a little intense."

"Such a shame," he said lightly, "that you can't choose your family like you choose your friends."

Suspecting a deeper issue lurked in his words, Cindy smiled. "I'm sure parents feel the same way occasionally about their kids."

He laughed suddenly. "You're probably right." Distracted by the conversation, she involuntarily moved closer to his body. Eric took up the slack immediately, his hand splaying across her bare lower back. "Now, about tomorrow," he whispered.

"What about tomorrow?" she asked, fighting the urge to lower her head on his shoulder. He smelled so good, damn him. He moved with such grace. And his feet were so intriguingly huge.

"Since I'm the reason you'll have the day off, I think the least you can do is spend some of it with me."

Secretly thrilled, Cindy pretended to relent with a sigh. "And what did you have in mind?"

"Sleeping in."

She missed a beat and stepped on his foot.

"Ow!"

"Sorry, I told you I'm not a very good dancer." She couldn't be sure he meant he wanted to sleep in *with her*.

"So we'd have to get a late start," he said, picking up where he left off.

"I have Christmas shopping to do. Not exactly the most *engaging* pastime."

He smiled wide. "The company will be engaging. You'll be shopping all day?"

"No. I thought I'd walk the Golden Gate Bridge— it's invigorating and the view is great because there's no fog this time of the year."

"Sounds wonderful. I have some shopping to do

myself, and in all the times I've been to San Francisco, I've never seen the Golden Gate."

Suddenly nervous, Cindy stalled. "Did I say the view was great? I meant to say 'gray.' Blah. And the bridge is not really golden, you know. Kind of rust-colored. Actually, there's no gate, either. Come to think of it, the bridge isn't all that special."

"I believe you're trying to talk me out of going," he said in a low voice, winking at her for what seemed like the hundredth time. "Which is very naughty, considering I'm the reason you're getting a day for fun and frolic."

The song changed to the upbeat "Rockin' Around the Christmas Tree," and Cindy allowed him to swing her into a fast waltz, laughing with every dip. After a few spins, she started feeling the alcohol bleed through her system. "I'm getting light-headed."

"If we stop now, I'll have to find something else to keep my hands busy."

At his whispered words, Cindy's breasts tingled. "Okay, one more song." She had the deliciously dangerous feeling she was spiraling out of control, but she couldn't deny she was enjoying the ride. He alternately brushed his body close to hers, then away for a spin. At last the song ended and everyone applauded.

"You're a very good dancer," she remarked as they walked off the floor.

"I haven't danced in ages," he said, almost to himself. "My kid sister used to make me jitterbug with

her in the kitchen." With a blink, he seemed to return to the present. "You're pretty light on your feet
yourself." He winked.

There was that wink again—maybe he was getting drunk, she thought, concern creasing her forehead. The last thing she needed in her life was a
man who sold sex toys and had a drinking problem.
Then she chastised herself—this was only a potential fling, not a relationship. And she could relax her
standards a bit for a fling.

They stopped by the buffet and piled their plates
high with quiche and sausage balls and fruit, then
joined Manny, Samantha and Sam's date seated
around a table. Eric excused himself to go and get
fresh drinks.

Samantha, stunning in a long green dress, had invited a Trekkie friend who apparently thought "black
tie" meant the type of tennis shoe laces to be worn.
Manny looked incredibly bored.

"Cheer up," she whispered.

"Easy for you to say," he muttered back. "You're
getting laid tonight."

Her mouth dropped open. "I am not."

"I'll betcha Mr. Quinn thinks you are."

"Simply because I danced with him?"

"No. Because you've been winking at him every
twenty seconds."

"What are you talking about?"

"How are the lashes?"

The *winking.* "Oh, my goodness, Manny—you're right. I've been winking at him nonstop. He probably thinks I'm being fresh."

Manny smirked. "I'd say 'fresh' would be a safe understatement."

"Knock it off, here he comes."

"So, Cindy, how's the Christmas tree in the lobby progressing?" Sam asked.

"The decorators said they'd be finished by morning."

"That's great. Oh, and how are things going with our difficult Mr. Stark?"

Cindy sighed. "I made sure he'd be off the premises tonight. I hope he doesn't have any other bizarre room experiences to report." She smiled at Eric as he rejoined them. Sam's date pulled her to the dance floor.

"I heard the tail end of your comment," Eric said, popping a grape into his mouth. "And speaking of bizarre, I've been meaning to mention a rather strange incident."

"What?" Cindy asked. Manny leaned forward.

"This is going to sound crazy," Eric said, shaking his head, "but I think someone stole a pair of pajama pants from my room and replaced them with a new pair, same color, same brand."

Cindy swallowed hard, refusing to look at Manny. "Really?"

"Yeah, sounds nuts, huh?"

"Insane," Manny agreed, nudging her knee.

"The thing is," Eric continued slowly, "the pants were a gift—probably expensive, too—but I never cared for them." He laughed. "The pervert who took them obviously wanted something worn, but little did he know, he didn't have to replace them."

Now you tell me. "Eric," she said, playing with the end of her napkin, "if these, um—pajama pants, did you say?"

He nodded.

"If these pajama pants are the same color and same brand, what makes you think they're not the same pair?"

"Because," he said simply, "my initials were monogrammed on the pocket."

"Your initials?" she squeaked.

He bit into a tiny quiche, nodding. "Odd, huh?"

"I might go as far to say 'warped,'" Manny declared. "Desperate, sick, disturbed—"

Cindy gouged him in the ribs. "If there's anything the hotel can do—"

"I'm not looking for compensation," Eric said. "I just wanted you to know you might have a weirdo on the loose."

She conjured up a watery smile. "Thanks for the tip."

The hours slipped away. She drank and ate and danced with Eric until she was giggly and exhausted—and more turned on than she could have imagined. Her apprehension increased as the minutes ticked away. Surely they would share another good-night kiss, but what if he suggested more? Should she explore the unbelievable chemistry she detected between them? She smiled at him and, feeling languid, rubbed her foot against his leg.

In the middle of telling a funny story, Eric jerked, then cut his eyes to her.

"Hey," Manny said sternly. "Hands on the table, Cindy."

Everyone laughed, and to her astonishment, Eric actually blushed. Suddenly Joel appeared. "Eleven-thirty, Cindy. Ready to play Santa Claus?"

Cindy blinked. "Santa Claus?"

"Don't you remember? You said you'd do it the other night after you set one of my tables on fire."

Cindy stared, her memory sliding around. "Oh, yeah, I did say something about being Santa." *When I presumed I'd be coming alone.*

"Follow me," he said. "The suit's in the back."

Just when she thought she'd get through the next few hours with a scrap of dignity. She glanced at Eric, and he winked. Propping up her lazy eye with her index finger, Cindy sighed and slid out of her seat.

"No way," she said, looking at the outfit.

Joel lifted his finger. "Ah, ah, ah. You already said you would, boss."

"But *you* said I'd be wearing a Santa suit."

"This is a Santa suit."

"Joel, it's a long-sleeved minidress with fur around the edges."

"Well…it's red."

She crossed her arms.

"And look, there's a pair of black boots with it."

"They're thigh-highs!"

"And the hat—don't forget the hat," he said, dangling a red stocking cap with a white ball on the end.

"Who bought this ridiculous getup?"

A tolerant expression came over his face. "The lady who runs the gift shop came across it in a clearance catalog. I don't think she realized what she ordered. She paid for it out of her own pocket."

Cindy sighed, her shoulders dropping. "If you're trying to make me feel like a dog, it's working." Joel smiled triumphantly. "You'd better be glad I've been drinking," she declared. "And I am *not* wearing those boots."

"Okay, okay. The thing looks a little big for you," he said, holding up the red dress. "At least it won't be skintight."

She yanked it out of his hands and pointed toward the door. "Scram."

"I'll get the gifts ready—everyone is going to love this!"

"Ho, ho, ho," she mumbled, waving him out of the supply room. She shimmied out of her dress, then hung the black gown on a hook next to a mop. The fuzzy white hem fell just below her knees, the furry cuffs down to the tips of her fingers, and the dress bagged around the waist. Spotting a wide plastic black belt on top of the preposterous boots, she wrapped it around her middle and cinched up a couple of feet of fabric.

Feeling like a complete fool, she set the cap on her head, and flipped the white cotton tip over her shoulder. At a tap on the door, she took a deep breath and stepped outside. Joel stood holding a bulging red velvet bag, grinning ear to ear.

Cindy lifted a finger. "Not a word."

He pressed his lips together and handed her the bag.

Eric watched for Cindy's return, but he heard the roar of laughter before he actually saw her. When she came into view, he grinned and joined the ranks of those around him. She didn't look nearly as amused to be wearing the baggy red dress, obviously made for a much taller, more buxom Santa. She was a good sport, though, and made the rounds, passing out envelopes to all her employees while the DJ played "I Want a Hippopotamus for Christmas."

From the good-natured ribbing she received, it was apparent to him that Cindy's bubbly personality made her popular with the employees. Unfortunately, in his experience, well-liked managers were not always the most efficient, because they let personal relationships influence their decisions. He swallowed a large mouthful of his drink. Which was precisely why he had to maintain a proper distance from Cindy, at least until he finished his job at the Chandelier House.

Of course, he acknowledged wryly, if he recommended that the hotel be sold, or that Cindy be replaced, that personality of hers might undergo a quick change from bubbly to boiling.

When she stopped at their table, Cindy made sheepish eye contact, then handed Manny and Sam identical envelopes. "You're in luck this year. You get the same gift regardless of whether you've been naughty or nice."

"Speaking of nice," Eric remarked, toying with the cotton ball on the end of her cap, "love the outfit." A vision of her wearing nothing but the hat flashed through his mind.

"I wanted to make sure no other woman at the party would be wearing the same dress," she said with a mock-serious face. "I'm almost finished. Will you still be here when I get back, or are you completely humiliated?"

He laughed. "I'm completely humiliated, and I'll be here when you get back." Sam and her date hit the dance floor again, leaving him alone at the table with Manny. Eric's gaze strayed to Cindy as she finished passing out the envelopes, and his body swelled in…anticipation.

"Cindy's a gem," Manny said crisply, interrupting his musing.

Eric started, then turned to the concierge and nodded. "She's quite a lady."

Manny leaned forward. "Just so you know, she told me why you're here." His tone was even, his expression serious. "Normally I couldn't care less what a person does for a living, but in this case, it matters because Cindy matters. You'll be leaving in a few days and Cindy's the one who will have to deal with the fallout." The blond man pursed his mouth, then said, "Cindy means a lot to me, sir. I don't want to see her get hurt."

Rubbing the condensation off his glass, Eric pondered the man's words. He heard the wisdom, but hated the implication. "I don't want Cindy to be hurt any more than you do."

"Good," Manny said, pushing away from the table. "At least we see eye to eye on one point. Good night."

"Manny." Eric pushed himself to his feet. "If you wouldn't mind waiting a few minutes, would you stay and give Cindy my apologies? I think I'd better call it a night."

"No argument here," the man said curtly. "Merry Christmas, Mr. Quinn."

Eric didn't miss the dig, calling him by his registered name. "Yes, merry Christmas, Manny." Funny,

he thought as he left the bar, this was the first time
he could remember ever wishing he was anybody
but himself.

CHAPTER EIGHT

"GONE?" CINDY BIT HER lower lip, trying to hide her disappointment.

"He said to tell you he was sorry," Manny said. "But he had to call it a night."

She plucked at the neckline of the black gown she'd changed back into. "Well, after all, it was just a date. You know, to show Joel."

Manny clucked. "You like this guy, don't you?"

Grimacing, she rolled her shoulders. "I don't know. It's hypocritical to make my living off people like Eric, then hold his profession against him. But I have to admit it does bother me that he makes a living selling plastic rear ends. How does a man like Eric find his way into that industry?"

"Maybe he was a porn star."

Her eyes bulged. "You think?"

He shrugged. "He's got the looks for it."

"Oh, my God, you're probably right. I might as well put a casket by the phone for my mother to fall into."

"It was just a thought, Cindy. Don't bury her yet."

She sighed. "It's just that otherwise he seems so... perfect."

"Well, trust me," Manny said, "no man is perfect."

She squeezed his shoulders. "You are."

He grinned. "Well, excluding me, of course. How about I walk you back to your room?"

Cindy sighed, looking around the deserted bar. "No, but thanks anyway. I'm going to check a few things in the back, then go to bed." She managed a smile. "At least I get to sleep in tomorrow."

"Hey," he said softly. "Are you okay?"

She nodded. "Sure."

"If this guy breaks your heart, I'll break his nose."

"Not a chance," she assured her friend. "I'll see you tomorrow." But as she watched Manny leave, Cindy acknowledged that she had been looking forward to talking to Eric alone, even if it was only during the few minutes' walk back to her room. Even if he only shook her hand good-night...well, okay, she would have preferred a grinding, full-body kiss, but beggars couldn't be choosers.

If truth be known, she was hurt that he hadn't said good-night. Wasn't it just her luck that the first man in years she was attracted to couldn't conjure up enough desire for her to even make a lousy pass?

Cindy picked up the sack of extra gift certificates she would give out tomorrow to those who missed the Christmas party. She slung the bag over her shoulder, then waved to the team of cleaners who had emerged to put Sammy's back in order. She stepped into the corridor, paused, then turned in the direction of the stairs. After climbing fifteen flights, she reasoned, she'd be so tired, she wouldn't lose a minute's sleep thinking about Eric Quinn.

Just as she grasped the door handle, the strains of music reached her ears. Cindy stopped and cocked her ear. Someone was definitely playing the piano that had been moved from the bar. Curiosity won out and she followed the tinkling sound down the long hall to the Asteroid Room.

Part of a larger ballroom, Asteroid by itself was roomy enough to host a dinner party for a hundred guests. She opened the door silently to find the room cast in darkness. The unmistakable melancholy notes of "I'll Be Home for Christmas" wafted out, and the pianist wasn't half-bad. The piano had been pushed to the far corner of the room with its back to the door, obscuring the identity of the player.

Intrigued, she crept closer, recognizing the soft glow spilling around the sides of the piano as candlelight. The player missed a note, but covered well. Cindy's heart pounded as she circled closer, squinting when she recognized the outline of a man. Then she gasped and the pianist stopped abruptly, his head swinging around.

"Eric!" she exclaimed softly. "I heard the music and I...I mean, I had no idea you were in here or... geez, you're really good."

His tuxedo jacket lay folded over the top of the piano, and his bow tie hung down the front of his open-throated shirt. A half-burned candle sat on the ledge above the keys, casting soft light over the ivory and his long-fingered hands. His chuckle reverberated in the room. "I haven't played in years. I found the piano and...well, I didn't mean to disturb anyone."

"Play as long as you like," she said quickly, walking backward. "Good night."

"Cindy."

She stopped.

"I'm sorry I bailed on you at the party."

"It's fine," she said. "Really."

"I had a good time."

Her heart lifted slightly. "So did I."

He looked as if he wanted to say something else, then he cleared his throat and gestured toward the keys. "Any requests before you go? Trying to keep my hands busy, you know."

"Well," she said, lowering the red sack of envelopes to the floor, "I've always been partial to 'Blue Christmas.' How's your Elvis impersonation?"

Laughter rumbled from his throat. "A little rusty."

"Okay—you play, I'll sing." She walked to the piano.

He slid over on the padded bench and smiled broadly. "Have a seat."

Cindy settled onto the seat next to him, keeping a safety zone of a few inches between them. He started playing and she sang, *"I'll have a blue… Christmas…without you."* He leaned his ear closer as if he couldn't hear her, so she belted out, *"I'll be so blue…thinking…about you."*

He grinned. "You're really terrible."

"I know. *Decorations are great…on a green—*"

He stopped playing. "I don't think those are the words."

"Those are too the words."

"Decorations of *red* on a green Christmas tree."

"You play and I'll sing."

"Okay."

"Decorations of red…on a green Christmas tree… won't mean a thing, dear—"

He stopped playing. "Won't *be the same,* dear."

She motioned for him to keep playing. *"If you're not here with me.* Harmonize—this is where the girls go 'ooh-ooh ooh-oohwoo.'"

He laughed so hard he could barely play and finally Cindy succumbed, too. Their shoulders brushed, triggering a bolt of awareness through her. Eric's fingers tripped over the keys lightly, playing the song with a honky-tonk swing. Cindy sang to the end, then yelled, "Big finish—everybody sing!" and Eric crooned the last refrain with her. Cindy clapped and whistled while he tinkled out a resounding finale. "You're amazing!"

A self-deprecating laugh escaped him. "You *must* be inebriated."

Feeling dreamy, Cindy leaned on her elbow and faced him, struck by his strong profile in the semi-darkness. "I mean it. The fact that you can put your hands on these keys and make recognizable sounds is remarkable. Did your mother teach you to play?"

"No," he said quietly, still playing a soft, ambling melody. "My father. *He* was amazing." Respect colored his voice. "Couldn't read a note of music, but he could play the most complicated concertos by ear." The melody he played took on a haunting quality. "I was never as good as he was—never wanted to be. I enjoyed playing for my mother and my sister, and to impress girls." He laughed softly. "It made my dad nuts that I didn't love playing as much as he did."

"You argued?" she probed gently.

"More times than I can count," Eric admitted, his gaze still on his fingers. "I wanted to make money, lots of it, instead of winding up teaching piano lessons out of my home."

"Is that why you aren't close?"

"There are other reasons, but yeah, basically, it boils down to my old man being disappointed in the way I make a living."

Cindy resisted the urge to ask why he didn't just sell pianos. Eric was a grown man and undoubtedly knew his choices and the ramifications of those choices. "You should call him," she said simply.

"It always turns into a disagreement." He suddenly stopped playing, plunging the room into eerie silence. "You know, the first sales bonus I received on my first job was for four thousand, six hundred and thirty-eight dollars, and twenty-five cents." He glanced up and caught her gaze, his expression rueful. "I went to the piano store in the mall and blew the entire check on the nicest piano I could afford and had it delivered to our house for Christmas, for my dad."

"That's the most incredible thing I ever heard," she said, tearing up.

"Except he didn't want it." Eric laughed sadly. "He told me I was materialistic and didn't know what was important in life. That was over fifteen years ago, and that damned piano is still sitting in the family room, pushed up against the wall. To my knowledge, it's never been played."

Cindy brought her fist to her mouth as the tears welled in her eyes. "When was the last time you saw your father?"

"Last spring I went home for my niece's birthday. I stopped by to see him for a few minutes. It wasn't pretty."

She shook her head. "He must love you very much to have reacted so fiercely to your choosing, um—" she searched for a euphemism "—a business career over music."

One side of his mouth lifted. "I suppose that's one

way of looking at it." Then he straightened, obviously
ready to change the subject. "Last call for requests."

Her head still spun from his revelations. "Play
your favorite Christmas song."

He smiled, a welcome transformation. "That's
an easy one." He played a dramatic opening, then
launched into a bluesy "Santa Claus Is Coming to
Town." "Bring it home, Cindy."

She sang loudly, bumping his shoulder until he
moved with her side to side. *"He's making a list, and
checking it twice, gonna find out who's naughty or
nice, Santa Claus is coming to town!"* They finished
the song in rollicking style, laughing and clapping.

"That was fun," she declared.

"I'm glad you came to investigate," he said, lowering the wooden key cover. He picked up the votive
candle as if to blow it out, then stopped. "Well, well."

Cindy glanced up, and her pulse leapt. Hanging from the top of the piano was Jerry's mistletoe.
Thank you, Jerry, wherever you are.

Slowly Eric set down the candle, then turned toward her, his expression unreadable. "It would be
a shame to waste the mistletoe, don't you think?"

Cindy pursed her lips and nodded. "A l-low-down
d-dirty shame."

He leaned closer, his gaze riveted on hers. "You
look beautiful tonight."

Her throat constricted. "Well, technically, it's tomorrow."

Eric brushed his lips against hers lightly. "Then you look beautiful tomorrow." He tilted his head and Cindy closed her eyes just as his mouth covered hers. At first his lips were firm and gentle, cautious and sweet. But when she offered her tongue, he deepened the kiss with a groan. She leaned into him, her skin tingling for his touch.

He tasted of rum and grapes, he smelled of English Leather and starch. Her breath caught in her chest, until she had to break the kiss and gasp for breath in a decidedly unsophisticated manner.

He glanced away and swallowed. "I guess we'd better get going."

She nodded, struggling for composure.

Eric stood and shrugged into his jacket, then picked up the candle. Cindy rose on shaky knees, then followed him out of the room, picking up the red sack of envelopes. In the corridor, Eric blew out the candle and set it on a banquet table. "I'll walk you to your room," he said, taking the sack from her.

"That's not necessary."

"I know, but it's the least I can do for skipping out on you."

"Oh, I'm sure you had your reasons," she said congenially.

"I did." They strolled toward the elevator. "At the rate we were going, I was afraid I'd end up asking you to spend the night with me."

Cindy tripped, and he grabbed her arm. "And you were afraid I'd say no?" she asked nervously.

"No," he said with the barest hint of a smile. "I was afraid you'd say yes."

Smooth line. "Eric," she asked as the elevator arrived, "do you have any experience in the film industry?"

A look of puzzlement came over his face. "Film? No, why?"

"Just wondering," she said happily, pushing the button for her floor.

He seemed so relaxed on their walk to her room, Cindy's awkwardness evaporated. He'd obviously liberated himself by deciding not to ask her to spend the night with him. After she unlocked her door, he set the red sack inside, brushed her cheek with his lips, and said, "Good night, Cindy. Thank you for a truly engaging evening."

Remembering her intent to seize the moment, Cindy touched his sleeve, her heart thudding. "Eric, did you leave the party because you're still worried about how I feel about your, um, job?"

He considered her words for a few seconds, then nodded. "That's part of it."

She slid her hands up the lapels of his jacket. "Then maybe this will alleviate that part of it." Curling her fingers around the back of his neck, she pulled his mouth down to hers for a slow, sensual kiss. His arms immediately encircled her, his hands splaying against her naked back and pulling her against him. She felt his hardening desire for her and her body responded in kind. Next week her job would be on the line, this week she deserved a little fun.

She drew back and looked into his ice-blue eyes. "Eric, spend the night with me."

He swallowed, then ran his hand through his hair.

She held up one hand. "I'm going into this with my eyes wide-open."

"Cindy, are you absolutely certain?"

In answer, she grabbed him by the lapel of his jacket and dragged him inside.

Once he passed the threshold of her suite, Eric blocked out all the reasons why he shouldn't spend the night in her bed and concentrated on all the reasons he should. His mind shut down and his body took over.

They stumbled through the hallway, tugging at each other's clothing in the near darkness. They shed their shoes in the sitting room, his jacket in the second hall, his pants in the doorway of the bedroom. Cindy fumbled with her zipper and Eric obliged, standing behind her, his breath catching as he reached around and slid his hands over her flat stomach. The dress whooshed to the ground, then she turned in his arms, naked from the waist up.

Standing in the window light of her bedroom, she was simply breathtaking. Slender and long-limbed,

her breasts firm and round like two peaches waiting
to be plucked from a shapely tree. He wrapped his
arms around her waist and pulled her against him,
reveling in the feel of her. She pulled at the hem of
his T-shirt and soon the hindering garment joined
the others scattered about.

Eric was drowning in his desire for her, undoubtedly fueled by the fact that he shouldn't have her.
But she felt so damned wonderful next to him, her
skin as smooth as the ivory keys of his chosen in-
strument. He swung her into his arms and carried
her to the bed, lowering her gently. Taking ragged
breaths, he rolled down her stockings, overcome by
the sight of her lying beneath him, clad only in teeny
black bikini panties. She arched her back, pushing
her breasts in the air.

Eric practically dived into the bed. He wanted to
make love to her leisurely, but she reduced him to the
likes of an inexperienced teenager, hungry for every
inch of her, and unsure where to begin. His raging
erection strained against the front of his boxers, but
he knew he'd come undone if he felt her bare skin
against his arousal. He kissed her mouth hard and
nipped at her neck, then stroked her nipples, playing
her until the music of her moans reached his ears.

Rolling her beneath him, he lowered his mouth
to a perfect breast, and laved the plump nipple while
she drove her hands through his hair. Her body, her
moans, her scents drove him blind with need. He

pushed her flimsy panties down her thighs, swallowing hard at the sight of her tangled dark nest. He groaned and gritted his teeth for control.

She tugged at the waistband of his boxers and he hesitated only because he knew it would be over soon if she unleashed him. Then with a frustrated moan, he stilled her hands.

"What's wrong?" she gasped against his chest.

Embarrassment coursed through him. So determined was he not to let the night end this way, he'd left protection in his room. "I seem to be a bit, um, unprepared for the moment."

Sudden realization dawned. "You mean a rubber?"

He cleared his throat. "Yes."

How odd—she figured he carried condoms like business cards. Her desire-drugged mind raced. Of the pack of twelve she'd bought years ago, eleven were still buried somewhere in her bathroom cabinet, but she'd never trust them. Then she remembered the box of sex samples under the bed. Cindy hesitated, embarrassed at the thought of rifling through the box of torrid toys in front of Eric. A second later she realized that not only would he recognize every trinket, but he would probably be able to rattle off the product code. And what better way to prove to him that she was okay with his line of work? "I might have one."

Eric brightened considerably.

Sliding out of bed, Cindy knelt and pulled the

suitcase-size box from under her bed. She opened the lid of the carton, recalling with jarring clarity the diversity of the products she'd given a perfunctory glance.

"Wow," Eric said, standing behind her.

She rummaged through the bounty, and not wanting him to know how inexperienced she was with the tricks of his trade, handed him the products she thought might be useful.

"Coconut body liqueur...textured condoms..." She held up an interesting-looking battery-powered device and raised her eyebrows in question.

Eric shrugged and added it to the pile.

"Chocolate-flavored whipped cream...crotchless panties?"

Eric passed on the whipped cream, but fingered the minuscule panties. "Maybe later?" he asked.

She nodded and bent back to her task.

Suddenly Eric was kissing her neck, and rubbing his hard chest against her bare back. "Um, Cindy," he whispered. "Don't you think we have enough equipment for the first go-around?"

She smiled lazily. "Get the lamp, would you?"

"No way," he said, pulling her back to the bed. "I want to see you."

"And I," she breathed, pushing down his underwear to free his erection, "want to see you." She took in the size of him, then bit her lip, covered him back up and shook her head. "I don't think it'll fit."

His laughter filled her ears, apparently pleased with her assessment. "I'll stop whenever you say."

But of course she didn't stop him. She lay trembling against him like a virginal coed, wanting him so much it frightened her. They broke the seals on the flavored potions and proceeded to paint and consume each other's bodies until they both panted with restraint. She wrestled with the condom package until he took it from her and opened it, then handed the condom back to her. With shaking fingers, she placed the condom over the oozing tip of his straining shaft.

"The other way," he prompted with a smile.

She glanced down to find that yes, indeedy, she had the thing flipped. "Oops," she said, knowing her cover was blown. She wasn't a sophisticated sex kitten—she couldn't even roll on a condom.

"Let me help," he said, putting his hand over hers, pinching the top of the condom. "I have a feeling," he said with a groan as her hands encircled him, "I'm going to need extra breathing room."

He eased her back to the pillows and settled between her knees, covering her like a big, warm blanket. Her body sang with exhilaration from the feeling of his skin against hers. The light hair on his chest teased her breasts as his hands entwined with hers above their heads. With the moment of reckoning near, Cindy had nearly lost her capacity to speak. Instead, she let her body converse with him, responding to his kisses, nips and caresses with expressive shudders, contractions and yielding.

"Ladies first," he whispered, then began making love to her with his hand, his arousal branding her thigh throughout. Within seconds, he had her straining against him, moving with a slow, probing rhythm. Months of pent-up sexual energy and the heady presence of the man above her sent her quickly over the edge with shameless abandon. Their moans mingled as she slowly descended.

He withdrew his powerful hand and she instantly felt his shaft at the door of her desire. She ran her hands down his back, clutching his buttocks, inviting him inside. He advanced slowly, his heart thrashing against hers, his teeth clenched. Her knees opened slowly to give him full access and he filled her with one long moan. Cindy threw her head back and arched into him with ecstasy, crying aloud. He slipped his hands under her hips, undulating into her body with agonizing slowness and shocking depth.

She clawed at his back, matching his rhythm, tightening around him instinctively to draw the life fluid from him. Their rocking tempo increased to a frenzy of movement and sounds. Cindy sensed his approach and when he shuddered his release, swelling emotion pulled her over with him. He cried out, his face a mask of pleasure-pain, then lowered his face to her neck.

Gasping for breath, Cindy stroked his back softly

and felt an odd stirring in her chest. Stark fear forced her to lighten the moment. "I'm glad you changed your mind about spending the night," she murmured.

His deep laugh rumbled against her neck. "So am I." He propped himself up on his elbow and smiled devilishly. "And the night is young."

Cindy's toes curled with anticipation. "Now about that gadget with the battery pack…"

CINDY HOVERED BETWEEN sleep and consciousness for long, languid minutes. Imbedded into the fluffy mattress, her body ached pleasantly. Slowly she opened her eyes, although her left one felt a bit sticky. The events of the previous evening flooded over her. Eric still slumbered, facing her and breathing shallowly through his mouth. Awake, he was gorgeous, but asleep, the man was a god.

When she remembered the way he had held her, a warm, fuzzy tingle spread over her limbs. Their familiarity staggered her. She turned on her side to watch him. Tender, fun, sexy. She sighed. If only Eric's job was more…ordinary. Of course, she reminded herself, his vocation explained why such an eligible man remained eligible. Apparently, all the good ones were either taken or made their living selling blow-up dolls.

She wasn't sure why she was complaining. She should be grateful that her uneasiness about the man's job kept her from falling head over heels in love—

Cindy jerked back. Love? Manny had once said love was best saved for cashmere and Dom Pérignon. Pain exploded in her head, reminding her of how much she'd had to drink at the party. And coconut body liqueur did not contribute to a fresh morning mouth. She lifted a hand to her tingling scalp, only to encounter a tangle of wiry hair. Groaning inwardly, Cindy wondered how scary she must look right now.

Keeping an eye on Eric, she slid out of the bed and limped across the carpet, wincing at her stiff muscles. She wore the yellow crotchless panties, and they had found their way into uncomfortable crevices. Their clothes were strewn from chair to chair, and all surfaces in between. Bottles of flavored potions littered both nightstands and the memory of their consumption brought warmth to her cheeks. And a nurse's cap from the sampler case hung over the edge of a lamp shade—now *there* was a week's worth of journal entries.

She yanked a short terry robe from the bench at her vanity and pulled it around her, then leaned forward for a glimpse in the mirror. Cindy gasped, covered her face with both hands and peeked through her fingers.

Her hair sprang in indiscriminate directions. Medusa with a serious case of bed head. A strip of eyelashes stuck to the center of her forehead like some kind of weird tattoo. She plucked at it, managing to loosen one end.

Before Cindy could decide what to do first—dive into the shower or simply leave—the phone rang. Eric stirred. Cursing under her breath, she lunged to the nightstand on her side of the bed and pounced on the phone. It was only eight-thirty, for heaven's sake, and this was supposed to be her day off!

"Hello," she snapped, turning her back to the bed and walking as far across the room as the cord would allow.

"Um, good morning?" Manny sounded sheepish.

"This had better be good," she whispered sharply, cupping the mouthpiece.

"You're not alone?" he asked, his voice tinged with concern.

"As a matter of fact, no, I'm not."

"Oh, brother. Quinn isn't warming your sheets, is he?"

"That's none of your business."

"I totally agree, but I have a bit of news that you might find, er, eye-opening."

She turned to look back at the bed. Eric lifted his head and glanced around the room, then smiled when he saw her and rolled onto his side to watch her. Instantly, her nipples pebbled and her thighs twitched with the memory of his weight on her. "What is it?" *He's married, he's a felon, he has seven children in Iowa.*

Manny cleared his throat. "Well, I hadn't gotten around to disposing of his pajama pants yet—I thought I might cut them up, you know, maybe make pillow covers or something out of the fabric."

Eric lifted himself with flexing biceps and piled the pillows against the headboard. The nubby blanket slid down past his waist, but he didn't seem to mind. And neither did she.

Her heart thrashed in her chest. "I don't care what you do with them," she told Manny sweetly. "But I do wish you would get to the point."

"I found his monogram on the pocket, Cindy, and I did some checking. The man in your bed is Eric Quinn, all right—Eric Quinn *Stanton*."

The air left her lungs. Her vision narrowed to the handsome man lounging on her bed, fragrant from her body's scents, smug with the knowledge that not only had he duped the naive general manager, but he'd bedded her, too. Humiliation crashed over her, with mortification close on its heels. A hot flush singed her skin from feet to forehead.

"Cindy, are you there?"

He'd lied to her. Lied in order to get next to her, to win her over, to blackmail her—who knew the extent of his motivations? Of all the unmitigated gall. She had a good mind to take those inflated gonads of his and give them a hearty twist. The phone slipped out of her hand and she took one determined step toward the bed, her muscles propelled by calm fury.

Eric absently watched the phone fall to the carpet, completely distracted by Cindy's approach. He swept her tousled appearance with a smile and lustily wondered if she'd be willing to fulfill his morning urges like she'd fulfilled him last night. He hated to push, but the woman was addictive. Her sex sampler kit had been a delightful surprise. Without a doubt, they were horizontally compatible. He smiled. For a few seconds last night, he could have sworn they levitated off the bed.

"Did you sleep well?" she asked from across the room.

He nodded contentedly against the pillow, then glanced behind her. "Don't you need to hang up the phone?"

"No."

A smile crept up his face. She obviously didn't want the phone to disturb them again.

"You're pretty good," she said quietly, stepping closer.

He allowed himself a sliver of pure male satisfaction. "I'd like to think we were good together."

She sauntered closer, her hips swinging. "Oh, I guess I should take some of the blame—I mean credit—for what happened."

Something in her too-seductive expression set off warning bells. "More role-playing?"

She stopped by the bed, then leaned over slowly and opened the drawer in her nightstand.

"Nurse and doctor again?" he asked, craning his neck.

Still reeling from last night's adventures, he couldn't imagine what she could be springing on him now. "I'm open to just about anything," he pressed on nervously.

But when she withdrew her hand, he blinked, because she held a can of *mace*. "Except pain," he said, sitting up straighter. "I am not into pain."

Cindy's expression turned lethal as she aimed the can directly at his melting manhood. "The only game going on here, *Mr. Stanton,* is the one you've been playing, and it stops now."

Baffled, Eric pressed his back into the mound of pillows. "I don't know what you're talking about."

Her eyes narrowed. "Are you or aren't you Eric Stanton?"

He blinked. "Of course I am."

"Don't lie to me—huh?" She straightened slightly.

"Yes," he declared hotly. "I'm Eric Stanton!" Had she lost her mind?

Her mouth tightened and the can shook. "You aren't even ashamed enough to try to deny it?"

Astounded, Eric felt his jaw drop. "Why should I deny it? You've known my identity almost from the beginning."

Now *she* looked amazed. "What?" And angry. "How dare you? All along you led me to believe you were Eric Quinn, adult toy salesman. Get out of my bed and get the *hell* out of my room."

Incredulity settled in even as he made small, methodical moves to extract himself from her bed. He spoke slowly, keeping his eye on the nozzle of the mace can. "Adult toy salesman? Where did you get a cockamamie idea like that?"

"From you, you…you shyster!"

"Shyster?" Eric backed out on the opposite side of the bed, suddenly wondering if she was unstable. All too aware of his nakedness and glad to have the bed between them, he held up one hand and laughed softly. "Cindy, put down the mace, okay?"

"You'd better start making tracks, Stanton."

"I have to get dressed."

"Ten seconds, then I start spraying every appendage you've got."

"Cindy—"

"Ten…nine—"

"Wait!" He stooped to grab his pants, then jerked them on as he stumbled across the room.

She followed him, taking aim. "—eight—"

"I don't understand," he protested, grabbing clothes as he trotted through her bedroom. "Last night we—"

"—seven—"

"—had incredible sex—"

"—six—"

"—many times, in fact—"

"—five—"

"—and now—" He jogged backward through the hallway, shrugging into his tuxedo shirt.

"—four—"

"—you're ready to—" Eric passed through the sitting room in a blur.

"—three—"

"—disable me!" He backed up against the door, half dressed, his arms full of clothes. "Can't we discuss this?"

"—two—" She assumed a firing stance.

He whipped around and undid the dead bolt and chain with lightning speed.

"—one."

"I'm gone!" he shouted, throwing open the door and diving headfirst into the corridor. He landed with a thud, followed by the sound of her door slamming.

Eric rose on his elbows and groaned at the smarting carpet burns on the undersides of his arms. He heard a noise and turned his head to see two white-haired women standing in the hall, staring.

He smiled tightly and pushed himself to his bare feet, then gathered up his tux jacket, his boxer shorts and one sock. "Morning, ladies." Stepping aside, he gave them a friendly nod as they passed, wide-eyed.

When they rounded the corner, he cursed, feeling like a pervert. Mystified and irate, he walked back to Cindy's door and rapped loudly. "Cindy, open the door. Dammit, Cindy," he whispered harshly through the door. "At least give me my shoes."

But apparently, she was not in the same generous mood she'd been in last night when she'd—oh, hell. Eric set off in the direction of the stairs, painfully stubbing his toe on the carpet. When he heard the sound of her door opening, he turned back, relieved she had changed her mind about talking to him. He barely had time to duck before one large hard-soled shoe bounced off the wall behind him. The second shoe clipped his shoulder, then her door slammed again.

Confounded, Eric stuck his sockless feet into the stiff shoes, and shuffled toward the stairs, dragging his pride behind him.

CHAPTER NINE

AFTER GOING TO THE TROUBLE to make a pot of coffee, Cindy passed on her morning dose of caffeine since she already had the shakes. She clung to the full mug anyway, taking comfort in something she could actually get her hands around, unlike her current predicament.

A fresh wave of self-castigation kept her rooted to the stool at the breakfast bar. She craved a long, numbing shower, but she couldn't bear to go back into the bedroom, to see the remnants of her lovemaking with...that man. And to think she'd actually flirted with the idea of falling for him. She gritted her teeth, trying to banish the memory of the intimate things she'd done with him and *to* him. And the "Box o' Sex Toys" she'd unveiled, trying to impress the "trinket man" when all the while...

She groaned, blinking back tears. How could she have been so stupid? The man had come to study her staff, to scrutinize her operation, to test her professionalism, and last night she'd played "Santa and the naughty elf" with him. When she thought of the ridiculous props she'd worn, entering the witness protection program actually seemed liked a viable alternative to facing Eric Stanton—or her staff.

What would her employees think of her cavorting with the enemy? Would they label her a traitor? And how fast would word spread to headquarters? Panic seized her anew. Had Eric Stanton already reported what undoubtedly seemed like lascivious behavior toward guests? Perhaps she'd been too hasty to eject him from her room, sans a shower and his shoes.

At the sound of a discreet knock on her door, Cindy inhaled deeply, summoning courage to face Eric if he'd returned. She smoothed a hand over her haphazard hair, not that it helped—or mattered— then padded to the door, her heart pounding. She looked through the peephole, nearly collapsing with relief to see Manny's grim mug staring back at her. "Are you alone?" she called.

"Yes. Are you?"

She swung open the door, then nodded miserably.

Manny sighed. "I couldn't hear everything on the other end of the phone, but it sounded bad. Is the receiver still off the hook?"

She shrugged. "I forgot about the phone."

"Sorry to have been the bearer of bad news," he said as he moved inside.

To her horror, she welled up with tears. "Oh, Manny, I couldn't have dreamed up a worse nightmare."

"I should have figured it out," he said, pulling her into a comforting hug.

"*I* should have figured it out," she exclaimed. "I should have realized Eric wasn't hanging around just to spend time with me."

Manny frowned. "Hey, don't sell yourself short. And don't waste time dwelling on what you can't change."

She inhaled deeply and raised her chin. "You're right. I have to get a grip and concentrate on damage control."

"Attagirl."

She exhaled. "Want some coffee?"

He checked his watch. "Sure, I've got a few minutes left on my break."

"Okay," she said, pouring the hot liquid into a cup for her friend. "Let's go over what *we* know he knows about the hotel and about me."

"Well, for starters, he knows we're shorthanded in the salon."

She frowned, then nodded.

He ticked off the items on his fingers. "He watched you stab yourself with a clipboard, the scarf incident in the elevator you told me about and the fire in the dining room."

Her confidence started to slide.

"He was there when the tree got wedged in the front door, plus he came to the party last night, watched everyone get drunk and saw you dress up like a Christmas Playmate to pass out gifts."

She slouched on her stool.

"He knows something strange happened to his pajama pants. And let's not forget," Manny said, then jerked a thumb toward her bedroom.

She closed her eyes. "Oh, God. Don't remind me."

"By the way," he said lightly. "How was it?"

Cutting her gaze to him, she considered lying, then sighed. "Un-freaking-believable."

He grinned. "Really?"

"I think I passed out once."

"Darn."

"Yeah, it's a shame he turned out to be a conniving, lowlife, corporate scumbag who came here to dig up dirt on me."

"Well, how did he act this morning? Was he sorry?"

She scrunched up her face. "No, the jerk had the nerve to act surprised—he said I'd known his identity all along."

"But didn't he tell you he sold adult toys?"

She nodded, then stopped, replaying their elevator conversation. "He said he was in sales, and when I asked him what kind, he answered 'trinkets and things.'"

A frown wrinkled Manny's forehead. "And from that comment, you assumed the man sold X-rated playthings?"

Cindy scoffed. "No. Then I asked if he was here for the trade show next week, and he said something like 'As a matter of fact, I *am* preparing for next week.'"

Manny sighed. "Except he really meant he was preparing for his ream team to arrive at the Chandelier House for a good going-over."

"Well, *now* I know that, but with the condoms and all—"

"What condoms?"

She rubbed her temples. "When I was in his bathroom washing up, he told me to get a couple of bandages out of his toiletry bag. I unzipped a pocket, and out fell enough contraceptives for China."

"Which is interesting, but not particularly incriminating."

"It was other things he said," she insisted, then snapped her fingers. "He told me his father didn't approve of his line of work."

Manny shrugged. "Another blanket statement."

"But there's more!" The words tumbled out as she remembered them. "Last night we were talking about convention groups and I said something about the adult toy people—no, wait, I said 'his people' would be arriving shortly."

He held up his hands. "His people *will* be arriving shortly."

"Then he said he was glad I knew what he did

for a living and hoped I understood why he had to be discreet."

"Bingo! From that point on, he thought you knew he was Stanton."

She gaped. "But if I knew he was Stanton, why would I have invited him to the party?"

"To butter him up, ply him with liquor."

Nodding in dismay, she said, "He did say that people tended to treat him differently once they knew the truth about him." She felt the blood drain from her face. "He said he was glad to see his line of work wouldn't interfere with our 'friendship.'"

"And you said?"

She stared at him. "I told him I was open-minded."

Manny drained his cup and set it down with finality. "Well, at least now we know how the mix-up occurred, and that Stanton didn't bed you under false pretenses."

"No, he simply thought I knew who he was and would sleep with him anyway."

He shrugged. "Probably not the first time it's happened to him."

She stopped, suddenly remembering the questions he'd asked about the chandelier. Nausea clutched her stomach. How much had she divulged?

"I'd better get back to work," he said, pushing away from the bar. "The decorators are supposed to have unveiled the tree by now. Will I see you later?"

She nodded numbly. "I'm going to call a quick

staff meeting as soon as I shower and do something with my hair."

"In that case," he said with a wink, "I'll see you in the spring." Manny gave her forehead a sympathetic rub, then placed her wayward false eyelashes in the palm of her hand.

Cindy sighed. "I guess I'd better get used to wearing these things."

Manny tilted his head. "Don't you have a pair of reading glasses somewhere?"

She sniffed and nodded, cheering slightly. "Good idea. Maybe they'll hide my black circles, too."

He touched his thumb to a loose tear, then smiled. "Just you wait. Stanton will be gone by Christmas and you'll forget this ever happened."

Touched, Cindy watched Manny leave, then leaned heavily against the wall. "Gonna find out who's naughty or nice," she whispered.

ERIC TOWELED HIS HAIR DRY, mulling over the events of the last few hours. If he understood the scene in Cindy's room this morning, she had been under the impression that he was some kind of adult toy salesman. Admittedly, he'd first told her he was in sales, but how she had concocted the rest of the story was beyond him.

His best guess was that someone on her staff—probably the concierge—had discovered his identity and called to deliver the news, not realizing he occupied her bed. On the other hand, if Manny had designs on Cindy for himself and suspected Eric had spent the night, the timing of the phone call might simply have been a bonus.

Regardless, the misunderstanding meant one thing—they'd slept together and he alone had known it would pose a conflict of interest. Last night's justification that Cindy also knew the ramifications now fell flat. He should have conducted himself like the professional he was reputed to be.

Eric finished dressing, still stupefied over how he had let himself be drawn into Cindy Warren's bed. He'd been propositioned by women more beautiful and more determined, but never had he succumbed to temptation during an assignment. Eric cursed— he was getting sloppy.

Feeling like a heel, he slowly rehung his rumpled tuxedo in the closet. He had to talk to Cindy, to try to explain…what? That he had assumed she was the kind of woman who would sleep with the man sent to evaluate her and the hotel? He sighed, then looked down as something crunched under his shoe. He knelt and picked up two broken pieces of one of Cindy's earrings which must have gotten tangled in his clothing. Not surprising, considering their frantic progress to her bed.

Regret washed over him. Fortunately, the break along the narrow part of the long translucent teardrop appeared to be clean. Perhaps a jeweler could repair it. He hoped so—it was the least he could do to make up for his behavior last night.

He'd promised Lancaster an update call this morning, but considering what had transpired, he needed to clear his head and decide what to do next. He had compromised his objectivity and the trust of the general manager, not to mention the trust of a "good woman," as Jerry had called her. Great, just what he wanted for Christmas—guilt.

Flashes of their lovemaking plagued him. She had pushed buttons he hadn't known he possessed. Oh, the silly games were fun, but when he closed his eyes, what he remembered most was the total abandon on her lovely face as she climaxed with him buried inside her. At the ripe old age of thirty-six, he was no sexual novice, but no woman had ever bared her vulnerability to him that way. For a few seconds, she had passed complete control of her body and soul to him. She had trusted him, only to discover this morning that he wasn't the person—or the man—she'd thought him to be.

And she was right, of course. He wasn't a lovable man—hell, his own father preferred not to have him around. He had no business entertaining thoughts of spending time with Cindy Warren. She ran a hotel for misfits, ignoring corporate policies and making a laughingstock of what could be a stately property. He and Cindy Warren might be in perfect harmony between the sheets, but when it came to business, they were way off-key.

He wrapped the broken earring in a tissue and tucked the package inside his shirt pocket. Cindy didn't answer her phone, and he couldn't think of an appropriate message to leave, so he simply hung up. Perhaps he would catch her in the lobby and talk to her before she left the hotel.

Opting for the stairwell so he could smoke half a cigarette on the way, Eric slowly descended to the lobby. His temples throbbed with a nicotine headache, and his lower back hurt from either the strange mattress or the high-spirited ride he'd given Cindy the Naked Elf last night on a trip around the world. He gritted his teeth and snuffed out the cigarette. Hell's bells, what had he gotten himself into?

From Mr. Oliver's rigid posture behind the concierge desk, he assumed the man had indeed placed the ill-timed wake-up call.

"Good morning, Mr. Stanton," the blond man said in a crisp tone, confirming his suspicion. When Eric neared, the man leaned forward and whispered, "I ought to punch your damn lights out."

Eric blanched at the man's verbal attack, then angered. "Mind your own business, Oliver."

"We had an understanding last night when you left the party."

Eric chewed the inside of his cheek. "Cindy made the pass."

Manny scoffed. "She didn't know who the hell you were!"

"Well, I thought she did."

The blond man looked disgusted. "So is this standard procedure for you, Stanton?"

"I'm going to overlook that comment because I know how much you care about Cindy." Eric clenched his teeth. "Now, have you seen her?"

Manny's mouth tightened. "Yes."

When he didn't elaborate, Eric asked, "Where can I find her?"

The man's blue eyes gave away nothing. "I believe she's taking a day of vacation."

"So she's already left the hotel?"

"Can I help you, Mr. Stanton?"

He turned to find Cindy standing five feet away, looking more composed than he felt at the moment. Dressed casually in a pair of slim jeans, white turtleneck and a man's boxy plaid sport coat, she looked like a coed. She'd stuffed her too-curly reddish hair under a green velvet newsboy hat, but a few strands had managed to escape down her back. The round wire glasses were new, and flattering. No one would have guessed this serene-looking woman had spent the better part of last night naked and writhing beneath, beside and on top of him.

"May I help you, Mr. Stanton?" she repeated coolly.

Eric walked toward her, stopping at a professional

distance. Striving for a level tone, he said, "Cindy, I'd like a private word with you."

"Sure," she said, surprising him. "Except it will have to wait until after my staff meeting." She glanced at her watch, then gave him a polite smile. "I'll be back in fifteen minutes—perhaps I can address your concerns then." She signaled Manny, then strode toward the elevator.

Not sure what he expected, Eric stood rooted to the spot. "Ms. Warren," he called.

She turned.

He suddenly wanted to see her smile again. "I thought you were due a day of fun and frolic."

Her expression remained unmoved. "Something came up," she said simply, then kept walking.

Watching her retreating back, Eric experienced a foreign twinge...loss? He coughed and thumped his chest, deciding that smoking on an empty stomach had given him heartburn. He wheeled in the opposite direction and went in search of coffee, pondering Cindy's impending staff meeting.

...*TWENTY-FOUR, TWENTY-FIVE, twenty-six.* Cindy stopped counting her steps at the elevator and began counting the seconds until the car arrived. In her pocket, she'd clicked the end of an ink pen in quick succession so many times, she'd practically worn out the button. Counting always helped calm her, and if ever she needed a soothing ritual, it was now. In five minutes she would admit to her staff that not only was Mr. Eric Stanton on the hotel premises, but she'd unwittingly ensured him anonymous access to her employees. As for the access she'd given him to herself, well, that was beyond belief or understanding.

"Goodbye, Ms. Warren."

She spun to see Mr. Stark approaching her, suitcase in tow. Stifling a groan, she painted on a smile. "Are you leaving, Mr. Stark?"

"Yes, headed home earlier than I'd planned." He tipped his hat. "Thanks for the great tickets last night. The rat incident aside, I must say, I enjoyed my stay."

"That's wonderful," she said tightly.

He folded a business card into her hand. "If you ever decide to remodel, give me a call and I'll take some of this junk off your hands."

"I'll do that. Have a nice trip home." As soon as he disappeared toward the door, Cindy flipped over his card. Reginald Stark, Antiques. She grimaced.

Manny walked up just as the elevator doors opened. "Perfect performance," he murmured. "Don't let Stanton know you're rattled."

"Rattled?" she said airily, stepping inside. "Who's rattled?"

"Here," he said, handing her a new ink pen. "For when the one in your pocket falls apart."

She shot him a grateful smile, then sighed. "Do

you want to hear the worst part about last night? I lost one of my earrings."

"Did you check the bed?" he asked dryly.

"Yes, smart aleck, I did. It's not in my room. I think I might have lost it when I put on that stupid Santa dress at the party. I checked the bar, but no luck."

"Joel and I will look for it," he soothed.

"I think this might be the worst week of my life," she said as they approached the meeting room. "Do you think the staff will stone me?"

"They'll come around when they realize he hood-winked you, too."

"Oh, now I feel better."

"Don't torture yourself. This was all one big mis-understanding. If he was good in bed, count your blessings."

"Unless this affects his review of the hotel in a bad way. Talk about performance anxiety."

"So call corporate human resources and tell them what happened—you thought he was a guest."

"And then everyone in the home office will think I'm seducing guests on a regular basis."

"That's ridiculous, Cindy. My goldfish get more booty than you do."

"*I* know that and *you* know that, but extended ab-stinence is difficult to prove." She glanced around, then lowered her voice. "Especially after Mr. Stan-ton and I set land records for speed and endurance last night." She groaned. "Manny, I don't know what it is about this man, but just when I think I can't do anything more idiotic around him, I amaze myself."

With her heart pounding, she walked into the boardroom and greeted her staff already seated around the table. She decided to stand, eyeing the distance to the door in case she needed to make a quick getaway.

"This must be important," Joel piped up, "considering you're supposed to be off today after bringing a *real, live date* to the party." A titter traveled around the room, stopping at Manny, who studied the ceiling tile.

Her cheeks flamed with memories of just how alive Eric had been last night—and just how much she'd wanted to kill him this morning. Still, she dredged up a wry smile. "I am planning to do my Christmas shopping later, but, um—" She cleared her throat. "First I want to discuss a personal matter with you."

Amy, sporting a white breathe-easy strip on her red nose, leaned forward. "Is everything okay, Cindy?"

She nodded vaguely, glanced at Manny, then plunged ahead. "I b-believe most of you met the gentleman who escorted me to the party last night."

"Oh, my God," Sam said, leaping to her feet. "Eric proposed, didn't he?"

The room erupted while Cindy nearly swallowed her tongue.

"You're getting married?" Joel exploded. He began clapping and hooting.

Approaching hysteria, Cindy waved her arms. "Wait!"

The door in the back of the room opened and, to her abject horror, Eric Stanton walked into the melee.

Manny silenced the room with a two-finger whistle.

Everyone turned to stare at Eric.

He indicated the door. "I'm sorry to interrupt. I knocked." Edging closer, he said, "I have a feeling I'm the reason this meeting was called."

Unable to maintain eye contact with him, Cindy nodded, practically numb. "You might as well come in." She waved everyone back into their seats, her mind spinning.

Joel frowned. "So are you and Eric getting married or what?" He yelped in pain and jerked back, eyeing Manny directly across the table.

She wished for something sharp to throw at Joel, then gripped the edge of the table. "First of all," she said with deadly calm, "I'm not getting married anytime in the foreseeable future. And second—" She inhaled and swept an arm toward Eric. "Everyone, may I introduce Mr. Eric Quinn *Stanton*."

He stepped up and glanced around the group, falling short of a smile. "Good morning. As you have previously been briefed, my review team and I will be conducting a routine study of your operations at the request of your parent company. I met most of you last night. Hello to the new faces."

Jaws dropped. Eyes bulged. Adam's apples bobbed. She watched as incredulity transformed to confusion, then accusing gazes swung back to her.

"Ms. Warren didn't discover my identity until—" He caught her gaze and she silently begged him not to say "this morning" with all its lewd connotations. "Until a short while ago," he finished.

Cindy glanced back to the group. "As we discussed, the rest of Mr. Stanton's team will be arriving soon, but on Saturday instead of Monday. According to my schedule, they will be on the premises for five days, leaving on Wednesday the twenty-third." She looked to Eric for confirmation.

He nodded.

"Until that time," she continued, "I'm sure you will extend every courtesy to Mr. Stanton as he directs the review." She herself had certainly gone above and beyond the call of duty. Cindy picked up her clipboard to signal a welcome end to the meeting. "That's all I have. If you haven't met Mr. Stanton, please introduce yourself before you leave."

Cindy walked around to the other side of the table to avoid Eric and glanced at her watch.

"Ms. Warren."

At the sound of his voice, she stopped. And so

did everyone else. Cindy turned back to find Eric flanked by a few of her employees, apprehension clear on their faces. "Yes?"

One dark eyebrow rose slightly. "You said we could have a word after the meeting."

Damn. "I'll be in the lobby near the Christmas tree." She made a hasty exit without waiting for his response.

Amy trotted up next to her on the way down the hall. "I'm sorry, boss."

Cindy frowned. "Why are you sorry?"

"If I hadn't pinpointed Mr. Stark as the corporate spy, you might have suspected Eric before you—" She broke off abruptly.

Cindy sucked in a breath. As far as she knew, only Manny was aware that Eric had spent the night in her bed, and she planned to keep it that way. "Before I what?"

"Before you asked him to the party," Amy finished, looking sorrowful. "Don't blame yourself, Cindy. He used you to get close to us."

Her friends scrambled to assure her they didn't blame her. When they arrived at the lobby, Amy slipped away. Joel started to make his escape too, but one of his two beepers sounded.

He pushed a button and lifted the radio to his mouth. "Joel here, what's up?"

Manny's voice crackled over the tiny speaker.

"Trouble at the Christmas tree—you'd better get here quick. And bring Cindy."

Cindy strode toward the front entrance with Joel right behind her. Her steps faltered as they rounded the corner. "What the—?"

Black. The blue spruce was dressed in black from top to bottom. Black ribbons, black ornaments, even a black star on top. Horrified, Cindy could only stare. Guests passed by and winced.

Joel gasped. "Who ever heard of black Christmas decorations?"

"Get the decorators back here," she ordered, then pointed to a knot of people gathering on the sidewalk, some with signs. "And security. Looks like we've got a picket forming. We just may have offended every religious group in the city."

"Oh, Stanton will love this," Joel muttered.

"I'll cut him off and take him out the side entrance," she offered, handing him her clipboard.

"You're a trouper," Joel said, clapping her on the back.

"I'm an idiot," she mumbled as she clambered back to the elevator to wait for the man she never wanted to see again. As she lingered, Cindy evaluated her situation and concluded she was definitely up the creek without a paddle. But she didn't have long to berate herself. Eric stepped off the elevator and nearly smiled when he saw her. Gloating, no doubt. She swallowed the pride she had left—

less than a mouthful—and offered him a flat smile. "Have you eaten breakfast?"

His forehead wrinkled slightly, then cleared. "No."

"I thought we could walk to a diner to have that word in private."

He pursed his lips, evoking thoughts of her mouth on his. Cindy shook off the memories, thinking tomorrow would be easier since she wouldn't be reminded of their lapse every time her sore muscles moved. "Fine," he said, sweeping his arm toward the front entrance.

"Um, the side exit is closer," she said, moving in the opposite direction.

"HAM, HASH BROWNS, two biscuits, gravy and a side order of grits." Cindy handed the menu to the waitress with a nod. "I'm starved."

Amused, Eric tugged on his ear—he couldn't deny they had worked up an appetite. "I'll have the same."

When the waitress left, he lifted his coffee cup. Where to start? He wished he knew what she was thinking, but she'd barely spoken a word to him during the stroll to the restaurant, despite his best attempt at small talk. She looked so fetching in her little green hat and scholarly glasses, Eric wished he could strip away the murky circumstances and carry her back to her disheveled bed. He splashed coffee over the edge of his cup. "Cindy, we obviously need to talk."

"Me first," she said, unsmiling, then cleared her throat. "Mr. Stanton—"

"I'm Eric, remember?"

She gripped her coffee cup with those wonderfully familiar hands. "Maybe," she said evenly, "but you are not the person I thought you were."

He set his jaw, and nodded in concession.

"Mr. Stanton," she began again, her voice stronger. "Let me start by saying that I'm not in the habit of…of fraternizing with male guests. In fact—" she dropped her gaze "—last night was the first such incident." She returned her gaze and lifted her chin before she continued. "I have no excuse for my behavior, but I sincerely hope you won't hold my regrettable lapse in judgment against my staff."

Eric pursed his mouth. Regrettable?

"That's why," she said, pressing on, "if you feel obligated to report this incident to headquarters, I'm asking you—" she hesitated, then wet her lips "—no, I'm *imploring* you to wait until the review of the hotel has been completed. If I'm removed as GM now, employee morale will suffer and the profit margins on holiday events might be compromised. I want the Chandelier House to present as healthy a bottom line as possible."

His respect for her ratcheted up yet another notch. "Ms. Warren, I have no intention of bringing this, um, awkward situation to the attention of anyone at Harmon, although it had crossed my mind that you might be the one filing a report."

Her forehead wrinkled. "Me?"

"Yes. Especially if you thought I might threaten to divulge or withhold certain details about the operation of the hotel unless you, er, you know."

"Slept with you again?"

He nodded.

"Would you?"

For the first time he wished he was more of a people person, more intuitive, because her greenish eyes were clouded with emotions he longed to decipher. "No," he said quietly. "I'd never blackmail my way into your bed."

Her mouth twitched, but she remained silent.

"Which brings me to why I wanted to talk to you," he continued. "I'm sorry I misled you into thinking I was someone else. For the sake of discretion when I'm undercover, I'm usually vague with personal details, but I don't deliberately try to deceive people I'll be working with, especially not the general manager. I truly thought I had already blown my cover." He sighed. "And I've never indulged in this kind of liaison before either."

She studied her hands, then lifted her gaze. "I owe you an apology for accusing you of tricking me. In hindsight, I jumped to wrong conclusions based on that vague information."

"I'm sorry you're embarrassed—"

"Please," she cut in. "Let's stick to how this situation will affect your handling of my hotel and staff."

"Okay," he agreed, having slammed into the personal brick wall she'd erected. "I have two propositions—" He stopped and laughed uncomfortably. Cindy didn't even blink. "Um, make that two *solutions* I want to put on the table."

She nodded, unsmiling.

"First, I can remove myself from this project entirely—"

"I like that one."

Eric sighed with resignation. He couldn't blame her for being angry, but he didn't want her to make a decision that might adversely impact the hotel. "Except I have a sneaking suspicion that if the review is delayed, some executive at Harmon looking for a promotion is going to ax the Chandelier House without a fair shake."

"Why?" she asked, spreading her hands. "We've maintained a healthy margin, no thanks to Harmon. They're pocketing our earnings and doling out nickels and dimes for expansion and repair."

"The hotel is bad for their image," he said bluntly. "You're familiar with Harmon's strategy to cater to the corporate traveler—your guest demographics are way off the chart."

"So let them sell us," she said, pounding her fist

on the table. "We'd be better off in the hands of someone else."

"Cindy," he said, resisting the urge to cover her hand. "It's not that simple. If Harmon puts your hotel on the block, they'll do it piece by piece—first the antique furniture, then the fixtures, then the building itself. And chances are, the building could be bought for the land alone and the structure bulldozed."

She inhaled, then exhaled noisily. "And the alternative?"

"I stay on the project and if the books are as healthy as you say, I could at least present Harmon with a fair business case for keeping the hotel. A positive review won't keep them from selling, but it will at least make a divestiture more difficult to justify."

"That's it?"

He locked his gaze with hers and spoke sincerely. "I can't make any promises."

A scoff escaped her lips. "You mean my best hope for saving the hotel is for you to stay and perform the review?"

"In my opinion, yes."

"And what if you screw me?" One corner of her mouth lifted, but her eyes remained flat. "Again?"

Eric squirmed, knowing he'd put them both in an ethical position more awkward than any position they'd conjured up in her bed last night. "Cindy, I'm not in the business of wrecking people's lives."

"That's not what I've heard."

The remark hit him like a sucker punch, but he didn't flinch. "You'll have to trust me on this one."

Her mouth tightened. "It looks as though I have no other choice, Mr. Stanton." She pushed herself to her feet, her face pinched and pale. "I guess I won't stay for breakfast. I lost my appetite. And since I'm going to be forced to see you for the next few days, Mr. Stanton, I think I'll take this opportunity to avoid your company."

"Cindy—" he said, half standing and putting his hand on her arm.

She pivoted her head to stare at his hand, which he removed after a few seconds of silence. Cindy slung her purse over her shoulder, then walked away.

CINDY DIALED THE NUMBER twice, hanging up both times before the phone could ring on the other end. With a heavy sigh, she leaned her head back on the comfy chair and stared at her bed. With no effort, she could picture Eric lying nude amidst the covers, his rakish smile beckoning her. She closed her eyes, allowing herself the sinful pleasure of reliving the more vivid sensations of their lovemaking before the inevitable, crushing return of humiliation and self-reproach roused her from her daydream.

Resigned, she picked up the phone and redialed the number, almost hoping no one would answer. But when her mother's voice came over the line, Cindy acknowledged a decidedly juvenile sense of comfort she hoped she'd never outgrow.

"Mom? Hi, how's everything—hmm? Oh, the party was fine—what? Well, the date didn't turn out exactly—no, Mom, he didn't take advantage of me, in fact—huh? No, I doubt if we'll be going out again—the Donna Karan. Yes, the black one. My hair? Well, I've been doing some experimenting—oh, no, I like it. Hmm? A little shorter—no, it's not ruined. Everyone around here is talking about it. So how's everything—Eric...Eric Quinn. Right, with a Q. No Quinns in Manassas? Well, it's a big place—Mom, it doesn't matter because he was only—what? Ham will be fine. No, Mom, Manny is not Jewish. No, you don't have to buy him a gift—size large will be fine, I think. Right. I just called to say hello—yes, Christmas Eve. Uh-huh. Uh-huh. My love to Dad... Love you, too. Okay...Okay, bye-bye... Okay, bye-bye."

Cindy replaced the phone and shook her head, then smiled warmly, her spirit on the mend.

CHAPTER TEN

"I'M SORRY, MR. STANTON," the jeweler said, shaking his head. "I can't fix it, and there's no way I can find a replacement."

Eric's shoulders drooped. "When I left it here two days ago, the woman said it would be no problem."

"Again, I'm sorry, but my wife didn't realize, and neither did I at first, that this earring isn't glass—it's vintage crystal."

Irritated, Eric scrubbed his hand over his face. Cindy hadn't exactly warmed up to him in the last couple of days, and he was hoping the gift would help repair their strained relationship. *Like the piano you gave your father?* He squashed the unsettling thought.

The jeweler turned the pieces over in his hand, his expression regretful. "Beautiful piece—looks like it might have come from a chandelier."

He stopped and squinted at the man. "A chandelier, did you say?"

"Uh-huh. Now *that* would be some piece, a chandelier made from this caliber glass."

Eric poked his tongue in his cheek, his mind spinning with possible scenarios. After securing the broken pieces in his pocket, Eric left the shop and found a pay phone. He punched in a number slowly, feeling a stab of longing when a familiar voice came over the line.

"Pop? It's Eric."

"I know that," his father snapped. "I only got one son, you know."

Eric bit his tongue, then asked, "How are you doing?"

"Bored to damned death—not that you care."

"Pop, that's not true—"

"I got your postcard from San Francisco. You out there hacking up another company?"

"No," he answered patiently. "Dad, did you get a chance to check out the chandelier on the postcard?"

"Sure—recognized it right away. It's a French design—À Merveille."

"À Merveille," Eric murmured. "'To perfection.'"

"Right. I did a little research. This particular model was custom-made in the twenties—the three originals took months to make. It was copied in lesser materials quite a bit in the forties and fifties. And the chandelier on the postcard appears to be a good copy, except for a missing piece, probably broken."

Eric's pulse picked up. "Tell me about the missing piece, Dad."

"The original had a small spiral of crystals hanging from the center."

From which at least one pair of earrings had been fashioned? "Do you have any idea what the original might be worth?"

"I wrote it down—one point three million."

Eric clutched the edge of the phone booth. "Really."

"Uh-huh. But the copies are only worth between twenty and thirty thousand. Not chump change, but not enough to retire on. Why the sudden interest in a light fixture?"

"Just trying to estimate a book value," Eric lied, to gain time. "Dad, I need a picture of the original chandelier."

"Christmas is only a few days away. Can't you get the book then?"

Eric pinched the bridge of his nose. "Actually, I need that photo right away, and I, um...I'm not going to make it home for Christmas this year."

There was a brief pause on the other end. "Why not?"

Because I don't want to argue with you the entire visit and hear about how much money I wasted on that damned piano. "Something came up at work."

"Okay by me, but Alicia and the kids will be disappointed."

"I'll call her and try to plan a visit after New Year's." He sighed. "Will you send the book?"

"Sure. What's the address?"

Eric pulled out Cindy's business card and read the hotel address to his father, thinking it sad that two of the people he cared about most would just as soon not be around him. Then he stopped. Cared about most?

CINDY HELD HER HEAD BACK, looking straight up at the tree. "I think you're right," she said to Manny. "Those veil decorations are definitely melting."

Her friend scoffed. "A Middle Eastern theme— aren't those addle-headed decorators aware that most people in the Middle East don't celebrate Christmas? In fact," he said flatly, "maybe I'll move there."

"Oh, don't be such a Scrooge," she said lightly. "We've managed to have a decorated tree for—what? Four whole days now. Have Amy call the decorators and tell them to take off everything but the lights— that way it'll still be festive when the rest of the review team arrives today."

"You're nothing if not optimistic," her friend noted. "Speaking of the review team, I haven't seen Stanton lurking around today. Wonder where he slept last night?"

She offered a rueful smile. "As long as it wasn't with me, I couldn't care less."

"Just checking," he said, his low voice rich with innuendo.

"What's that supposed to mean? I've gone out of my way to avoid that man these last few days." She'd even resisted the urge to hand-deliver the shirt she'd bought to replace the one she'd burned.

His pale eyebrows shot up. "My point exactly."

"I don't want anyone thinking I'm…I'm, you know."

"Still infatuated with him?"

Her jaw dropped, then closed. "Not *still*…not ever!"

"That's what I meant," he said smoothly.

"Well—" Flustered, she scrambled for words. "I take issue with the term 'infatuated.'" Her arm flailed of its own volition. "Being infatuated implies the existence of…some type of emotional involvement, of…of some kind of personal attachment. Anything between me and Stanton was purely physical."

"Just a one-night stand," Manny said, nodding.

A frown pulled down the corners of her mouth. "Right."

He smiled and exhaled noisily. "What a relief to hear you say that. I can't imagine a worse match than you and Eric Stanton."

"Right." She worried the inside of her cheek with her tongue. "What makes you say that?"

He scoffed. "Cindy, you're so fun-loving, and he's so…*anal*."

A fond memory of him playing the piano washed over her. "Eric has his less serious moments."

"And you value tradition, people. That man won't

lose a wink of sleep worrying about the employees here."

She worked her mouth side to side. "But he said he'd try to help us make a case to Harmon."

"Why would he do that? Harmon is paying him untold dollars to oversee this review because of his hard-ass reputation. And you think that Stanton is going to help us because he's undergone a sudden change of heart?" He gave her a dubious look. "This is the same man, Cindy, who climbed into your bed knowing he'd be evaluating you on job performance. What makes you think you can put your faith in him now?"

Hurt stabbed her from all sides. "You're right." Deep down, she'd known all those things about Eric—so why did hearing the words aloud bother her so much?

He handed her a plastic bag he'd been holding.

"What's this?"

"*Stanton's* jammies."

Her eyes widened. "Why did you bring them back?"

Manny shrugged. "I don't know—I couldn't bring myself to throw them away, and it seemed icky to hang on to them."

"Icky?"

"Another word for 'I don't want this on my conscience, girl.'"

She clamped the bag under her arm. "Like I don't have enough on mine."

"Well, I feel better about giving back the pants knowing that Stanton doesn't mean anything to you."

She swallowed. "Thanks. I have to go. I have an appointment with our new hairdresser in the salon." She held up a finger. "Don't say a word."

He made a zipping motion across his mouth with his finger, turned on his heel and headed back to the concierge station.

Cindy turned toward the salon, anticipating a few minutes of peace and quiet to mull her recent restlessness.

"Whew, that perm really stripped your color," Matilda, the new hairdresser, said emphatically. "Let's try shade number twenty-eight B, chocolate coffee."

Cindy settled into a salon chair, frowning in puzzlement.

"Dark brown," the woman clarified.

"Ah. Good—back to my original color." She glanced at her hair in the mirror. "Is it safe to color so soon after perming?"

"I'll apply a conditioner first."

"Okay, you're the expert...aren't you?"

Matilda nodded, while in the background, Jerry shook his head.

"Just match my eyebrows as closely as you can,"

Cindy declared, ignoring the barber. How hard could it be to open a bottle of dye and pour it on?

"Okeydokey."

At least her hair would be back to its normal color by the time she met the review team. While the stylist painted on goopy hair dye with a brush, Cindy's thoughts strayed to pending catastrophes. She longed for the days when they weren't enslaved to a corporate master, when they didn't expend so much energy watching their p's and q's. "How much longer?" she asked the hairdresser.

"Time to rinse," the woman said, yanking Cindy's head back into a sink and nearly drowning her in her attempt to wash away the residue. After a knot-raising towel dry, Matilda plugged in a blow-dryer.

Except when she flipped the switch to the hair dryer, the lights blinked, then went out, pitching the salon into total darkness. "Did I do that?" Matilda cried.

"I don't think a hair dryer could do this," Cindy said. The low-watt generator lights came on. "It would take a huge power draw, something like a..."

"Like a Christmas tree?" the woman asked.

"Yeah," Cindy said, nodding, then gripped the arms of the chair. The Christmas tree—had the decorators added more lights once they stripped the melting decorations?

She launched herself out of the chair and fled for the lobby.

"POWER FAILURE," ERIC murmured, grasping the rail along the three-story staircase landing. He immediately wondered if Cindy was at the source of the calamity and smiled to himself, surprised that the mere thought of her evoked that odd twisting feeling in his chest. Guilt, probably. He held a small pair of binoculars through which he'd studied the chandelier hanging a few yards in front of him for a good fifteen seconds before everything went black.

Emergency lights came on, supplementing the thin daylight streaming in around the front entrance. Eric had a fairly good view of the activity in the lobby. Newly erected scaffolding held a dozen workers, some of whom had been removing items from the tree while others had been adding strands of lights. Someone with a pronounced lisp yelled for everyone on the scaffolding not to move. A knot of six guests came through the front door, dressed professionally and pulling sleek suitcases. His team, he noted, cursing the bad timing. Eric descended the long stairway in the semidarkness.

As expected, Cindy came flying onto the scene, almost literally, since she sported some kind of cape that flapped behind her. Her hair sprang wild and wet around her. Eric approached his team, shaking hands and explaining the recent turn of events. With a start, he realized he was becoming numb to the hotel's minidisasters. Within a few minutes, Cindy had coordinated an evacuation of workers on the scaffolding and announced that the electricity, which was off in a two-block radius, would be restored soon.

He waved to get her attention and gestured her over. She resembled a drowned cat with her huge greenish eyes and her wild, wet hair that looked almost…no, it was probably just the low lighting that made it look purplish. From the gray cape he assumed she'd been "salonus interruptus" when the blackout occurred.

"This is Ms. Cindy Warren," he said to his team, "general manager of the Chandelier House." That she occasionally moonlighted as Nurse Lovejoy, he kept to himself. "Ms. Warren, meet the Stanton & Associates review team members who have been assigned to evaluate your property."

She blanched, then recovered quickly as she exchanged greetings with his stoic-faced team. "We apologize for the inconvenience," Cindy said with a big smile. "Lights are being rounded up as we speak so that everyone can find their way around the hotel. Ah, here we are. Eight lights over here, please."

From a box, a young man passed out pale cylinders to the group, then moved on. Eric studied the object in his hand, frowning.

"Ladies and gentlemen…" A voice he recognized as Samantha Riggs's came over a bullhorn. "We are providing all guests with a combination glow-in-the-dark flashlight/vibrator, batteries included, compliments of Readynow, one of our vendors for the adult entertainment trade show that will begin on Monday. If you're still visiting with us at that time, we invite you to drop by the show. Oh, and please bring photo ID."

Eric shot Cindy an amused glance as she stared at the contoured flashlight cradled in her hands, closed her eyes and mouthed something heavenward. He suppressed a smile. "Ms. Warren, I was hoping you'd join us for dinner in the restaurant, say around seven? Hopefully the lights will have been restored by then."

She nodded and smiled shakily. "We can hope, can't we?"

"It's purple," she moaned, looking in the mirror.

"'Eggplant' sounds so much more fashionable," Manny declared.

"Why does this keep happening to me?"

"It's a conspiracy, Cindy. What did the hairdresser say?"

"By the time I got back to the salon, Jerry had sent her home."

"Hmm. And did Jerry have any advice?"

"He gave me a paper sack to wear on my head. I asked for plastic so I could suffocate myself."

"You have to admit it's very trendy. Some people would pay top dollar for this look. It's not half-bad, actually."

"Manny, I'm supposed to have dinner with Stanton and the rest of the review team in one hour. I look like one of the Spice Girls."

"Is this just a shmoozy meeting?"

"I think so, although Eric mentioned he wanted to talk to me afterward."

"Uh-oh."

"Relax. He said it was about the hotel, although he didn't give me any specifics." She gave him a wry smile. "And with my wet head and wearing that plastic cape, I was in such a hurry to get out of there, I didn't question him."

"I heard the rest of the review team arrived during the blackout."

"When else? I'm sure they were very impressed with my getup, not to mention the vibrating hostess gifts."

"Oh, well, it can't get any worse."

"Please don't *say* that."

"At least the lights are on now."

"Which is a good thing, else no one would be able to see our totally bare three-story Christmas tree."

"That's the spirit."

"Do you think the green hat is too casual for dinner?"

"Yes." He picked up a lock of her wine-colored hair. "Don't you have a dress this color?"

She nodded.

"How about a head wrap? Blue would be nice."

"I don't have a blue scarf."

"Hmm." He pursed his mouth as if an idea had struck him.

"What?"

"Where are the jammies?" He spied the paper bag in a nearby chair and pulled them out.

"Oh, no." Cindy held up her hands. "I am *not* going to dinner with Eric wearing the pajama pants I stole from him wrapped around my head."

But his hands were already at work. "Think of it as a three-hundred-and-fifty-dollar scarf. Fold under the waistband, hide the stain, tie the legs in back, tuck, tuck, tuck, and *voilà!*"

She opened her mouth to protest, but he guided her face to the mirror. She looked…good, exotic even. Creating a four-inch strip around her hairline and ears, the makeshift scarf held the curly purple hair away from her face, forcing it to spill up and over the pale fabric. "Dammit, Manny, how do you do that?"

"Resourcefulness," he said, snapping his fingers.

"But what if he recognizes it?"

"If he were gay, I'd say don't risk it. But straight, hungry, horny and under low lights—are you kidding?" He laughed. "Besides, this is *too* perfect."

Frowning, Cindy looked at her reflection and let out a sigh. "I don't have a good feeling about this."

CHAPTER ELEVEN

STANDING NEXT TO THE long dinner table, Eric lifted his hand in a final wave as the members of his review team filed out of the restaurant. Strange, but he hadn't noticed before what incredibly dull company his associates were. Of course, he suspected the hours had dragged because he was longing to talk to Cindy alone. She'd chosen the seat farthest from him, so he hadn't been able to engage her in conversation. "Thanks for agreeing to stay awhile longer."

She nodded curtly, her expression guarded, as it had been each time he had caught her gaze throughout the meal. "You wanted to talk to me about a hotel matter?"

When she started to reclaim her seat, Eric's mind raced to come up with a venue that would offer privacy without the connotation of either of their rooms. "How about if we go up to the roof to take in that great view you told me about? I hate to admit it, but I'm dying for a smoke."

She pressed her lips together, hesitating.

"And I don't want to risk our conversation being overheard," he added.

Her eyes narrowed slightly. "I thought you said you wanted to discuss the hotel."

"I do, but I believe you will appreciate the privacy."

Concern furrowed her forehead. "I'll need to stop by my room to get a jacket."

"You can use mine," he offered. "I won't keep you long."

In answer, she picked up her bag and walked to the hostess station, where she signed for their meal. Eric couldn't stop himself from devouring the swell of her hips beneath the thin fabric of her slim burgundy dress. Her hair, which was actually an odd, lovely contrast to her green eyes, would take a little getting used to, but— What was he thinking? He wouldn't be around long enough to get used to *anything*. Spending the night with Cindy would undoubtedly be a fondly recalled memory, but little more. Once he put a little space between him and the Chandelier House, he would recover his edge.

"You made a good impression on the team," he said with sincerity as they strolled toward the elevator.

She laughed softly. "With the utter chaos surrounding my introduction this afternoon, I had nowhere to go but up."

He waved off her concern. "I told everyone they'd get used to seeing you like that."

"Gee, thanks."

Eric laughed. "I meant, they'd get used to seeing you in the middle of things, taking charge, no matter what."

She turned wary eyes his way. "That's my job, Mr. Stanton." She walked into the elevator car, claimed a front corner and depressed the top floor button. Her posture remained uncompromising.

Hating the formality, the distance and the awkward tension, he watched the floors light as they climbed. Strange, how they had gone from being strangers to acquaintances to lovers, and now back to mere acquaintances.

They reached the top of the building in short order. Cindy removed a handheld radio from her bag and asked the operator to notify security that the silent alarm for the roof door would be tripped. Eric followed her down a hallway, up a flight and a half of stairs, and through the heavy metal door covered with warning stickers.

Cindy looked forward to the openness of the roof after being in close confines with Eric for the past few hours. A gusting breeze enveloped her as she stepped outside, the December chill raising gooseflesh on her skin, despite the long sleeves of her dress.

She shivered involuntarily, then started when

Eric's jacket appeared around her shoulders. The warmth from his body still emanated from the silky lining, and the faint scent of English Leather drifted up to tease her. "Thank you," she murmured, then stepped away from the stairwell enclosure toward the center of the roof.

"Nice," he observed, scanning the view.

She had to agree. At this height, the world was a soothing mixture of calm silence with faint undertones of traffic far below. The wind sent the ends of her hair skimming across her face and dancing in the air. She patted the pseudo-scarf, experiencing a stab of alarm that it seemed much looser. Oh, well, the wrap seemed intact for now, and Eric had told her the discussion wouldn't take long.

Her heart pounded in her ears, drowning out the wind. The only reason she could think of for his wanting to talk in private was to rehash the impact of their night together on the review, and she didn't want to talk about it again. Wasn't it enough that the encounter was never more than a few seconds from her mind anyway?

She tried to distract herself by absorbing the wonderful view, which remained breathtaking no matter how many times she made this pilgrimage. A myriad of lights from homes, cars and Christmas decorations studded the landscape in three directions as far as one could see. To the west, of course, lay the bay, offering its own nighttime spectacle.

"Beautiful," Eric said, turning to look at her.

Despite the circumstances, Cindy found it difficult to make eye contact with the man and not be affected. Not only was he undeniably handsome, but she also knew intimate secrets about the powerful body standing little more than an arm's length away. The awareness of their physical compatibility pulled at her like a vacuum. "Mr. Stanton," she said hurriedly, "I need to get to bed early tonight."

The words hung in the air between them.

"Alone," she amended quickly, then stopped and took a deep, calming breath. "Maybe you'd better just dive right in…. Into whatever you wanted to talk about, I mean." To cover her growing uneasiness, she smiled cheerily into the stiff breeze and rambled on. "You know, I'm so glad we've been able to get past that little indiscretion and move on to building a business relationship based on—" she spit out a hank of hair that the wind blew against her mouth "—mutual respect."

Eric nodded, his expression unreadable. Then he stepped forward and reached for her. Terrified at the zing of desire in her stomach, she held up both hands to ward him off. "Stop right there, buster." Her body responded shamelessly even as her indignation ballooned. "How dare you lure me up here under the guise of business when all you had on your mind was…was copping a feel!"

He halted, his eyes wide.

Hurt loosened her tongue, making her want to give pain in return. "Haven't you ever done it on a roof, Mr. Stanton? Does it turn you on? Didn't I give you enough material the other night for a few weeks' worth of locker-room talk?"

He frowned and nodded toward his jacket. "If you're finished, there's something in the left pocket, wrapped in a tissue. I believe it's yours."

Slightly deflated that he hadn't brought her to the roof to feel her up after all, Cindy reached into the pocket and withdrew a wad of tissue.

"Careful," he warned.

She gently unfolded the tissue, at first confused by the bits of glass winking in the moonlight. Then she sucked in a breath. "My earring," she said softly, wincing when she saw the two pieces.

His tie whipped in the wind, curling around his neck. "It must have fallen into the pocket of my tux or gotten hung on my clothes somehow," he explained. "I stepped on it accidentally. I'm so sorry."

"That's all right." But she could hear the hurt in her own voice.

"I wanted to have it repaired, but the jeweler told me he couldn't replace it."

Her head jerked up. "Jeweler?"

"He told me it wasn't glass, as I'd thought, but vintage lead crystal."

She met his gaze, looked away, then glanced back,

her knees weakening. "Um, yes, as a matter of fact, it is crystal."

"He also said it probably came from a chandelier."

"Did he?" Stuffing the broken earring into her purse, she walked past him and over to the shoulder-high concrete edge, her mind spinning.

"He told me an intact chandelier made out of this crystal would be extremely valuable." She could tell from his muffled voice that he stared at the opposite horizon. How perfectly symbolic, she realized.

Cindy wet her lips, blinking against the wind, which was much stronger here on the perimeter of the roof. "I suppose it would be," she said over her shoulder. She gasped as the scarf fell slack against her hairline and a leg of the pajama pants whisked in front of her face, riding the wind like a flag. She snatched the leg and straightened, using both hands to try to repair the damage.

Eric still stood with his back to her, hands on his hips. He obviously didn't know how to broach the next question, which made Cindy a nervous wreck. How much did he know? How much should she tell him?

The head wrap fell around her neck. She panicked and whipped it off in a motion she knew would leave burn marks on her throat. Holding the garment in front of her in a ball, her mind raced. Her purse was too small. She had no pockets of her own. He still had his back to her. Her heart thudded.

"Cindy."

She held the wadded-up pants over the edge and dropped the bundle, then spun and gave Eric her seemingly undivided attention as he crossed the small distance between them. "Yes?"

"Did that earring come from the chandelier hanging in the hotel lobby?"

"The earrings were p-passed down in my family," she said quickly.

"And I remember you saying that your grandfather was one of the original owners of the Chandelier House, isn't that right?"

She inclined her head. "You have a good memory." *Dammit.*

He stepped closer, then pinned her down with his gaze. "Cindy, *did* that earring come from the chandelier hanging in the lobby?"

"Eric," she said, laughing softly, "I'm not an expert on chandeliers."

"No," he said quietly. "But my father happens to be."

She swallowed. "Your father?"

"He's a retired master glassblower. I sent him a picture of the chandelier. According to his research, if it's an original French *À Merveille,* it's worth a fortune."

"I can't recall what the chandelier is worth," she said, her voice sounding high-pitched even to her own ears. "But I'll make sure someone in account-ing gets that information to you."

"I checked the books," he said calmly, "and I don't think they're right. Cindy," he said, stepping even closer and leaning forward, "I'm giving you one more chance to tell me everything you know about that chandelier. If you don't, I'm going to call Har-mon, tell them my suspicions, and suggest the piece be appraised."

She evaluated her options—including jumping—but none of them seemed viable. Finally she angled her head at him. "And how do I know you won't call Harmon anyway?"

His mouth tightened. "You don't."

She sighed and turned back to the view. Eric joined her, resting folded arms on top of the concrete wall. Wetting her lips, Cindy said, "My grandfather loved this hotel. He said the chandelier symbolized the greatness, the uniqueness of the place. While he was still part owner, he had the center piece removed from the chandelier and commissioned these ear-rings for my grandmother. I inherited them, along with the wonderful story about the three original chandeliers being sold for the war effort and replaced with glass copies."

With a soft laugh, she said, "I honestly didn't suspect the one in this hotel might be one of the originals until after Harmon bought the Chandelier House."

"What made you suspect it wasn't a copy?"

"I had a chance to visit the hotel in Chicago where one of the other two *À Merveille* originals once hung. That chandelier had an extra central spiral that our chandelier doesn't. Out of curiosity, I made the trip to Hollywood and the copy there also has the center piece."

He shrugged. "So maybe the center piece was removed from your copy to make it look like the original."

She smiled, her lips dry and tight. "My thoughts exactly—until I poked around in my grandfather's personal journals. At the last minute, instead of donating the chandelier, he made a hefty cash donation to the war effort, an amount that exceeded the value of the original chandelier at the time. The copy was hustled away on the black market, and no one was the wiser."

He shook his head slowly. "That's an amazing story."

"And sad," she noted. "That cash donation drained my grandfather's resources and he ended up selling his interest in the hotel, even though he continued to love the place. He wrote that it was his secret, knowing the magnificent chandelier reigned over the place in his absence."

"And why didn't you notify someone?"

"Because I knew Harmon would probably sell it to the highest bidder and replace it with a cheap copy, if they replaced it at all. And our talk the other day at breakfast only reinforced my resolve to keep quiet."

"Cindy," he said quietly. "That piece should be in a museum."

She frowned, turning to face him. "It belongs here."

Eric shook his head. "It's not right, Cindy. Harmon owns that chandelier and they should be told how much it's worth."

She stared at him. "And you're going to tell them?"

He sighed and held up his hand. "I didn't say that— I need to think things through."

"I'm trusting you." To her horror, her eyes filled with tears. "I'm trusting you to look past the capital gain and do the right thing, Eric." She looked up at him, hoping for reassurance, but saw only indecisiveness in his expression.

Cindy turned and gripped the top of the cold concrete wall. She hated needing something from him... hated feeling so vulnerable...hated thinking she could be responsible for over two hundred employees losing their jobs. "It's my fault," she whispered. "I brought all this trouble on the hotel. I should have conformed to the corporate mandates. Now we'll be sold or closed and the chandelier will be lost, too." Cindy brought her hand to her mouth to stem a humiliating sob.

"Hey," he said softly, turning her to face him.

She inhaled deeply to regain her composure, loath to meet his gaze. "Cindy, don't take this review personally—you did what you thought was best for your employees. It won't be your fault if Harmon decides to divest the Chandelier House."

She looked into his eyes, aware of the warmth of his hands on her arms, even through the fabric of his coat. "You mean if *you* decide, Eric?"

He faltered, then nodded curtly. "It's strictly business, Cindy."

"How can you do this?" she asked, searching his face. "Don't you care that a few words from your mouth can change the lives of so many innocent people?"

His head dipped until their eyes were level. "We both have a job to do. We can't let emotion interfere."

She looked into his eyes, frustrated that with everything on the line, he could still have such a physical impact on her. His mouth mesmerized her, too vividly bringing back the memory of his lips on her body. Let emotion interfere? He taunted her. She lifted her chin. "That's not the way I operate, Mr. Stanton. The Chandelier House is more than an entry on a profit-and-loss statement. If I could afford to, I'd buy this place myself."

His expression softened and he lifted one hand to smooth her unbound hair back from her cheek. "And if I could afford to, I'd buy this place for you." As if in slow motion, Eric pulled her to him and wrapped his arms around her, tucking her head beneath his chin. Enclosed in his warm coat and strong embrace, Cindy closed her eyes and relaxed against him. Gradually, the comforting hug gained momentum. Eric ran his hands up and down her back and she folded her arms around his waist, delaying the moment she'd have to release him.

Eric drew back slightly, cupped her chin in his hand and lifted her mouth to meet his. She inhaled deeply just before their lips touched, because she wanted the kiss to last a long time—through the night, past the review and into the new year. His mouth moved on hers with an aching sweetness. He flicked his tongue against her teeth and gave her his own breath when she needed air. Her knees buckled and she fell against him, moaning and straining for his touch.

Eric moved his mouth to her neck, nipping at the sensitive curve until waves of desire set every nerve ending on edge. His hands moved inside the jacket, cradling her hips with one large hand, supporting her back with the other. Effortlessly he lifted her against him, sliding her down oh-so-slowly over his chest, his stomach, his swollen arousal.

"Cindy," he whispered. "You make me want to do crazy things, like make love to you right here."

"We shouldn't," she murmured, more for herself than him. Yet she felt herself succumb to the titillating temptation of making love with him under the stars, with the wind whipping over their bodies. She massaged his erection through his slacks, eliciting a frustrated groan from Eric.

He pulled up her dress and slid his hands inside her panties, grasping her bottom and rubbing her against him. Teasing her nest from behind, his fingers urged her to open and give him better access. With a sigh she leaned into him, gasping when he inserted his fingers into her wet folds. The angle of his probing drove her wild and within seconds, they adopted a rhythm, him thrusting, her sliding back to meet his hand. The cool air on her exposed skin, and the sounds of his encouraging whispers billowed her higher and higher, until she trembled around his fingers in a shuddering pinnacle.

He showered her face and neck with kisses, caressing her body with both hands, murmuring her name. Wanting to pleasure him and since her legs were still weak from her own release, Cindy lowered herself to her knees and unfastened Eric's belt. With his help, his monster erection was soon freed. A little intimidated by the size of his shaft, she trailed kisses and licks up and down before tentatively taking the tip into her mouth.

Eric plowed his fingers into her hair and threw his head back as a long moan escaped from his lips. She advanced carefully, taking him into her mouth with utmost care, grasping the base with her hands and falling into a slow tempo of massage. He could have been in agony or ecstasy from the sounds of his groans, but he let her set the pace. She stroked and devoured him while the wind whisked between them. At last he gasped her name, warning her of his impending flood, giving her time to retreat if she desired.

Suddenly a floodlight lit the sky, illuminating Eric's head and shoulders above the concrete wall. He jerked around. "What the—?"

Cindy froze, then dragged herself to her feet, struggling to rearrange her clothing. Eric did the same, under considerably more duress. She glanced over the edge straight into a beacon of blinding light.

"Stop!" the head of hotel security bellowed through a bullhorn. A crowd of several dozen had gathered on the sidewalk. "For God's sake, don't jump! The police are on their way!"

"What the devil is going on?" Eric growled.

She stared down at the street. "I think *he* thinks there's someone up here going to jump."

"Believe me," he said, running a hand through his hair, "I'm tempted to jump, just to wring that idiot's neck!"

"Pete!" she yelled down through cupped hands. "Nobody's going to jump!"

"Cindy? Is that you?"

"Yeah, Pete, it's me."

"What happened to your hair?"

She looked for a brick to drop, but seeing none,

yelled, "Call the police and tell them it was a mistake. I'll be right down."

"Okay." He sounded dejected.

The light was extinguished, plunging them back
into semidarkness. "I have to go," she said, the impact of her lapse suddenly dawning. "Or else someone will come for me."

"Hey," he said quietly, pulling her close for a quick
kiss, "I was about two seconds away from coming
for you."

But the tawdry way she'd behaved shamed her.
Her hands started trembling. They'd groped like
frenzied animals, with no emotional involvement—
at least not on his part. With a sinking feeling, Cindy
realized that somewhere between "What's wrong
with long, straight hair?" and "I was about two seconds away from coming for you," she'd fallen for
Eric Quinn Stanton.

"I have to go," she said forcefully, breaking his
embrace and shrugging out of his coat.

A frown marred his smooth forehead. "What's
wrong?"

"Nothing," she said coolly, feeling like the world's
biggest fool. "Like you said, we both have a job to
do." She turned and strode toward the door, mortified by her heart's revelation in light of all that had
transpired.

What was it Manny had said? *Falling in love will*

be an agonizing event with a man who represents
everything you hate.

Manny…right again, dammit.

MANNY LOOKED IN the plastic bag she held open, then
gaped at her. "You threw the pajamas off the top of
the building?"

She shrugged. "How was I to know they'd snag
on someone's window? Security thought there was
a man on top of the building getting ready to jump."

"Little did they know there was a man on top of
the building who was *being* jumped."

"Hardee-har-har."

"Where did you get these?"

"I filched them from security—it took me four
days of sneaking around to find them."

He looked at her as if she was insane. "Okaaaaaaay.
I'm almost afraid to ask where you're headed now."

"To the furnace room," she declared. "I'm going
to burn these things so they can't get me into any
more trouble." Her stomach rolled with queasy fear.
"Stanton said he'd give me a preview of the final report this afternoon at four. And although it doesn't
seem likely that I'll have yet another catastrophe before he leaves, I'm trying to limit the possibilities."

"At least the tree is taken care of."

"Right. What could be more harmless than plain
old candy canes?" She checked her watch. "Got to
run—I'm due at the salon."

Manny clucked. "What else could you possibly have done to your hair?"

"I'm getting it fixed this time. New stylist."

He shook his head. "You never learn, do you? Besides, I've heard a lot of people say they think the color is cool."

Cindy nodded. "Complete strangers have stopped me to ask about my hair, but I just don't think I can live with it."

"You or your mother?"

"Both."

He fidgeted. "Cindy, are you nervous about the report?"

"Sure," she admitted shakily, "but I'm trying not to worry about it." Trying not to worry about losing her job, or the chandelier being sold, or the entire hotel being auctioned off, or being in love with Eric, or why bubbles form in leftover glasses of water.

Manny patted her hand. "You're doing a bang-up job here and if Stanton and his people can't see it, they're blind."

"Thanks."

"And I hate that man for putting you through the wringer."

She gave him a careful little smile. "Don't blame Eric, Manny. Everything I'm going through, I brought on myself." And to her mortification, her eyes filled with tears.

He brought his hand to his head in a helpless gesture. "Oh, God, you're in love with him, aren't you?"

She nodded, wiping her eyes. "A fact I am not
proud of," she added. "But don't worry, I'll be over
him by New Year's." She tried to laugh it off. "Besides, I may have a change of heart when I hear his
report this afternoon."

"He's a fool if he doesn't realize how lucky he is."

She sniffed and gave him a grateful squeeze.
"Thanks. I'm glad you're going home with me for
Christmas."

"Me too. Speaking of which, I have to run a couple of errands early tomorrow, so I'll meet you at the
departure gate."

Falling in love with Eric Stanton—how stupid
could she be? she thought morosely as she tramped
downstairs to the furnace room. A corporate hack
with no real ties to his family, and no appreciation
for the things in life that were really important, like
preserving the integrity of the Chandelier House.

Using a mitt, she opened the door of an aged furnace and stuffed the pants into a bed of coals, grati-
fied when they caught instantly and began to burn.
She watched the tiny white monogram of EQS fold
in on itself, then disintegrate. Then she made herself
a note to turn in a security report for Eric's missing
pants, just in case he checked her paperwork.

At the salon, Cindy did a double-take at the line of

men, women and teenagers waiting to get in. "There she is," yelled one. "That's the exact color I want!"

Confused, Cindy walked in to find Matilda furiously working on clients in three separate chairs. "You're a hit," she told the woman, amazed at the crowd.

"No, you're the hit," the hairdresser said. "Most of these people are here for exotic coloring jobs because they saw your hair."

She touched her purplish tresses. "Really?"

"Yep. We could make a fortune specializing in coloring, head shaving and stuff like that."

With their clientele, Cindy couldn't believe they hadn't thought of it before. She grinned. "That sounds terrific."

"Great. Oh, Jerry is waiting for you in the back."

"Thanks." Cindy wound her way to the back where Jerry had staked out a small sink. "I owe you big for this," she said, sitting down.

He snapped the cape, then draped it around her shoulders. "It's my Christmas present to you," he said with a smile, then raised an eyebrow. "Even if you have been naughty."

She frowned. "Don't believe everything you hear."

He leaned down, his gaze boring into hers in the mirror. "And what if it's something I see with my own eyes?"

Glancing away from his knowing expression, she said, "I have no idea what you're talking about."

He shrugged. "You make a good couple, you and the Stanton lad."

She shook her head, but recognized the futility of arguing. "Jerry, did you have any idea that Quinn was Stanton?"

He nodded. "I knew that day in the salon when you first cut your hair."

"He told you?"

"Nope—I just knew."

She sighed. How like Jerry to sit back and watch people just to see what unfolded. She shot him a lethal look, but he simply spun her away from the mirror and picked up a pair of shears, chuckling beneath his breath.

CHAPTER TWELVE

ERIC SCANNED THE REPORTS each of his review team members had provided on every aspect of running the hotel from linen inventory to customer service to leaving Sweet Tarts on the pillows. The phrase "unconventional, but effective" appeared over and over. In all, his associates had confirmed his conclusion that the Chandelier House was a finely tuned nuthouse with a profit margin Harmon could only dream about for some of their "pet" properties.

Unfortunately, the Chandelier House didn't score well on Harmon's predetermined checklist for the corporate direction. So, although he'd composed several pages about the viability of the property, the crux of his recommendation had to answer one question: Did the Chandelier House meet the profile of a future Harmon property?

Eric tossed down his pen and crossed his arms. The answer was obvious to the point of hilarity, but Cindy's pleading green eyes kept getting in the way. In a weak moment, he considered the scenario of recommending that Harmon keep the property—

his reputation would be compromised, they would think twice before retaining him again and they would likely go against his recommendation in any case. And even if Harmon did keep the hotel, they'd forever be pressuring Cindy and her staff to conform—or more likely, replace her with a more corporate-minded general manager.

He stroked his chin, frustrated because never before had he labored over the delivery of such a logical directive. The words he'd spoken to Cindy on the roof kept haunting him. *If I could afford to, I'd buy this place for you.* He couldn't afford to, but he had the contacts to assemble investors who could, and possibly the clout with Harmon to convince them to sell the property intact instead of piece by piece. Resigned but considerably cheered, he typed up the report on his laptop. At least he'd be able to walk away from this assignment knowing he'd treated all parties fairly.

Fairly? What a joke. He'd bent over backward... for the sake of Cindy Warren.

But could he walk away? Definitely. He had no business diddling with the comely woman—if he needed proof, he had to look no further than the disconcerting report he'd just prepared. His team had left this morning, and tomorrow was Christmas Eve. He'd decided to fly to Atlanta and spend a few days looking for a condo. The Southeast was pleasant this time of year, and New Year's in Atlanta was hard to beat.

And he was bound to find some Southern belle who could take his mind off Cindy Warren. She'd spent the night with him, then ignored him for days, then spilled the beans about the chandelier and begged him to keep a million-dollar secret. Then the next thing he knew, they were both half-naked on the roof and howling at the moon. Had she participated only out of hope he'd keep quiet about the chandelier? And after they'd been interrupted, she'd decided to play hard to get again. To keep him on a chain? Hot, then cold, then hot and cold again. Was that her game? If so, then...then...

Then it seemed to be working.

Gritting his teeth, he typed in a half page of text about the chandelier, then changed his mind and deleted it. Eric cursed and slumped back in his chair. He'd vowed never to let a woman get in the way of doing a good job, and he never had—until now. Falling for Cindy had scrambled his brain.

He jerked his head up. Falling?

Eric pounded his hand on the desk, then attacked the keyboard again, typing furiously. After a few minutes, he absently patted his pocket for his cigarettes, then remembered he couldn't smoke in his room. Begrudgingly, he grabbed a package of Sweet Tarts and popped a couple, then resumed typing.

Falling for an eccentric, soft-hearted, nostalgic,

crazy-haired woman who would have him in knots every day of his life? He hit the caps button, then typed N-O W-A-Y.

MANNY SQUINTED, TILTING his head from side to side. "Your hair really looks wonderful. You should have cut it sooner."

Cindy lifted a hand to her short, wavy, blessedly dark brown locks, then punched him in the arm. "Now you tell me!" She was happy to spend a few minutes clowning with her best friend—especially now, when her stomach churned over the impending meeting with Eric. Laughably, she was more nervous about facing Eric Stanton the man than Eric Stanton the hotel mutilator.

Fifteen minutes before the appointed time she headed up to the boardroom, wanting to appear calm and collected when Eric arrived—for once. She turned on the lights and made herself a cup of hot tea, then assumed the authority seat at the end of the table, facing the door. She gulped her tea, trying to drown the butterflies in her stomach, but only managed to dribble on her best white blouse. She swore, then buttoned her jacket. For five minutes she practiced her busy, on-the-edge-of-her-seat pose for when he came in, and her jaunty-hair-toss-and-ease-back-in-the-chair-confidently maneuver for when he sat down. Then she raised her seat four inches and lowered the one to her right by four inches to give herself a feeling of superiority.

At the sound of approaching footsteps, she quickly assumed the pose, scrutinizing a memo she'd memorized. A light rap resonated through the room. She glanced up and, ignoring the catch of her heart at the sight of him, she waved Eric in, then immediately looked back to the memo and jotted a note in the margin.

"Do you need more time?" he asked, lowering himself, to her consternation, into the chair to her left instead of her right.

"Um...no," she said after an appropriately occupied pause. She closed the folder and set down her pen, then carefully tossed her hair and slid back in the chair. Except the chair tilt didn't lock. A leisurely split second passed during which Cindy experienced that sick feeling of knowing she was going over backward. Her eyes bugged and her arms flailed as she fought desperately to regain her balance, but to no avail. Eric lunged for her, but he couldn't move fast enough to keep her chair from slamming against the floor.

Her head bounced twice, but the rest of her seemed to be okay, thanks to the death grip she'd maintained on the arms. She sat in the chair perfectly aligned, apart from the fact that she was looking at the ceiling.

Eric's face appeared over her, tight with concern. "Are you okay?"

"I'm fine."

An amused smile broke over his face as he helped her up. Burning with humiliation, she leaned against the table and gingerly touched her forehead. She felt light-headed, but then again, she *was* down a few pounds of purple hair.

"No wonder it tipped over," he said, inspecting the chair. "Someone raised it too high and threw off the center of gravity." He pushed her power chair aside and replaced it with the one she'd lowered. "Try this one."

She cursed silently, but her head hurt so much, she dropped into the proffered seat, not caring when she sank so low his knees were at her eye level.

Eric knelt and peered into her face. "Are you sure you're all right? Can I get you a glass of water?"

"No, thanks," she mumbled. With her luck she'd probably drown herself. Cindy caught the fragrance of his strong soap, and she noticed he'd nicked his square chin while shaving. She wanted him. She loved him. She despised him. "Let's just get this over with."

He studied her face, his eyes guarded, then he nodded abruptly and reclaimed his seat. She looked up at him from her dwarfed position, her heart thudding. Eric opened a leather portfolio and read aloud. "This document serves as the official report from

Stanton and Associates concerning Harmon Hospitality property number eighty-five, the Chandelier House, located at—" He stopped and pursed his mouth, closed the portfolio, then slid it toward her. "You can read it at your leisure, Cindy. I'll hit the highlights."

From his close body language and hesitancy she didn't have to guess the contents. "Go on."

He pressed his lips together, then said, "My final report contains a recommendation that Harmon sell the Chandelier House. I'm sorry. Professionally, I had no choice."

She sat immobile, struck by a profound sense of sadness. Aside from the fact that her beloved hotel would likely be quartered and auctioned, Eric simply didn't get it. Some things were worth more in sum than the total of their parts, market price be damned.

He pointed to the portfolio. "Overall, the review team found this property to be well-run. The hotel's worst distinction is being purchased by Harmon in the first place. It's all in my report if you care to read it."

Cindy swallowed carefully. "Perhaps later."

Eric folded his hands and leaned forward. "In case you're wondering, I didn't disclose the alleged history of the chandelier."

She smiled tightly. "But when the hotel is put up for sale, unlike when Harmon stole the place two years ago from a group of granny investors, every last spoon will be appraised."

He conceded her point with a nod. "I decided the only way I could make an objective business evaluation was to proceed as if you hadn't told me."

"But I did," she said slowly. "I *did* tell you the story of the chandelier, so it *should* have influenced your decision. The history of this hotel should be preserved, especially when you consider that the Chandelier House is well into the black."

"For now."

"What's that supposed to mean?"

"That in five years role-playing groups and vampires and tattoos might be out of vogue."

"So? Other special-interest groups will emerge."

He threw up his hands. "The long-term customers Harmon needs to cultivate are large and midsize corporate—"

"You made your point, Mr. Stanton." Cindy fought to maintain her composure. "This meeting is over." She spun around in her low chair, turning her back to him and biting back tears of disappointment.

She heard him push away from the table and walk across the room. A few seconds of silence passed and she thought he must have left quietly. Then he spoke from the doorway. "Cindy."

She looked at him over her shoulder. "Yes?"

"I'm sorry if I ruined your Christmas."

Egotistical S.O.B.—at least he'd be easy to get

over. "Mr. Stanton, you don't have that much power in my life."

From the squaring of his jaw, she knew she'd scored a point. "Then let me say it was very nice, um, working with you, despite the misunderstandings."

She blinked.

"And just one more thing," he said.

She waited.

"Your hair looks nice." Then he walked out.

Cindy laid her aching head back on the chair and wished for the hundredth time that she'd never heard of Eric Quinn Stanton.

Her beeper sounded. Massaging the knot on the back of her head, she punched a button on the hand-held radio. "Cindy here."

"It's Manny. Can you stand one more Christmas tree crisis?"

A groan started deep in her chest and eased out. "How could five thousand candy canes possibly be hazardous?"

"If hordes of street people are shaking the tree to knock down the candy."

"I'll be right there."

ON THE WAY TO SAMMY'S for a stiff drink, Eric heard a commotion in the lobby and investigated the noise. The sky rained candy canes. Teams of shabbily dressed people were grabbing up the candy and stuffing it in bags, hats and pockets. The limbs within reaching distance were picked clean. Four large men hugged the trunk of the tree, taking turns shaking it to dislodge the stubborn hangers-on.

Eric shrank to a secluded corner to watch. As expected, the newly shorn general manager arrived on the scene in record time, dismantled the tree-shaking team, and ordered maintenance to erect scaffolding—again. The remaining candy was to be removed and placed in a bin just inside the entrance, free for the taking.

She'd done it again, he acknowledged. Danced into a crisis and handled it beautifully, dousing tempers and making everyone happy. As he watched her, Eric once again experienced the swelling in his chest he'd begun to associate with seeing and thinking about Cindy Warren. She was a delightful woman— witty, charming, beautiful and honest. Her employees loved her.

And he loved her.

With a jolt, Eric admitted he had indeed fallen for the wrong woman at the wrong time. Some of her most irresistible qualities—eccentricity, aplomb and chutzpah—were the very ones he knew would eventually drive him stark raving mad. He needed order in his life. He liked being surrounded by practical, predictable people.

Which was why he and his father couldn't get along, he supposed. His father was unconventional. He preferred the process of making music and art to owning it. If his father had a choice, he would rather have been the creator of the chandelier than the heir to its value. That philosophy had been behind the hurtful things he'd said when Eric had purchased the piano so many years ago.

Eric watched as Cindy surveyed the workers and, apparently satisfied that her instructions were under way, slowly climbed the sweeping staircase. Dressed in her standard green uniform she seemed unremarkable, but he knew better. He knew that beneath the sensible skirt lay a pool of desire he craved more than he could ever have imagined. And what about the heart that beat beneath the buttoned-up jacket? Did she have any feelings for him other than malice? It was just as well, he decided, that their jobs had hindered their physical involvement before emotional barnacles started forming.

She stopped at the top of the stairs and wrapped her hands around the railing. Then she simply stared at the magnificent chandelier. Eric wondered what could be going through her mind—was she thinking of her grandfather? Of all the employees and guests who had walked through those double doors? She waved as the maintenance men carried away sections of the impromptu scaffolding. The street people and a few guests lined up to take candy canes from the bin set near the entrance. The tree, tall and naked and completely abandoned, flanked the staircase, swaying slightly.

Swaying?

Eric emerged from his hiding place, his steps quickening. He glanced up and saw the expression on Cindy's face. She, too, suspected something was wrong. "The tree is falling!" she screamed, shooing stragglers with animated gestures. "Get out of the way, the tree is falling!"

He pulled back a few spectators, then watched in stunned amazement as the tree leaned, then gained slow momentum on its way down. The top branches grazed the chandelier, sending it rocking violently. Eric dragged his gaze from the scene to look for Cindy. She stood on the landing, her hand over her mouth, her eyes riveted on the swinging chandelier.

The gigantic tree landed with a fantastic whoosh, sprawling across the lobby in a spray of needles. Remarkably, no one had been in its path. But Eric knew spraying crystal would not be so kind. "Everybody down!" he yelled. And sure enough, with a sickening twist of metal, the magnificent fixture spun loose and fell on top of the tree, splintering into thousands of pieces.

CHAPTER THIRTEEN

CINDY OPENED HER EYES, practically swollen shut after a night of endless crying. It was Christmas Eve morning, and she'd never felt so miserable in her entire life.

She'd thought the meeting with Eric would be the lowlight of the day, but the falling Christmas tree and the crashing chandelier had outdone that horrible meeting. Luckily the tree broke the fixture's fall, but she wasn't sure how or if the chandelier would ever be completely restored. For the time being, the remnants had been carefully gathered and stored in countless boxes.

Eric was one of many who had helped with the cleanup last night, but she'd been careful to stay as far away from him as politely possible. If her overwhelming grief for the shattered chandelier had an upside, it was the fact that it numbed her to the biting sadness of knowing Eric was not the man she'd thought him to be—the kind of man who could love her, eccentricities and all, the kind of man who wanted to build and preserve people and places and things, not tear them down in the name of corporate cloning.

She dragged herself to the edge of her bed, her head spinning with the events of the last several days. Her life had gone from upbeat and fairly stable to downtrodden and perhaps *living* in a stable if she lost her job. And her heart…well, maybe she'd get a new one for Christmas. An unbreakable one.

On impulse, she picked up the phone and dialed her parents' number.

"Hello, Mom? Merry Christmas—hmm? No, we'll be there in a few—what? I've got a bit of a cold—no, I don't have a fever—Mom, I need some advice… Mom, are you there? Good, well, remember the man from Manassas? Right, with a Q. Well, actually, it's an S…"

ERIC STRODE INTO THE health club and absently climbed on a vacant treadmill, surprised when he realized that Manny Oliver was running on the neighboring machine.

The blond man had a muscular build, tall and lean. Sweating profusely, he nodded curtly at Eric, then checked the display monitor and slowed down.

"Getting in your workout early," Eric observed.

"Got a plane to catch in a couple of hours," Manny explained, his tone not overly friendly.

"Going home for Christmas?"

"Yeah," the man said, "with Cindy."

Eric balked—so she *was* having a relationship with her concierge? The realization shocked him because she didn't seem the type to...not that it was any of his business. He'd been battling guilt all morning over not seeing his family for Christmas. Now his heart squeezed painfully as he imagined Manny and Cindy sharing a good old-fashioned holiday. He increased the speed of the machine to a brisk jog as intense jealousy pulsed through him. "I hope the two of you have a nice Christmas together," he managed to say.

Manny's eyes never left his own display. "Well, Mr. Stanton, I'd say you sort of nixed that now, didn't you?"

Eric didn't miss the thinly veiled hostility. "Look, I didn't realize you and Cindy were involved."

Slowing to a walk, Manny shook his head, smiling ruefully. "Cindy and I aren't involved, Stanton."

Eric's heart lifted, surprising him. Then remembering the man's comment about him ruining their Christmas, realization dawned. "I guess Cindy told you about my recommendation to sell the Chandelier House. I'm sorry, but that's my— Hey!" Manny pushed him from the machine with one strong shove. "What the hell are you doing?" Eric thundered.

The blond man's face was a mask of calm disgust. "Cindy told me everything in the final report was positive, you jerk. Sounds like she was trying to spare me." He scoffed. "You're a chickenshit, Stanton. You don't deserve her, and she doesn't deserve what you've put her through, professionally *and* personally. Excuse me, sir, but I'd better leave before I pop you in the mouth and lose my job."

Dumbfounded, Eric watched the man walk away, wiping the sweat from his wide shoulders. A slow revelation crept over him, shaming him. Manny was right. He *was* afraid to reach out to the people in his life he cared about—Cindy…his father.

His mind spun with scenarios. Harmon would collect insurance money for the booked value of the chandelier. Even restored, the piece would never be as valuable as before, except to Cindy. A smile crept up Eric's face. He just happened to know a bored glass expert who might be willing to tackle the painstaking process of rebuilding the precious antique. Perhaps the project would also give him and his father the time to repair their own bruised relationship.

But first, he had to talk to Cindy and tell her how he felt. Desperate times called for desperate measures. "Oliver!" Eric called. "Wait up."

The concierge stopped, his towel draped around his neck. "Stanton, I really don't want any trouble."

Eric ignored him, rushing to explain what he had in mind.

Manny shook his head and started to walk off. "That's crazy, man."

"I know it's crazy," Eric said, following him and

throwing his hands in the air. "But our entire relationship has been crazy." He pushed his hand through his hair. "This ordeal has thrown me for a loop." He knew he was rambling, but he couldn't stop. "I mean, when you think about it, it's pure happenstance that our paths even crossed."

Manny stared at him. "Happenstance?"

A flush climbed his neck. "You know—luck, serendipity."

"I know what it means, it's just that— Never mind." Manny sighed. "If this backfires, Cindy's going to kick both our asses."

CINDY CHECKED HER WATCH, scanning the crowd for Manny. He'd promised he wouldn't be late, but where was he?

"Last boarding call," the gate attendant announced.

Unbidden tears welled in her eyes when she realized that on top of everything else, she'd miss spending Christmas with someone she really cared about. She picked up her carry-on bag and shuffled toward the gate, looking over her shoulder one last time. No Manny in sight.

As she sidled down the crowded aisle, she steeled herself to hold her tears until she at least found her seat. Then she'd have several hours to purge before arriving home. She had to admit she was anxious to see her mother. Their phone call this morning had been such a turning point in their relationship. Her mother had actually listened and sympathized, woman to woman.

The seat next to her sat vacant, dashing her hopes that she'd somehow missed Manny in the crowd. Cindy stowed her bag, then dropped into her seat, exhausted.

"Hi."

Cindy rolled her eyes upward, then froze. "Eric?"

Devastating in dark slacks, red sweater and a sport coat, he smiled, looking…tentative?

She straightened in her seat. "What are you doing here?"

He stretched overhead to stow the familiar black leather toiletry bag. "I bought the seat next to you."

Her heart squeezed. "Manny sold you his seat?"

"Yeah," he said, lowering himself into the vacant spot. "Well, maybe *traded* is a better word." His mouth stretched into a wry smile. "He's on his way to Atlanta."

She nodded slowly. "He used to live there and still has friends in the city." Still, she was hurt that he hadn't informed her of his change in plans. She took a deep breath, wondering how she'd get through the next few hours. Determined to make the best of the situation, she smiled. "I guess this means you talked to your father."

"As a matter of fact," he said cheerfully, "I did.

Things are going to be much better between us, I think."

"That's great," she said, and meant it.

The intercom beeped and the captain informed the cabin that due to heavy runway traffic, their takeoff would be delayed for forty-five minutes. A series of groans rose from the passengers, including Cindy. The flight couldn't be over soon enough.

"Well, perhaps that will give us time to talk," Eric said.

Cindy cut her eyes over to him. "Talk?"

From the pocket of his coat, he withdrew a small package wrapped in silver metallic paper and red string ribbon. "This is for you."

She gaped, her heart pumping. "For me? Why?"

"Open it," he urged.

With trembling hands, she uncovered a slim box imprinted with the name of the finest jeweler in the city. She raised wary eyes to Eric, but he nodded for her to lift the lid.

She did and gasped. Two perfect diamond teardrop earrings lay against the black velvet, winking back at her in breathtaking splendor. "Oh, my goodness," she exclaimed, swallowing hard. She traced the outline of one with a trembling finger, then turned to him, shaking her head. "Eric, I can't accept these."

"But I ruined your other pair."

"That was an accident."

"Okay, then I love you."

"And besides, these are much too expensive—" Cindy stopped and wet her lips. "You what?"

"I love you," he whispered. "I talked Manny into trading tickets so I could spend Christmas with you. And you wouldn't believe the strings I had to pull to do it." He leaned toward her and captured her lips in a sweet kiss, but Cindy, too stunned to respond, sat stone-still. He pulled back, his expression clouded with disappointment. "I messed up, didn't I? I'd hoped you had feelings for me, too." He laughed softly. "Other than animosity." He sighed and fell back in his seat. "Manny warned me you'd whip us both for this stunt."

Her body stung with jumping sensations—happiness, fear, confusion. "Eric," she said carefully, closing the lid of the box. "I am in love with you." At the hopeful look in his eyes, she added, "But it takes more than love to make a relationship last. Basic values, similar goals, family ties." She smiled tentatively. "Remember, I'm going to be out of a job soon."

Eric grasped her hand and proceeded to tell her of his hopes for buying the hotel. Cindy listened with dawning joy, her heart soaring. "And I can't think of a better person to run the whole show," he said with a smile. Then he added, "As long as you don't fraternize with the male guests."

He claimed another kiss and Cindy warmed to

him, moving closer, refamiliarizing herself with his taste. When the kiss ended, she frowned slightly. "You give me a pair of unbelievable diamond earrings and I'm supposed to fall into your arms?"

His eyes crinkled with merriment. "Is it working?"

"Absolutely."

He studied her face, smiling at her short halo of dark hair. "I think I fell in love with you the moment that woman cut your hair."

She leaned on the armrest, propping up her chin with her hand. "Then I guess it's a good thing I didn't take your advice. Are you ready to meet my family?"

"Yes. Are you ready to meet mine?"

She bit her bottom lip. "I think so. Do you think your dad will like me?"

"The woman who got me playing the piano again? I'd say that's a safe bet."

Reeling from sheer bliss, Cindy sat back in her seat. Within a few hours, the most miserable Christmas Eve of her life had turned into the happiest.

Eric reached into his pocket and withdrew a slightly crumpled sheet of paper.

"What's that?"

"When I checked out, the reservations clerk gave me a copy of the security report on my 'switched' pajama pants."

Her pulse kicked up slightly at the mere mention of the problem pants.

He pressed his lips together, almost smiling. "Cindy, this report has your signature on it."

"That's because I filed it."

"Really?" He leaned forward. "How did you know the color of the pants?"

She almost panicked, then relaxed and swallowed. "W-well, I remembered seeing them hanging behind your toiletry kit when you offered a bandage for my hand."

He nodded and glanced back to the sheet. "And this note about the monogramming on the pocket. How did you know that?"

She meant to laugh softly, but it came out sounding somewhat tinny. "Don't you remember? You told me and Manny at the Christmas party that your initials were on the pocket."

His forehead wrinkled slightly. "Funny, but I don't remember mentioning the specific letters."

She manufactured an animated shrug and gave him a thousand-watt smile. "I assumed the monogram was your full name, EQS."

"Really?" he asked, his eyebrows high.

"Uh-huh." She nodded uncontrollably.

"And how did you know the monogram was—" he referred to the report "'—straight across the pocket edge'?"

Perspiration moistened her upper lip. "Um, a lucky guess?"

"Ah." He folded the sheet of paper and stuffed it

inside his jacket pocket. "Just one more thing, my dear," Eric said, tipping up her chin with his finger. "How is it that you happened to know the *color* of the monogrammed letters?"

She bit her lip, her mind racing. Then she smiled and leaned forward, running her finger down Eric's nose seductively. "I have an idea," she said. "Why don't we go to the lavatory and finish what we started on the roof the other night?"

He grabbed her finger. "I think you're trying to change the subject."

"Is it working?"

"Absolutely."

Clasping his hand, Cindy jumped up, and trotted toward the bathroom with him in tow. After they jammed themselves into the tiny cubicle, Eric laughed. "You," he said, shaking his head, "are very naughty."

But when her lower lip protruded in a pout, he grinned, kissed her hard, then leaned his forehead against hers and whispered, "Which is what makes loving you so very nice."

* * * * *

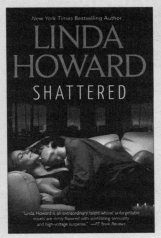

JUST CAN'T GET ENOUGH
ROMANCE
Looking for more?

Harlequin has everything from contemporary, passionate and heartwarming to suspenseful and inspirational stories.

Whatever your mood, we have a romance just for you!

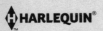

HARLEQUIN®

American Romance®

He's out to get her back

In the fifteen years she's been gone, Bella Biondi forgot how sexy Travis Granger could be. And she can't afford to remember. She's back in Briggs to seal a real estate deal, that's all. No more tears or heartache, no reminiscing, *definitely* no kissing. However, Travis has other ideas. He's sure he can crack the wall Bella's built around herself. She's the girl who loves Christmas in ranch country even more than he does.

Look for
Christmas with the Rancher
by MARY LEO

Available December 2014
wherever books and ebooks are sold.

◆ HARLEQUIN®

SPECIAL EDITION

Life, Love and Family

Coming in December 2014

A BRAVO CHRISTMAS WEDDING

by *New York Times* bestselling author

Christine Rimmer

Aurora Bravo-Calabretti, princess of Montedoro, is used to the best of everything—including men. So when her crush, mountain man Walker McKellan, becomes her bodyguard, Rory is determined to make him hers. There's just one catch—Walker doesn't believe he's right for Rory. Can royal Rory make the Colorado cowboy hers in time for Christmas?

Don't miss the latest edition of
***THE BRAVO ROYALES** miniseries!*

Available wherever books and ebooks are sold!

HSE65854

When it snows, things get really steamy...

Wild Holiday Nights
from Harlequin Blaze offers something sweet, something unexpected and something naughty!

Holiday Rush by Samantha Hunter

Cake guru Calla Michaels is canceling Christmas to deal with fondant, batter and an attempted robbery. Then Gideon Stone shows up at her door. Apparently, Calla's kitchen isn't hot enough without having her longtime crush in her bakery...*and* in her bed!

Playing Games by Meg Maguire

When her plane is grounded on Christmas eve, Carrie Baxter is desperate enough to share a rental car with her secret high-school crush. Sure, Daniel Barber is much, *much* hotter, but he's still just as prickly as ever. It's gonna be one *looong* drive...and an unforgettably X-rated night!

All Night Long by Debbi Rawlins

The only way overworked paralegal Carly Watts gets her Christmas vacation is by flying to Chicago to get Jack Carrington's signature. But Jack's in no rush to sell his grandfather's company. In fact, he'll do whatever it takes to buy more time. Even if it takes one naughty night before Christmas...

Available December 2014 wherever you buy
Harlequin Blaze books.

HARLEQUIN®

Blaze

Red-Hot Reads
www.Harlequin.com

Holiday nights are heating up!

Lucy Vandenburg decides to end her dating dry spell in one naughty, uninhibited night with a sexy stranger. But the man she chooses turns out to be someone she knows all too well....

Don't miss

Oh, Naughty Night!

from *New York Times* bestselling author

Leslie Kelly

Available November 2014
wherever you buy Harlequin Blaze books.

SPECIAL EXCERPT FROM

HARLEQUIN

SPECIAL EDITION

Enjoy this sneak peek from
New York Times *bestselling author RaeAnne Thayne's*
THE CHRISTMAS RANCH, the latest in her
COWBOYS OF COLD CREEK miniseries.

***

The whole time he worked, he was aware of her—the pure blue of her eyes, her skin, dusted with pink from the cold, the soft curves as she reached over her head to hand him the end of the light string.

"That should do it for me," he said after a moment. In more ways than one.

"Good work. Should we plug them in so we can see how they look?"

"Sure."

She went inside the little structure at the entrance to the village, where she must have flipped a few switches. They had finished only about half, but the cottages with lights indeed looked magical against the pearly twilight spreading across the landscape as the sun set.

"Ahhh. Beautiful," she exclaimed. "I never get tired of that."

"Truly lovely," he agreed, though he was looking at her and not the cottages.

She smiled at him. "I'm sorry you gave up your whole afternoon to help me, but the truth is I would have been sunk without you. Thank you."

"You're welcome. I can finish these up when I get here in the morning, after I take Joey to school. Now that I've sort of figured out what I'm doing, I should be able to get these lights hung in no time and start work on the repairs at the Lodge by midmorning."

She smiled at him again, a bright, vibrant smile that made his heart pound as if he had just raced up to the top of those mountains up there and back.

"You are the best Christmas present ever, Rafe. Seriously."

He raised an eyebrow. "Am I?"

He didn't mean the words to sound like innuendo but he was almost certain that sudden flush on her cheeks had nothing to do with the cool November air.

"You know what I mean."

He did. She was talking about his help around the ranch. He was taken by surprise by a sudden fierce longing that her words should mean something completely different.

"I'm not sure I've ever been anyone's favorite Christmas gift before," he murmured.

She gave him a sidelong look. "Then it's about time, isn't it?"

***

Hope Nichols was never able to find her place in the world—until her family's Colorado holiday attraction, the Christmas Ranch, faces closure. This Christmas, she's determined to rescue the ranch with the help of handsome former Navy SEAL Rafe Santiago and his adorable nephew. As sparks fly between mysterious Rafe and Hope, this Christmas will be one that nobody in Cold Creek will ever forget!

Don't miss THE CHRISTMAS RANCH available December 2014, wherever Harlequin® Special Edition books and ebooks are sold!